A/R R.L. 4.4 Pts. 10

The *Summer* of *Letting Go*

Gae Polisner

ALGONQUIN   2014

Published by
Algonquin Young Readers
an imprint of Algonquin Books of Chapel Hill
Post Office Box 2225
Chapel Hill, North Carolina 27515-2225

a division of
Workman Publishing
225 Varick Street
New York, New York 10014

Excerpt from *Frog and Toad Together,* by Arnold Lobel. Text © 1971, 1972
by Arnold Lobel. Used by permission of HarperCollins Publishers.

"My Sharona" words and music by Douglas Fieger and Berton Averre.
Copyright © 1979 by Wise Brothers Music LLC, Small Hill Music,
and Eighties Music. International Copyright Secured.
All Rights Reserved. Used by permission.

LIBRARY OF CONGRESS CATALOGING-IN-PUBLICATION DATA
Polisner, Gae.
The summer of letting go / Gae Polisner.—First edition.
pages cm
Summary: Four years after her brother, Simon, drowned while
in her charge, Francesca, now fifteen, begins to move on after a summer
caring for Frankie, who seems to be Simon reincarnated, and getting
closer to her best friend's boyfriend.
ISBN 978-1-61620-256-9 (alk. paper)
[1. Death—Fiction. 2. Brothers and sisters—Fiction. 3. Best friends—
Fiction. 4. Friendship—Fiction. 5. Dating (Social customs)—Fiction.
6. Family problems.] I. Title.
PZ7 P75294Sum 2014
[Fic]—dc23   2013038536

10 9 8 7 6 5 4 3 2 1
First Edition

To my extraordinary parents,
Stu and Ginger.

To David and my boys,
Sam and Holden.

And, to the two best friends a teenage girl could
have had: my sister, Paige, who is still my best friend,
and Jennifer Hamlet, who is still my heart.

Part I

▊▖ *one* ▖▊

It's not even noon in not even July, yet already the sun bakes down hot and steady, making the air waffle like an oily mirage.

Lisette walks ahead of me, her blond ponytail bobbing happily, the stray strands lit gold by the sunshine that spills down through the fresh green canopy of leaves. Bradley holds tight to her hand, ducks to avoid the low-hanging branches. Prickles of sweat appear between his shoulder blades — dark gray spots against the pale blue cotton of his T-shirt that mesmerize me.

I shift my gaze to my spring green, no-lace Converse sneakers, wondering for the millionth time what it would feel like to have my hand in his.

As if he reads my thoughts, he turns for a second and smiles. My heart somersaults. *I shouldn't feel this way about Lisette's boyfriend.*

I duck my head and keep walking.

The path winds to the right. Lisette leans against Bradley into the curve, her shoulder bumping his, and he wraps his arm around her. I slow my pace and stare up through the sunny trees.

I hate summer to begin with, and it looks like I'm going to spend this one being a third wheel.

We reach the clearing that opens to Damson Ridge. Less than a minute from here to Lisette's house. Another five minutes to mine.

Lisette and I have made this trek from high school to home hundreds of times together, but today it feels different, at this hour, with Bradley Stephenson along.

We're out early for lunch in between final exams, this afternoon's test our last ever of tenth grade. Bradley's a junior, so he finished a few days ago. He's just being chivalrous walking Lisette home.

"Come on, Frankie!" She turns, still walking. "We need to hurry. We have, like, what, an hour?" But Bradley stops, sidetracked, at the edge of the path. "Are you kidding, Nature Boy?" she says. "You are so totally goofy."

I stop, too, so I don't catch up to them.

"What?" He holds out a leafy stalk he's pulled up by the roots. "It's sassafras." Lisette shakes her head and rolls her eyes, even as my heart melts. I love sassafras. My dad and I used to pick it from the fields by the elementary school, back when we did that sort of thing. "Suit yourself," he says, wiping the stem with the inside corner of his T-shirt and slipping it in his mouth. "Tastes like root beer."

"Ew, come on." Lisette pulls his arm. "I kiss those lips, you know. And, anyway, you may be done, but Frankie and I really need to eat something and get back

— 4 —

to school. I hear Shaw's final is crazy. We need sustenance. And I don't mean root beer sticks." She veers off the path toward her street and walks backward to face me. "You coming to my house, Francesca?"

"Nah, it's hot. I think I'll go home and change."

"You sure? It's fine by me." It's Bradley who says this, not Lisette.

"Yes, but thanks." I flip a wave and keep walking.

"Okay, see you back at school," Lisette calls. "Just one more to go, Frankie, and then we're free as birds for the summer!" She blows me a kiss before skipping away with Bradley.

I watch them disappear, my heart filled with longing, my life feeling anything but free.

• • •

When I'm about to turn onto our street, I perk up. Dad's car heads toward me. His silver-gray Jeep Grand Cherokee with the sunroof and the tinted windows. He shouldn't be home. He should be at work selling houses. I guess he had no clients this afternoon.

I smile and hold up my hand to wave, but the car turns right at the prior block instead of making the left onto ours.

I figure he spaced or something, so I wait, but his car never comes back around.

• • •

When I reach home, our driveway's empty. I must have been mistaken. Dad's still at work then, and Mom's where she always is: at her desk at the Drowning Foundation.

Fine. The Simon A. Schnell Foundation for the Prevention of Blah, Blah, Blah and Whatever.

After nearly four years, I still don't get how she spends her life there. I know she thinks it somehow "gives it all purpose," but the place only makes me feel worse about things.

I stop on the stoop, kiss my fingers, and touch them to Simon's stone frog. Inside, I make a lame cheese and mayo sandwich and stand at the kitchen window, eating.

As I'm about to head upstairs to change, Mrs. Merrill appears in her window across the street through the slats of her venetian blinds. They're parted just enough to make her out, though not clearly or completely. She moves to the center of the room, seems to talk on a phone, then walks to the window, presses a few slats down, and peers out.

I duck from view. I know I'm nosy, but I'm fascinated by the little I've seen of Mrs. Merrill since she moved in the summer that Simon died.

Dad was actually the broker who sold her the house, but Mom and I were never formally introduced. It's not like we were feeling too neighborly those days, and over the years, I guess, not that much had changed. Still, I've watched her working in her garden, taken by how pretty she is, but in a sophisticated, confident way like Angelina Jolie, not a pale, fragile way, like my mother.

Mrs. Merrill lets the blinds slip back and leaves the room, so I rinse my dish and turn to go upstairs, but she reappears a second later, walking quickly past the window. This time, she's not alone, but with a man—tall, dark hair, broad shoulders—who looks awfully like my father.

My heart stops, but in fairness, it's hard to make out much through the blinds.

I tell myself to chill, but my eyes dart back to our empty driveway, and my mind to the car I saw go by a few minutes ago. Did Dad park on the next street over and sneak in through her backyard?

I look at the window again, but Mrs. Merrill and the man are gone.

• • •

As I walk back to school, I try to shrug it off. Why would it be my father? If it was my father, and he needed something from Mrs. Merrill, he would have parked in our driveway and walked across the street. Plus, he barely knows her. Why would he park somewhere else and sneak into her house in the middle of a weekday afternoon?

I know the obvious answer even if I don't want to,

and all through Mrs. Shaw's English Honors final, questions circulate in my brain.

Dad has been acting funny lately, hasn't he? Too cheerful. But, of course, he's like that anyway—the only person in our family who is. But this is more than that. He seems *unusually* happy.

I try to keep my focus on my one remaining essay question about Homer and his poems, but it drifts to the poster on Mrs. Shaw's far wall. It's a scene from *The Odyssey*, which we read with *The Iliad* midyear.

The poster shows an old-fashioned illustration of Odysseus tied high on his ship's mast, a dark-haired siren trying to lure him with her song. In the poem, the sirens live on a magical island. Their song is enchanting but deadly, because the sailors who follow the music are led to dangerous, raging waters, where they die upon jagged rocks. Odysseus knows this, but he wants to hear them sing, so he orders his sailors to bind him there, while filling their own ears with wax.

On the poster, Odysseus strains against the ropes as the dark-haired siren reaches for him. A siren who looks uncannily like Mrs. Merrill.

What if it was my father in Mrs. Merrill's house? If it was him, don't I need to know?

If it was him, and I don't put a stop to it, there will be no hope left for my parents. I'm not naive. My parents' marriage has been teetering on the verge of destruction for years. They fight or, worse, they don't talk at all. It's not Dad's fault. Mom isn't herself anymore, and hasn't been one bit since Simon died.

Still, she's my mother, and she needs him.

She can't take more destruction.

She can't take one more person she loves being swept out to sea.

two

I sit up and adjust my bikini top, trying to stretch it across the spots it barely covers. It's snug only because it's one of Lisette's old hand-me-downs, and not for better reasons. She lent it to me last spring for a school car wash, and I grabbed what I could this morning. It's not like I own a fresh supply of bathing suits.

I yank the strings around my neck for maximum boost and retie them, my eyes shifting to where Peter Pintero towers like King of Summer atop his Hamlet Dunes Country Club lifeguard throne.

We're not members, at least not anymore, but I bribed my way in through Peter. He's in Bradley's grade, and I've seen him around, but other than that, I don't know much about him.

His eyes catch mine, and he squints at me funny, like he wants to know what the heck I'm doing here.

Well, it's none of his business what I'm doing here.

Besides, I'm not sure I even know.

I flip onto my stomach, with my head at the bottom and my feet where my head was before. Like this, I have a better view of Mrs. Merrill.

Lured by a siren to the pool.

She lies on a corner chaise on the far side of the deck, a wide-brimmed hat pulled down over her face. She hasn't moved in nearly a half hour. It was stupid to come here in the first place. I'd raced over without thinking after what had happened this morning with Dad.

I'd slept late again. I didn't have much on my agenda. With Lisette constantly busy with Bradley, I had no good reason to get up. For her, summer would clearly be fun, but for me, this summer would be what they always were: long, hot days that bore down, a constant reminder of the pure white absence of my brother.

An absence I am responsible for.

I went down to the kitchen before eleven. Mom was long gone to the Foundation. Surprisingly, though, Dad was still home, standing at the counter drinking coffee. Dressed not for work in slacks and a button-down, but for a day of leisure, in khaki shorts, an orange polo shirt, and deck shoes. He should have left hours ago.

"Morning, Beans!"

"No work today?"

"Yes, work." He sipped his coffee thoughtfully. "But no showings, so I thought I'd take it easy today." He ruffled my hair like I was twelve, then stared plainly across to Mrs. Merrill's house. Panic tightened my chest. "How about you?" he finally asked. "Any plans today?"

I mumbled something about hanging out with Lisette, even though I knew it wasn't true. I guessed I wasn't the only one lying. My dad never went in late, and never in deck shoes and shorts.

Dad put his mug in the sink and gave me a kiss good-bye. I watched him go. Other than Lisette, he was the only good thing I had left. If I lost him, if he left Mom—us—life would be unbearable.

As he backed his Jeep down the driveway, the knot that had taken up residence in the pit of my stomach last week when I thought I saw him with Mrs. Merrill twisted tighter. Something was definitely off.

I was about to call Lisette so she could tell me I was being ridiculous, but before I could, I saw Mrs. Merrill rush out her front door in a macramé cover-up, high-heeled sandals, and a straw sun hat, carrying a tote bag. She got in her car and sped off in the same direction as my father.

Odysseus's siren raced through my brain, which then went immediately to the country club. I mean, she wouldn't wear heels to the beach.

I ran upstairs, pulled on Lisette's old bikini, a pair of shorts, and a T-shirt, and shoved a five-dollar bill in my pocket. Of course, even if I was right and Mrs. Merrill was headed there, that didn't mean Dad was, too. Still, he had left, and she had left right after him, both of them dressed for a country club.

I had race-walked all the way to the club, the whole time telling myself how dumb I was being, even when I saw Mrs. Merrill's car parked up front in the lot. I scanned frantically for Dad's Jeep but didn't see it. Then again, he could have parked elsewhere.

I walked around the side of the club toward the back gate, my hands squeezing the sweaty bill I had grabbed before I left.

If my dad was doing what I was worried he was doing, would he really dare to do it here in broad daylight?

Still, I needed to be sure.

And, at the gate, for a mere five dollars, Peter Pintero had let me in.

• • •

Across the pool, Mrs. Merrill sits up. I put my head down fast, my nose pressed against the warm plastic of the chaise, but I'm pretty sure I'm mostly hidden by the tables and umbrellas. I breathe for a moment before lifting up a little to see.

She slides the straw bag from under her chair, the dim chime of her cell phone growing louder as she fishes it out and holds it to her ear. She nods and talks, all the while glancing over at the big, round clock on the clubhouse wall.

Eleven forty-five a.m.

She puts the phone away and stares off at the row of cabanas across from the back entrance to the club.

Is she waiting for someone?

After another minute, she lies back down and pulls her hat over her face again.

I look back up to where Peter sits. From this angle,

I can't see past the white, crisscross rungs of his chair. Just as well. He's a jerk. We both know if Lisette had been with me, he'd have let me in for free.

I let my gaze fall to the pool, to its calm, deceptive surface. I feel oddly drawn to it. It's been four years since I've stepped foot in a pool or the ocean. Why do I suddenly long to go in?

"Frankie!"

I bolt upright in time to see Peter's feet, then legs, then whole self come skittering off the lifeguard chair toward the ground.

"What? I . . . " But he's not yelling at me, rather at a small blond boy—not much more than three years old—who runs, arms raised, toward the deep end of the pool.

"Frankie, don't you dare! Do *not* do it, you hear?" But it's too late. The boy laughs and dives, disappearing headfirst under the water.

I jump up from my seat and race to the pool's edge, pulse pounding.

For a few seconds, I watch dumbfounded as the boy glides gracefully near the surface. Then he gasps, drawing a mouthful of water, and sinks promptly toward the bottom like a stone.

◼◼ *three* ◼◼

Everything stands still.

I watch, frozen, as his blond curls float upward while the rest of him plummets down. Bubbles escape his mouth, and his blue eyes blink up at me.

The air turns thick and dark, and a thousand panicked memories skitter like water bugs across the sunbleached landscape of my brain. *A bright summer day. The sparkling water. Simon, and the sand castle, and the waves.*

I should jump in. I should jump in now and save him. But my body won't move.

"Goddammit!" Peter shouts, shoving me aside. His body flies past me and sails in, lean and fast like lightning. I stare inept and silent as he descends.

Near the bottom, he catches hold of the boy's arm and drags him up toward the surface. The boy is not cooperative, kicks and bucks against him, but Peter holds on, his arm bent under the boy's chin to keep his head above water as he tows him expertly toward the shallow end. When he reaches the steps, Peter stands, panting, one hand gripped on the boy's arm, the other holding the railing. The boy coughs and laughs, twisting against Peter's grasp to break free.

"Frankie, geez, I mean it!"

A gray-haired woman comes up next to me and clucks her tongue as if she's wondering how I could just stand here watching the boy drown.

"Frankie, don't even think about it!" I snap my focus back to where Peter stands, out of the pool now and yelling some more. "Where in heck is your mother?" He looks around at the faces of the few spectators who have gathered. "Has anyone seen Mrs. Schyler?"

They shake their heads and start to walk away. It seems they've seen this part before. The gray-haired woman mumbles, "Where else?" and nods toward the clubhouse door, which swings open, releasing a petite blond woman in our direction.

She rushes at us, a frothy drink in her hand, a skewer of fresh fruit and a paper umbrella poking out from the top. She wears a red halter shirt and short jean shorts with red, open-toed, spiked heels. Her bright blond curls bounce in the sunlight. There's no doubt that she's the boy's mother.

When she reaches us, she squats down, teetering on her heels, giving Peter a bird's-eye view down her top.

"Oh dear, Frankie," she says, her eyes darting to Peter's apologetically. "I told you not to go anywhere. I left you in the TV room for three seconds . . ."

Peter, who's been trying to look stern, turns the color of her shoes. When he manages to look up, his eyes

catch mine and he rolls them at me, as if we're in ca-
hoots, which we are not.

"Mrs. Schyler . . ." he starts, but he can't seem to
get more words out. Instead, he gestures to a large sign
that reads, *Children Under 12 Must be Accompanied At*
All Times, the last three words underlined in fat black
marker.

"I know, I know, I'm sorry. He promised . . ." She
gives Frankie an exasperated look. "What did you
do, Frankie? Tell me." The fact that he's dripping wet
should be more than enough of a clue.

Frankie puts his hands on his hips and raises his
clear blue eyes up to her. "I swimmed!" he says proudly.
"I dived and I swimmed!"

Maybe it's the enormity of the relief I feel that makes
it seem so funny, or maybe it's just the boy's delivery
and the annoyed look plastered on Peter's face, but I
barely stifle a laugh. Peter gives me a dirty look. I see
the corner of Mrs. Schyler's mouth bend up into a smile
even as she tries to discipline him again.

"Frankie, it is not funny. You promised. You know
you could have drowned! Grandpa Harris is going to
have my head for this!"

She grabs his arm and pulls him in to her, and his
solid weight against her small frame nearly sends her
sprawling. Her drink goes flying, leaving a slosh of
snow white mush across the redbrick deck. Plus one
cherry, one orange slice, and a bright yellow paper
umbrella.

"Oh dear! Look what you've done now, Frankie!" she says.

"I swimmed, not drowned!" Frankie insists again, finally making me cave in and laugh. Frankie turns to me, eyes narrowed. "Who she?"

My cheeks light on fire. "Francesca," I stammer, embarrassed. "Francesca Schnell. But, um, everyone just calls me Frankie." I look at Peter, who shrugs.

The little boy takes a step closer. "Hey, I Frankie, too. Frankie Schyler. But Schyler is hard, so you can say Frankie Sky." He beams up at me, his blond curls blazing in the sun. And that's when I see it, how very much he looks like my brother. "Because," he says, "Simon is just like the sky."

Everything goes silent. The air disappears, presses in heavy, like a vacuum seal.

"Right?" he repeats, eyes fixed on mine. "Because Schyler sounds just like the sky?"

He's fixed it now, but I know what I heard. Clear as day, he had said, "Simon is just like the sky."

He waits for me to say something, but I can't get the words to come out. All I can do is stare back at him.

It's as if I am looking at Simon.

four

I turn my phone over on the kitchen table and tap the text message from Lisette so its words light up on the screen.

> Where u been? Headed to movie with B.
> Wanna come? p.s. No worries! His idea! ☺

It makes me feel pathetic.

Then again, if it was Bradley's idea, could that mean something? That he's the one who wants to invite me? I close my eyes and imagine us sitting side by side in the cool, dark theater. He slips his hand into mine.

Nope, I was right. I'm pathetic. He's probably just trying to be sweet.

I stare at the message until the screen fades and the words disappear, wishing I knew how to do the same. Fade away right along with them.

I walk to the sink and stare across at Mrs. Merrill's empty driveway, then our own. The whole street seems quiet and empty. Maybe I have disappeared.

In the months after I let Simon die, I spent countless

hours trying to figure out how to stop my breath and disappear. I'm not sure I wanted to kill myself exactly. All I knew was that I wanted to be gone. To be invisible, to slip away. I wanted to feel the opposite of how I felt, which was solid and weighted and frozen. I felt my own inescapable presence in every breath, every step, which seemed totally cruel and unfair.

I had read this story about a Buddhist monk who meditated himself into his own death. The story described how he'd sat under a tree and, knowing his body's physical demise was near, made his breath so slow and barely-there that he simply ceased to exist.

I wanted that. I wanted to cease to exist.

Every day after school, I would practice. I'd sit against the big old oak in our backyard, close my eyes, and inhale and exhale so slowly and so shallowly that I couldn't feel my breath at all. I would stay like that for what felt like hours, but whenever I'd finally open my eyes again, I'd still be sitting there, our house in front of me, everything intact except Simon.

Now I close my eyes and try to slow my breath like I did then, taking in air only through my nose. I keep the respirations shallow so that my chest barely moves, but I keep getting distracted by the face that looked so much like my brother's.

I picture the boy named Frankie Sky, the way he looked at me, over and over in my head. I hear his words, *Simon is just like the sky.* I must have misheard him. There's no way that's what he said.

It was just my nerves getting the best of me, seeing him go under like that.

I give up on breath-holding or anything remotely meditative, slide my cell phone over, and respond to the text from Lisette.

> Thanks, Zette. Think I'll pass. Weird day.
> Tired. Tell u about it later.

I wait a few minutes, but she doesn't text back, so I head upstairs to my room.

At the top of the steps, I freeze. Simon's door is open. Not fully, just the slightest bit ajar. Which shouldn't be that strange, except it is. Because Simon's door is never open. Ever. Only my mother opens it, and only my mother goes in. And neither she nor my dad is home.

It's not like there's a rule against his door being open. It's just unspoken, the way it's always been. In the weeks after he died, Mom went in there and cleaned out some things — I don't know what things — then closed the door and kept it that way. It seemed clear she didn't want anyone else to go in. But now, here it is, open, in the middle of the afternoon.

I stare at the narrow opening, my mind racing to the blond boy once again. But I shake the thought. Now I'm just being silly. Maybe Mom is home; maybe her car pulled in and I didn't hear it, and she snuck past me and is sitting in there on his bed.

A sense of urgency comes over me, the kind I always

feel when I remember that I'm the one responsible for how things are, so it's my job to keep my mother from breaking.

I take the few remaining steps to the door and push it open wider.

The room is empty. Sunlight spills in through the window, spreading baptismal rays across the pale blue carpeted floor. Dust motes dance in the swirling lines. Everything's peaceful and quiet. I force myself to walk in.

The room is pristine, sleepy. Sky blue walls the color of the rug, as if the whole room is suspended in air.

Simon is just like the sky.

I let my eyes fall to Simon's bed, to his navy comforter with the orange and green tree frogs. Next to that, his nightstand with the silly little lamp I'd forgotten. Simon loved that lamp because of the frog engineer, the small striped cap on his head. A red train circles the wooden base. You'd flip the toggle switch to make it go around.

Everything is intact, the way I remember it. For a second, I think about touching Simon's pillow, sitting on his bed, but seeing that frog engineer breaks my heart, so I duck back out, pulling the door closed tightly behind me.

Down the hall in my room, I kick off my shoes and lie on my bed, but I'm just too restless and get right up again. I take off my shorts and T-shirt, open my closet door, and stare at my bikini'd body in the mirror. I squint and twist around backward, trying to see myself the way someone else might. Like Bradley might. My legs are okay, and my butt, but the rest of me isn't impressive. I'm skinny like a stick. Straight hair, straight figure, all boring. My face is fine, but bland. And my eyebrows are too thick. "Like Brooke Shields," my father says, but I have no idea who he's talking about.

Lisette is so much prettier. No wonder she has Bradley and I have no one.

I squeeze my arms together to make my cleavage deepen like Mrs. Schyler's, give up, yank off the top, and throw it in the deep recesses of my closet. I get dressed again, walk downstairs, and stare out the kitchen window. Still no black Mercedes. Of course, Dad isn't home, either. Were they together? In the commotion of the blond boy's dive, I'd lost all track of Mrs. Merrill.

I check the clock. It's one forty-five p.m.

From these facts, I deduce absolutely nothing.

I sit at the kitchen table and rest my cheek on its cool surface. I think of Lisette, of her giddy remark a few weeks ago about how, now that we'd be juniors, we'd have so much more freedom this summer. So much more fun. I'd felt hopeful then, but that was before Bradley Stephenson, before she had wrapped him around her finger like she always does, and I was stuck all alone.

With or without Bradley, I should have known better. For me, there are never any good summers, only survivable ones.

I close my eyes and slide my cheek to a cooler spot, letting Lisette fade away and Frankie Sky slip back in. Hands on his hips, sunlit curls, bright blue eyes smiling.

So what if I don't know how it could be? I know it was Simon's face looking back at me.

■■ five ■■

I wake up early, determined to make something of my summer and stop worrying about foolish things I can't fix, to be normal and attempt to hang out with my best friend.

Or at least try to, when she's not completely pre-occupied with Bradley.

After all, that's what we are, best friends. And best friends don't require fancy plans. So I head over there, to Lisette's.

It's already sunny and hot, and I'm sweating by the time I reach her street. The Sutters' house is halfway down, a brick Colonial on a pretty grass hill, with white shutters and a giant brass cross on the front door.

I eye Lisette's bedroom window as I knock, but I can't see anything up there. A few seconds later, Andreas answers.

"Hey, Frankie." He gives me his typical look, tongue-in-cheek, ready to tease. "You trying to bust down the place?" Andreas is the younger of Lisette's two brothers, just graduated and about to head off to college in Boston. Lisette's older brother, Alex, is back from his junior year at UPenn. I've known them forever, so they're pretty much like family to me. "Geez, it's hot out, huh?" He closes the door behind me.

"Is that Bradley?" Lisette's voice drifts, hopeful, from upstairs, and my heart sinks.

Andreas shakes his head like she's lame. "You know her," he says. "One-track mind."

"No, sorry. Just me," I call.

"Oh, hey, Beans! What's up?"

The vision that's my best friend since first grade appears at the top of the stairs, smiling as she hops down them to meet me. I feel instantly better. She seems happy enough that I'm here.

I can tell from her outfit that her father isn't home. He's a pastor, and her stomach shows. Specifically, she's wearing a white cropped T-shirt that says *Pink* across it in silver script, and short jean shorts. She's barefoot, her toenails painted a raspberry sherbet pink. I feel boring in my shapeless green T-shirt dress.

"This is nice. New?" I flick the hem of her shirt as we head back upstairs. "I don't see you for a few days and you already have a new wardrobe? Oh, and since your ass will be totally grounded when your father sees it, can I borrow it for the rest of the summer?" Lisette laughs, but holds a finger to her lips because I've said the word *ass* in her house. "By the way, I would have called first," I add, "but . . ." Then I stop because I realize that whatever I was going to say would sound hurt on my part, or sarcastic.

She picks up on it anyway. "I invited you to the

movies, Beans." I give her a look like that invite was just sad, which it was. "I know, I know," she says, "but, honestly, you could have come."

"Whatever."

"No, seriously, I'm telling you, Brad likes you. He does. He's always bringing you up."

I look away fast. I don't want her to see how badly I hope that it's true.

"So, how was the movie?" I need to lighten up. I can't blame her because she has a gorgeous-but-somehow-also-smart boyfriend who I wish was my boyfriend instead.

"Okay, Beans, where are you? I said it was good." She waves her hand in my face. We've reached her bedroom, and clearly I haven't heard a word that she's said.

Other than my dad (and Mom, who doesn't anymore), Lisette is the only person who calls me Beans, and only in private, because she knows I'd be mortified if it caught on. Everyone would equate it with my being built like a string bean, even though it has nothing to do with my looks. My dad started calling me Beans when I was little. It came from Frankie, short for Francesca, which he had morphed into Franks 'n' Beans.

"It's cute," Lisette always says, "and anyway, you are in no way built like a string bean." Easy for her to say with her Victoria's Secret–perfect figure.

"Um, Francesca, I am so not kidding. Where are you?"

I finally focus on her, and she promptly rolls her eyes. I roll mine back and we laugh, but something feels off between us. Like we're disconnected—us on the outside, but inside we're some weird alien replacement of friends. Maybe it's because I haven't seen her in a while or told her the crap that's going on with Dad. Or about my visit to the club, and the boy, Frankie Sky, who looks so much like my brother.

I sit on her bed. She sits next to me and drapes her arm around my shoulders. "I've missed you, Frankie. What's going on?"

"Nothing much." I slip off my flip-flops and run my toes through her rug.

"Well, we need to fix that, don't we?" She twists her hair off her neck and lies down, letting her long locks splay loose around her face. She looks like a Sun Goddess Barbie I once saw in a doll-collecting magazine. I look around her room instead.

I've been in Lisette's room so many times, it feels like my own. Pale pink walls, darker pink carpeting. Antique white rocking chair that was her grandmother's as a girl. Desk across from that. Wrought-iron sleigh bed. And a giant rosewood cross above the headboard, hand-carved with ornate flowers and swirls. The cross has been there since I met her. Lisette minds it, but I think there's something pretty about it.

"Oh come on! What boy is going to want to feel me up under that?" she had asked last summer, when being felt up still seemed a faraway thing. Sitting here now, I'm guessing the answer is one handsome Bradley Stephenson.

I'm sure Bradley will want to feel you up under that cross, I want to say to her now. *I bet he already has.*

I'm dying to know if it's true—if Bradley has lain here on top of her, his fingers wandering up under her T-shirt as they make out, groping under her pink lace bra, caressing her picture-perfect breasts. Maybe more than just his fingers . . .

Envy fills me to bursting. I want it to happen for me. I long for it, even if the thought also terrifies me a little.

For a second, I let myself imagine Bradley's lips on mine, his strong hands slipping up under my shirt. Then I knock it off because I'm sure imagining my best friend's boyfriend like this is a sin of the absolute worst kind.

"Beans?" Lisette stares at me, but I don't answer.

The room has grown stuffy and warm. I feel overwhelmed by the need to be like we used to be, just the two of us. I don't like feeling so alone.

I should tell her everything, like I used to, all the weird, stupid stuff that's been going on. Even if it's nothing, at least it's news. But for some reason, I don't. I can't. And I can't explain why. It feels like there's a wall between us, invisible from her side, maybe, but still there, like one of those two-way mirrors.

Plus, why would I tell her about the boy named Frankie Sky? I saw him once, and it's not like I believe in angels or karma or reincarnation. Simon is dead. *Period.* That boy had nothing to do with Simon.

"Oh my gosh. Seriously, Beans, I'm starting to worry. What on God's green planet is up with you?"

I sigh and lie back so our arms touch. "Nothing. And besides, why do people call it green when there's way more water than land?"

"Excuse me?"

"Water. Water is blue, Zette. So the planet is mostly blue."

"Okay, fine, blue. God's blue planet, is that better? What on God's *blue* earth is eating you?"

I turn my head sideways and force a smile. It's not Lisette's fault that she has a boyfriend, and it's not her fault that I'm cranky.

"Hey, Zette," I blurt without thinking, "has your dad ever said anything about reincarnation?"

"Excuse me?" she says again.

"Reincarnation. You know, like coming back to life after death?"

She narrows her eyes, but I already know I sound crazy. "Um, no? It's not very 'Christian,' I don't think, that whole reincarnation thing." She makes air quotes around the word *Christian* to remind me that she doesn't share her dad's deep religious beliefs any more than I do. "Why are you asking, anyway? You sound like Bradley now." She sits up. "Beans, is everything okay?"

"Yeah," I say, my mind stuck on her comment about Bradley. "I'm fine, really. Never mind. It's stupid. I've just been thinking about my brother."

"Oh. I get it." She rubs my arm to console me.

"Forget it, Zette. Subject closed. Speaking of Bradley, tell me everything that's going on."

She flips onto her stomach, props up on her elbows, and studies me. Loose strands of her hair slip across my neck, tickling me. I make a face to let her know she shouldn't feel sorry for me about Simon, or about the fact that she has a life and a boyfriend and I don't, and wait for her to feed me information. Even though I don't know if I can really bear to hear it.

When she doesn't say anything, I say, "Come on, Zette, something juicy. I could use something juicy right now."

"All right, fine. He's good. Really sweet and nice, and maybe a little weird. What else is there to tell?"

"Weird how? He's, like, Mr. Popularity of the World."

"I know. He's totally hot. But he's goofy, too, I'm telling you. Like Mr. Nature and stuff."

"Like how?"

"I don't know. Like he saves bugs. Ants. And spiders and stuff." She shudders and sits up, legs folded Indian style. "He says they have souls. If there's one in his room, he carries it outside. I'm not kidding. He thinks it's bad karma to kill it. But, well, I guess it's sort of cute."

And then I get it, the comment she made about Bradley, and my brain goes whirling, because maybe he knows something about reincarnation. Maybe it's some karmic connection between us.

"Can you ask him?" I ask, sitting up too eagerly. "I mean the question about reincarnation?"

She stares at me hard and shrugs. "Sure. If you want me to, I guess. Now you're both weird, though."

I giggle. "I know. And, really, it's stupid, but, well, the other day . . . I just sort of need to know."

"Suit yourself."

She glances at the clock on her desk. "Oh, crap, speaking of Bradley, he's supposed to come over in a . . ." She stops midsentence, feeling bad that she's about to ditch me for him again. But it doesn't matter. I don't really feel like staying here anyway. I stand up and start to go, but she tugs on my arm. "Tell the truth, Frankie; is everything really okay?"

"Yeah, sure, fine." But even I can hear how unconvincing I sound. Still, what am I supposed to do, anchor her down when she has places to go and people to kiss?

I look at the crucifix. Forget virginity, in two months I'll be sixteen, and I've never been kissed by a boy. Not the French way or the regular way. It's painful how badly I want to be.

Her cell phone rings, jerking me from my thoughts. "Don't go yet," she says. "I still have a few minutes." She picks up and talks and giggles. It's clear in a second who it is. *Give me one minute,* she mouths to me.

I nod, but slide on my flip-flops and start toward her bedroom door, and when she turns her back, I slip out.

As I walk down the hall, my flip-flops make their rubbery slip-slap noise against my heels. Over that, Lisette's happy voice chases me all the way back downstairs.

six

I wander Lisette's neighborhood for a bit, then cut across the field to the elementary school and toward the playground. Except for a few preteen boys on the basketball court, the place is deserted. I sit on the swings and pump my legs. These are the same swings Lisette and I spent hundreds of recesses on, swinging so high we made the metal poles bump in and out of the foundation.

I swing low, dragging my toes through the worn sand trench beneath me. When I tire of that, I walk back and forth across the wood beam that Lisette and I used to pretend was a modeling runway.

"Eyes closed, back straight," Lisette would instruct, patting my butt with a long stick she found to use as a pointer. "Keep your toes forward. Perfectly lined up." It seemed so hard back then, to copy her and traverse the beam without falling. Now it seems stupidly easy.

I swallow back a lump in my throat. I miss Lisette. I miss us. I know I was just at her house, but we're not quite us anymore. Something is off between us. There's a crack turning into a chasm. It keeps stretching wider and wider.

My hand moves reflexively to my throat, to where

my half of our shared heart pendant used to be. But, of course, it's not there anymore. At the start of high school, we agreed they were babyish and put them away for safekeeping. Now, the empty spot makes me nostalgic for how we used to be.

A particular day pops into my head that I haven't thought about in a long time. It's a few months after Simon died and we're having a sleepover. It's a long weekend, and I'm there at the Sutters' house for the third night in a row, so it almost feels like I live there. I remember this, how I keep thinking I can pretend to be a Sutter, pretend I live with them and have two older brothers who love me, and not a baby brother who drowned.

Anyway, for most of the day we've been playing this dumb game we always play even if we're getting too old to play it. We're grown-ups, married, with jobs and make-believe husbands. After "work," we come home and make out with them, and Lisette even pretends to have sex. Then we clean and cook dinner and all sit around the table to eat.

Lisette's husband is always named Roger, and mine is always named Dan. Even though we know it doesn't make sense that we live together, we don't care, because that's what makes the game so much fun.

We're eating dinner and everything's going fine, until Lisette looks up from her plate over lit candles and her fake grape-juice wine.

"Oh my God! Roger!" she yells, and runs to where

Roger sits—well, now seems to be keeled over. She pulls at him and starts to cry.

Turns out, Roger is having a heart attack. Turns out, Roger has died. "Oh, dear God, just like that?" Lisette wails. "Right here at our kitchen table?"

For the next several hours, we weep, write eulogies, and have a big, sad funeral for which we dress in black, which her mother has plenty of, since her father does all the local ceremonies. It takes us all night. Most of the time we're giggling, but partly I'm secretly overcome with this terrible sense of loss, this feeling that Lisette is ending things and moving on without my permission.

Later that night in bed, I ask, "So, why did you do it, Zette?"

"Do what?"

"Kill Roger. You know."

She laughs. "I didn't kill him, Beans, he died. Didn't you see it? He fell right down on the table and died. I'm sure it was his heart. It just gave out. Must've been all the crappy food he ate. I begged him, you know . . . I can't help it if he died." I give her a look. "What? He should have eaten better then, right?" She smiles.

"Zette!"

"What? It's been, like, years, Beans. I got bored of him. He was a very boring man."

"You did? He was?" This information worries me. I'd never thought of Lisette as the type to get bored of someone, to just be done with them, especially when I didn't see it coming. "I mean, you made him up, Zette!

If he was boring you, couldn't you have fixed him? Or divorced him? Marry some new guy? I mean, what are we going to do now?"

Lisette must sense that at any minute I might cry, because she grabs the brush from her nightstand and pulls me over so that I'm sitting between her legs. She always does this when I'm upset, brushes my hair with her special abalone-shell brush.

Lisette says she loves my hair because it's straight like silk, instead of crazy and wavy like hers. But her hair is pretty, blond, and full of body, while mine is plain and brown. Still, it works, and the teary feeling passes.

The brush is precious because it's a part of a set her grandmother gave her for her birthday. An antique that comes with a mirror and comb. The shell mosaics on the handles are iridescent purples and blues and greens.

I always love when she brushes my hair because it makes me feel cared for without words. In the weeks after Simon died, it was one of the things that saved me.

"I told you, Beans," she says again as she strokes, "I didn't kill Roger. He died."

"Well, what if you get bored with me?"

"Don't be silly. I never would."

"But what if you do? What if you have a real boy-friend, or a real husband, and they're more important to you? Or what if you find a new friend? A better friend? A friend who doesn't have so many problems, like I do?

"You don't have problems, Beans." I twist and look at her. She rolls her eyes and turns me back around.

"You *don't*. I mean, your brother died, so of course that's hard for you. But you're fine. Besides, your hair is straight and silky and fun to brush, so how could I ever get bored with you?" She taps me on the shoulder, letting me know it's my turn.

We switch positions, and I hold her thick, gorgeous locks in my hands. "Well, promise me anyway that you won't."

"I promise. Plus, we have our hearts, remember?"

I grasp the half heart locket that rests beneath my nightgown. "Yes, I remember," I say.

• • •

I step off the beam and take the shortcut out of the playground, leaving our old kid ghosts behind. When I reach our block, I see Dad's car in the driveway. Two weeks ago, this would have made me happy. Now, it only worries me.

I slow my pace, my eyes shifting from our driveway to Mrs. Merrill's. Her black Mercedes is there, alone.

No big deal. Dad came home early. He's in our house. And Mrs. Merrill's in hers. He knows school is out. He wouldn't do something so stupid.

As I approach our house, relief floods me. Our front door is open. Dad's inside like I knew he was.

I head slowly up our stoop like my feet are stuck in molasses, stopping to kiss my fingers and touch them to Simon's frog, who's now covered by a periwinkle sea of forget-me-nots that shoot up around him each spring. I open the screen door and call for Dad, but no answer. A glass pitcher of Mom's unsweetened iced tea sweats on the kitchen counter. A few bloated lemon slices drift atop the weak brown mixture. Next to it, a glass of nearly melted ice.

I yell for Dad again. No answer. I turn and stare out the window.

I know like snow that he's in there.

I pour some tea into the glass of melted ice (still cold, so that's good—he couldn't have been gone long) and drink it down, trying to decide what to do. Then I head back out, my heart pounding so hard it hurts.

I cross the lawn. More molasses. When I reach our curb, I stop dead.

Mrs. Merrill's front door has opened. I can see Dad standing inside through the screen.

He's turned sideways, talking. He swings the screen open and waves at me. A stupid, casual wave.

My chest seizes with panic, my pulse banging inside my own ears.

The sun beats down hard. Dad smiles and starts walking, Mrs. Merrill's door closing behind him.

My life is falling apart.

Dad walks toward me, whistling some perky tune. He's still in his work clothes, a jar raised in his hand. I stare at the jar, all sorts of rants racing through my brain. *Breathe, Frankie, breathe. It's no big deal that*

Dad was inside Mrs. Merrill's house. Just don't let there be some dumb alibi.

He crosses the street to our side, holds the jar out to me, and gives me a cheesy smile. The fake Cheshire cat kind I hate. The one he uses to sell houses.

"Hey, Beans." He shakes the jar. White crystals shimmer in the sunshine. "I didn't realize you were back."

"What were you doing in there?" My voice is accusatory.

"We needed sugar. I borrowed some," he says, like I'm naive. He ruffles my hair.

My breath stops completely.

Maybe this will be the moment I finally fade away.

▪▪▪ *seven* ▪▪▪

The sun seeps through the leaves, baking me where I sit in the far corner at the Hamlet Dunes Country Club pool.

I'm here for one reason only, which is that there's a full box of Domino sugar in our cereal cabinet where it always is, in all its bright yellow glory.

I mean, borrowing sugar must be the lamest alibi ever.

In fact, in the four years that Mrs. Merrill has lived across from us, we have never once borrowed a thing from her. Not sugar, not cinnamon, not cooking oil, not eggs. Not even toilet paper. We're just not the borrowing type of neighbors.

Not to mention, Dad left for work late again this morning, in singularly unbusinesslike clothes. Right after which, Mrs. Merrill took off in her black Mercedes-Benz.

And there she sits, in her sunglasses and wide-brimmed hat, occasionally looking at the clock. But absolutely no sign of my dad. Which I wish I could read into, except I can't because it took me so long to get here. Because when I went downstairs this morning, my mother was sitting in the kitchen.

Now, why my mom—who should have been long

gone to the Foundation — was still home at ten a.m. on a weekday was beyond me. But there she was, reading the paper, a mug of hot tea pressed in her hands despite the ninety-degree day.

I tucked my bikini straps under my T-shirt and prayed the green top wouldn't show through. I had no good explanation for where I was going.

"Morning." I skirted past her.

"Francesca, good morning." She looked up and smiled, but not fast enough to cover the flash of disappointment that's always there when she realizes it's me.

It might bother me less if I couldn't remember the way she was before, but I *can.*

I remember how she'd sit on the floor and play jacks and board games with me. We'd bake muffins and eat them hot from the oven, snuggled up watching Saturday-morning cartoons.

I can still remember the feeling of us squished together on the couch while Simon marched around us with his plastic vacuum toy with the brightly colored popping beads. I try hard not to notice that we never do that anymore, not since Simon died. I tell myself I've gotten too old for such things, and it isn't because my own mother can't love me anymore. Or even call me Frankie, like she used to.

Anyway. I grabbed the English muffins from the fridge, popped one in the toaster, and sat down across from her.

"So, how come you're home?"

"Not sure. I overslept." Her eyes registered a speck of hurt, as if I'd accused her of something, which, I guess, maybe I had. It's just that she was never home after Dad left for work in the mornings. "Maybe it's the weather, the change of pace with summer. The Foundation's been quiet. I guess people don't like to deal with such issues in the summer, which, of course, is the most important time."

I looked away at the clock. I hated this part about the pools and drowning and the Foundation.

"Or maybe I needed a break," she added. "It's nice out. I thought I'd have breakfast with your father." I must've made some noise because her eyes took me in with surprise, as if she'd forgotten I was there. "It's just that I thought he was staying home, but apparently he had some business in the office this morning."

My heart sank deep, weighted by a steel anchor. It was as if Mom sensed something was wrong, too, and had stayed home to try to prevent it.

A tee-off-time page comes over the club's loudspeaker, pulling me back to the present. I glance at the clock. Eleven forty a.m. In ten more minutes, I'll give up this pointless Nancy Drew charade and go home.

I lie back down and let thoughts of Frankie Sky drift through my brain. Why do I wish he was here?

I stare over at the picture window of the clubhouse. The dining room tables have begun to fill, and I catch glimpses of waiters, of the hostess seating slow-moving old men in their plaid pants and polo shirts. I've been in there before—sleepy buffet breakfasts with my family during summers before Simon died. Now it's hard to remember. As if that were someone else, as if my life's been split in two. A reverse makeover. The Frankie before and after her brother died.

Across the pool, Mrs. Merrill stands. I cover my face again, my pulse ramping up for a change. One of these times, I'm going to give myself a real heart attack.

She puts on her hat and sandals and loads her belongings into her big straw bag as if she's getting ready to leave. I slouch lower, though I'm not sure she'd even know who I am.

She checks her cell phone and tosses that into the bag, too. Is she waiting for someone? Is that someone my father? If it is, and he comes here, what will I do then?

I concoct a vague alibi in my brain about this girl in my grade named Michelle Greenhut. I'm pretty sure her family belongs here. I'll say Michelle invited me but got sick and went home, and I was about to leave. It's not great, but Mrs. Merrill's in motion, so it's going to have to do.

I slink lower and watch her tap, tap across the brick patio, weaving her way between lounge chairs, cutting a path around the pool toward the cabanas.

I study her. Her cover-up is braided tan macramé,

with glittery gold flecks that shimmer in the sunlight. A chocolate brown one-piece with gold and turquoise medallions peeks through. The medallions jangle softly when she walks. Her legs are long and shapely. Her toenails are painted pomegranate red.

Everything about her is sophisticated.

She reminds me of an actress, and I wonder if she's ever been one. Maybe when she was younger, before she moved here with her husband. For the first time, I find myself really considering her — why she lives here in the suburbs of Long Island instead of somewhere exciting like Los Angeles or, at least, Manhattan.

She has no children. No dogs. Why would she choose to move here?

I watch as she slips a key from her purse and quickly disappears inside.

I count out the minutes waiting for her to reemerge. Five full minutes pass, but the door to the cabana stays closed.

Six minutes.

The sun bakes down.

I slide to the edge of my chaise and stare out over the pool. Where's Frankie Sky? Why isn't he here? Maybe his mother's been banned.

I let my eyes skim across the pool's blue surface. In the shallow end, a round white inner tube with red stripes bobs along like a giant peppermint, bumping against the sides. The water calls to me, calm and inviting. I wish I could just walk over to the deep end like Frankie Sky had done, reach up my arms, and dive in.

Simon slips past like a shadow, but I ignore it, willing him to go away. I used to know how to swim. One of these days I should force myself back in.

Out of the corner of my eye, I see Peter stand up and slither down from the lifeguard stand. It's 11:52. He walks across the deck to the back door of the club and goes inside. I glance toward the cabanas. Mrs. Merrill's door is still closed.

I stand up and walk nonchalantly toward it, stopping at the far end of the pool, as if I could hear anything from here. I don't want to look too suspicious, so I step closer to the edge of the pool and bend my knee just enough to dunk a toe in. The water sends a chill through my body.

I glance at the cabanas.

Nothing.

Which means my work here at the Hamlet Dunes Country Club pool is done.

I head back to my chair to gather my things to leave, but change my mind and walk decisively to the pool's edge and sit, knees bent to my chest. What do I have to rush home to?

I dunk one leg in, then the other.

Breathe.

I move my feet in small circles, making the water spin inward like liquid tornados. I could get caught in them, let them suck me under. One more chance to disappear.

I lean forward and sink my arms in, nearly up to my elbows. At least a third of me is technically in the water. I close my eyes and hold them there, letting the goose bumps prickle and the memories of my baby brother slip in.

▪▪▪ *eight* ▪▪▪

It's the beginning of summer, the middle of June. Mom calls a beach day, and we load all the stuff into the car.

Simon and I sing in the car. "The Wheels on the Bus," "Five Little Speckled Frogs," and "Bunny Foo Foo," which cracks him up.

Even though the air is bright and warm, when we reach the beach, the wind blows up hard and I shiver. Simon and I both have sweatshirts on. My hair whips my face, strands sticking to my lips and my eyelashes. The sand stings my ankles and calves. Simon runs ahead, nearly tripping in his not-yet-broken-in sandals.

"Let's stay back here for a bit," Mom says when we reach the soft, hot part of the sand. The ocean glistens before us.

We stop and shake the blanket out. Simon sits in the center to hold it in place, and I run back toward the dunes to collect the large rocks we use to keep the corners pinned down. By the time I get back, Simon has wandered off, desperate to get digging already.

"Simon, give me one minute, for Pete's sake!" Mom is exasperated because Simon always has the patience of a flea. She's rifling through her giant straw beach bag, the one with the colorful woven flowers. She retrieves suntan lotion, arm floaties, books, and the plastic container she prepared full of watermelon balls, cut strawberries, and green grapes, like a magician pulling scarves from a hat.

"But Fwankie and me are making sand castles!" Simon calls out. He stops a few feet away and waits for me to catch up.

"It's okay, I'll take him." I grab hold of his small, chubby hand and walk where he pulls me.

I'm good like this — always eager to help with Simon, to keep him from breaking into tears. He's a big fat baby, my brother, but I adore him. It took Simon so many years to get here, way longer than Mom wanted, so she calls him her "gift" when she talks to her friends about him.

"Watch him, Frankie!" Mom says. "I'll come when I get us set up over here."

"Okay!" I call back, but I don't need her help, which is good, because by the time Simon and I pick a spot to dig, she's lying next to Dad, face-planted, sleeping.

Simon and I park ourselves close enough to the water that, on his side, the ground is damp and easily packed, but far away enough that, across from him, my feet wiggle in hot dry sand.

I start the castle by dragging sand from the base up, pressing and patting with my hands. Simon works on carving out the moat. As we work, the sun gets stronger and the breeze from the water quiets down. I unzip my sweatshirt and toss it in the sand. Simon copies me, tossing his navy blue one with the green, rubbery iron-on of Kermit the Frog next to mine. The kid is obsessed with frogs.

"Don't need Kuhmit now, wight?" He pronounces *Kermit* and stuff weird like that because he still can't pronounce his *R*'s. Mom corrects him, but I secretly love how it sounds.

"Right," I say, and he gives me one of his giant, proud smiles.

We go back to piling and packing and digging. I've already got a pretty cool castle going, and Simon has a reasonable start to the moat, although on my side, where the sand is drier, the walls keep collapsing.

"We need some wetter sand, Pie Man," I say, because sometimes I call him Pie Man the way Dad calls me Beans. "If I put wet sand on it, it won't fall down so much."

I lean across and shovel some of the brown sugar sand from his side into my bucket, then drag it around to use at the base. Simon walks over and watches. I show him how to pack it tight with our hands to keep the castle walls from sliding down.

" 'Kay, I do it," he says, and copies me.

Soon the moat goes all the way around our castle. Simon sticks his arm in to measure, and it disappears up to his elbow. He smiles at me again, and I see a lightbulb go on in his eyes. He pulls his arm out and holds his pail to me.

"Want to fill it with water, Fwankie?"

"Sure," I say.

He takes my hand and we walk together to the water's edge. The waves crash up and freeze our ankles and shins. Simon shrieks and lets go and runs up the shore, but I like how the water feels on my feet, so cold that it nearly numbs my toes.

Simon comes back. We fill his pail and head up the beach, and he dumps the water into the moat. It fills momentarily, then bubbles back down into the sand.

"Hey!" He knits his brow, annoyed. "We need more now, Beans, see?"

I try to explain that the sand probably won't let it stay filled long because it has holes in it and the water will keep sinking away. But Simon doesn't believe me, or doesn't understand, so I keep going back for more with him.

After three more trips, and three more buckets of water that absorb quickly back into the sand, he finally seems to get it and agrees to give up on the plan. "It's okay without it. Really," I tell him. "We can just pretend."

We dig and build some more, but I'm getting hungry now. I glance over to the blanket where Mom and Dad are asleep on their stomachs, Mom's arm draped across Dad's back. I don't want to wake them, but my stomach's growling.

"Wanna get shells with me, Pie Man?"

"No." He grunts with effort, his arms buried down in the sand. "Finishing this moat."

"Okay, you want grapes? I'm going to go get some."

"Yes, gwapes, want some, Beans."

I walk backward for a while, watching him, making sure he stays put, head down, blond curls shining in the sun. Finally, I turn and walk toward my parents, stopping periodically to pick up shells that catch my eye.

My favorites are the reddish-pink ones that look like pleated fans, or the shimmery yellow or peach jingles, or the mini spiral whelks, when you can find them. Once I found a starfish, which was rare. But what I really want to find is a sand dollar, the flat white shells with the five-pointed star-flower made from teardrop holes.

Mom says that sand dollars are magic because the star stands for the Star of Bethlehem, the flower for the Easter Lily, and the five petals for God's fingerprints. If I find one, I'll give it to her as a present.

I kick at the sand because I know the best ones get buried, and I sing a song that Mom taught me, which pops into my head:

> *There's a lovely little legend*
> *That I would like to tell,*
> *Of the birth and death of Jesus*
> *Found in this lowly shell.*
>
> *On one side the Easter Lily,*
> *Its center is the star*
> *That appeared unto the shepherd*
> *And led them from afar.*

I can't come up with the rest of the verses, so I just sing those two, wishing I could remember my favorite part about the peaceful five white doves.

When I reach the blanket, I step over Mom's legs and grab the plastic container from her bag that holds the fruit we cut up this morning. She rolls over, looks up at me groggily, squinting in the sun, then rolls back, slinging her arm across Dad again. I quickly search her bag to see if there's anything else good hidden, a surprise she didn't tell us about earlier, like Goldfish or homemade cookies. When I don't find anything, I start back with the fruit toward Simon.

Except Simon isn't there.

He's not at our castle where I left him.

First, I think maybe I got turned in the wrong direction, so I look the other way down the beach, but that's not right, so I turn back, my eyes darting frantically toward the water.

Which is where he is, bending to scoop water with his pail.

"No, Simon!" I yell as he dodges a large wave that crashes along the shore.

Except, of course, he can't hear me. I stand frozen another second because I'm mad, but then I don't have time to be mad, because the next thing I know, another wave comes in, and Simon is down, and his body disappears under the water.

I break into a run, watching for the next wave to

cough him up, deliver him back onto land, but that one and the next one smash in empty-handed.

"Siiiimonnnn!"

I drop the fruit and dash into the surf as fast as I can. The coldness shocks me, but *there he is!* His small head pops up against the inky backdrop of another rising swell.

I fight the tug of the current, the vicious waves that trip me up and pull me flailing into the water after him.

His head surfaces again—thank God!—and I try to push toward it, but he disappears quickly under. I struggle and wait, getting my footing back before the next wave crashes in. I watch for his head to resurface so I know where to go, but it doesn't, he doesn't, and then there's nothing but roiling water.

• • •

I open my eyes and stare at the empty lifeguard stand where Peter Pintero still hasn't returned, and keep them open to stop the rest of the images from coming. It's the last part that's the most unbearable, the part I'd like to erase most. But then, as always, I close my eyes again and let it come, because I deserve it.

And there's really no stopping it, anyway.

• • •

I wait, blinking, wondering where to move forward, to swim, but I can't see Simon, and the waves fight me, knocking me back to shore.

Something clamps around my arm, my waist, dragging me away. I kick at it because I need to go get Simon. But it's my father who has me, and his voice is screaming, "Stop, Frankie, stop! Let me go!"

He's stronger than the water, and he pulls out of reach of the biggest waves and shoves me toward shore. Toward where my mother is collapsed in the surf.

I sit next to her, silent except for her sobs, and stare at the water that's taken my brother away.

It seems like forever that my father is out there, but I don't want him to come back, not until he's got Simon. But I do want him to come back, because all I can hear are my mother's wails, and I'm scared to be left alone with her.

Finally, Dad swims back empty-handed. Mom rushes toward him, throws her body into the water, pounds her fists against the waves. She's screaming, "No, no, no!" and for a split second, I think the water will envelop her and take her away from me, too.

But it doesn't have to. Trust me, she's already gone.

•　　•　　•

"Hey, Schnell, you deaf?"

I whip my head around. Peter Pintero's at the back door of the club, motioning wildly for me to come. Still, I point to myself in question.

"Yes, you, who else? I've been calling you for ten minutes!"

It's hard to resurface from the memories, but slowly everything comes back into focus. I walk toward Peter at the door. *Did he rat on me?*

Peter yells again. "Seriously, Schnell, I don't have all day! You're wanted inside, pronto!"

"I'm coming. I'm coming," I say.

I pass Mrs. Merrill's cabana, second-to-last, the end closest to the rear entrance of the club. Cabana #2. There's no sign of life in there. Either I missed her coming out or she's napping, or dead, inside.

When I reach Peter, I don't like the look on his face. Smug, like he's happy to see me get hanged. Then again, he's the one who let me in here. I could take him down, too, if I wanted.

"What's up?" I try not to sound guilty or scared.

"Search me. I don't ask questions. You're wanted inside, is all. Mr. Habberstaad's office. First door over there, left corner." He waves me through. I walk quickly, not looking back, trying to keep my mind from freaking.

"That's it," he calls when I stop at the dark wooden door, gold nameplate, black engraved letters: H. HABBERSTAAD. "Just knock. He asked for you. And good luck. Dude owns this place, you know."

■ *nine* ■

"Ah, young lady, come in. I'd like to have a word with you."

My knees shake, but I manage to propel myself forward to where Mr. Habberstaad sits behind a dark, ornate wooden desk. He's a big man, in his sixties maybe, balding, red-faced, jowly neck, bulbous chin. He points for me to sit down.

On his desk is a lunch tray—not an ugly, plastic, school cafeteria one, but a fancy, black, lacquered one with a silver dome that keeps stuff warm set off to the side. On the tray are a triple-decker sandwich (half eaten), a paper cone of French fries in a spiraled wire stand, and a glass of what looks like pink lemonade with a blue paper umbrella poking out the top. A second orange umbrella lies mangled in the corner of the tray.

He pulls the blue umbrella out of the lemonade and shakes it at me as he sips, then says, "I hate these damned things, don't you?"

I nod my head, even though I don't know if I mind them at all.

He narrows his eyes at me, and mine shift to the large picture window behind him that looks out over the pool area and cabanas. He must have seen me sitting there. My mind scrambles for information, specifically, whether I've ever learned the penalty for trespassing on private property. Will he call my parents or just the cops? Because, seriously, my parents are the far worse option. I cannot explain to my mother why I am here.

I race through my alibi—*Michelle Greenhut . . . stomachache . . . just waiting for my mother to come pick me up*—and start to stammer it, but Mr. Habberstaad waves a thick hand telling me to stop.

He takes a bite of sandwich, holds a finger up as he chews, and slides his desk drawer open. "You'll forgive me," he says, wiping his mouth with a napkin, "for doing this during my lunch. But I just happened to notice you there by the pool as it was being delivered." He sips at the pink liquid to wash the bite down. "So I sent the dashing Mr. Pintero out to fetch you. Anyway"—he pulls a small folded piece of stationery from the drawer—"you are Francesca Schnell, correct?"

"Yessir. I'm a friend of Michelle Greenhut's, and—" But he waves me off again, like he's totally uninterested in the details.

"No matter." He leans his heft across the desk with some effort and holds the paper out to me, nods. I take it but don't open it. "Mrs. Schyler asked me to inquire about you. She asked if I were to see you again, would I pass on this note, which I have done." He raises his brows as if waiting for me to say something, but then swivels his chair so that he's facing away from me, out the window. "You know this Mrs. Schyler I speak of?"

My brain tries to reverse and refocus now, because, yes, of course I know who he's talking about, but more importantly, it doesn't sound like I'm in trouble, let alone being arrested. My parents aren't being called. Mr. Habberstaad doesn't seem to care that I'm here at his club. He's merely summoned me because he was asked to by Mrs. Schyler.

"The mother of Frankie Sky, right?" He swings his chair back around, a confused look on his face, and I realize I've called him Frankie Sky. "I mean, Schyler." I add quickly, "The little boy who dived the other day." He knits his brow deeper, and it occurs to me that he doesn't actually know about that part. "What I mean is the little boy who comes here. With his mother. Mrs. Schyler. Yes, I do. I know who he is." I shut up and look down at the paper in my hands.

Mr. Habberstaad coughs a little, or maybe chokes on a bit of food. "Yes, that would be the very one. Excellent. Well, it appears that she, that Mrs. Schyler, is interested in hiring you to look after the child, which is a very good idea, indeed." He nods at the paper I hold, indicating I should open it. "A mother's-helper-type thing, is what she called it, I believe."

I unfold the note. At the top is printed in fancy script: *From the Desk of Brooke Schyler.*

"Lord knows," Mr. Habberstaad is saying, "we

would all benefit. The poor dear could use all the help she can get."

I nod to let him know that I'm listening, but all I keep thinking is that I'm the last person to ever help anyone, especially to be watching someone's kid. I should crumple the note and burn it so there's no temptation or hope, but instead, I let my eyes scroll down the rest of Mrs. Schyler's scrawled words. There's her telephone number and my name, like this: *Francesca or Frankie???* *Snail? Small? Snell?* And below that, it says, *Skinny girl. Pretty. Thirteen? Brown hair. Long. Don't think she's a club member. Thanks, Henry.*

I sigh, glad for the *pretty* part, but not so thrilled about the *thirteen.*

"I'm almost sixteen," I say to Mr. Habberstaad, but I doubt he cares much anyway.

"Well, according to Mrs. Schyler," he says, "the boy remembered you and liked you and asked for you by name. Apparently, he was fairly adamant." He chuckles at this. It's the first time I've seen him look friendly. "Anyway, do us all a favor and give the dear woman a call. Today, if you can. Before that child gets himself killed."

"Okay, sir, I will. And thank you." I stand to leave.

"Oh, Miss Schnell, one more thing."

My heart lurches. Is this the part where he calls my parents? "Yes?"

"Your family used to belong here, isn't that right?"

"Yessir?"

He's quiet for a moment. "I thought so. I thought I recognized the name. Well, good. Very good. Happy to see you here again. Go make that call, then, will you?"

"Yes. Thank you." I stand up and start to walk out before he can ask anything about my parents or why we're no longer members.

"Hold on a second." I freeze, waiting for the trouble part now, but he only slides open the drawer and retrieves another square of paper. "I almost forgot. I believe this is yours, too."

I take it, and he dismisses me with one more wave of his hand.

I'm relieved to be back out in the sunlight. As I return to the pool area, Peter Pintero watches me, a look on his face like he's dying to know the gory details about all the trouble I'm in. I shrug and proceed to my lounge chair. Let him wonder. He hasn't done me any favors.

I gather my things and head toward the back gate. Once outside, I sit on the curb and unfold the square of paper. As soon as I do, I get light-headed. I put my head on my knees and breathe to steady myself, then stare at the paper again.

Frankie play with me is written in wobbly print. But it's not the words that make me dizzy, it's what's under them.

A small green drawing of a frog.

ten

I sit on our stoop next to Simon's stone frog and clutch Frankie's crayon drawing in my hand.

Has something mystical conspired to lead me to Frankie Sky? Does it have something to do with my brother? Or is all of this nothing but coincidence?

I look across the street to Mrs. Merrill's. Was I meant to follow her to the club even if she has nothing to do with my dad? Because that's what I hope: that she has nothing to do with my father.

I mean, sure, I saw a car go by that looked like Dad's and a man who resembled him in her house. But I couldn't really see clearly, so there's a very good chance I was wrong. And, sure, he borrowed sugar from her even though there was plenty of sugar in the house. And, sure, I've seen her leave the house right after him when he just happened to be casually dressed. But there's been no sign of him at the club. In fact, as far as I can tell, my father has been nowhere near the Hamlet Dunes Country Club pool, or Mrs. Merrill's vacuum-vortex of a cabana.

So why do I keep being led there, if not for the boy named Frankie Sky?

I stare at the drawing again. It seems as if the little frog winks at me. But, no, that's just me going crazy. Or maybe the sunshine playing tricks. I fold the paper and put it in my pocket. Simon is dead. Simon is gone. Anything else is just tricks.

I try to think of something—anything but Simon, or questions with no answers—but only come up with more thoughts that drag me down. Like Lisette, who I barely see anymore, and Bradley Stephenson, who isn't my boyfriend and won't ever be kissing me or feeling me up under a pretty flower-carved cross. Or anywhere else, for that matter.

Which reminds me. I slip out my cell phone and send Lisette a text, trying to keep it casual before she truly worries I've actually gone out of my mind.

Hey, btw, did u ever ask B about reincarnation?

I wait a few minutes, but no response. I kiss my hand and pat the stone frog's head, letting my fingers linger on his rough, cool back, then I pull out the note with Mrs. Schyler's number and head inside to make the call. At least I'll have something to keep me busy this summer.

At first, I chicken out. Partly because I'm wondering if I should check with Mom before I call. But I can't bring myself to call her at the Drowning Foundation to tell her some stranger wants me to watch her little boy.

Besides, she's told me a hundred times to get a summer job. "We're not made of money, Francesca. It's not like it used to be."

As if she needs to tell me.

Still, I don't know this woman, Brooke Schyler, at all. Maybe I'll try Lisette one more time. But, of course, her voice mail answers.

"Hey, this is Lisette. Leave a message at the sound of the . . . *beeeeep.*"

Right.

"Hey, Zette, it's Beans. I left you a text. But, well, I had the weirdest day, so, well, and some other stuff. Anyway, just wanted to call and say hi and ask you something if you have a chance. So, call me back when you get this, okay?"

I stare at the note from Frankie Sky again—Frankie play with me—and before I can think better of it, quickly dial the number Mrs. Schyler gave me. The phone rings immediately, sending butterflies flitting wildly through my stomach. It rings five more times, but nobody answers, not even a machine.

I hang up, make a sandwich, and sit at the table. When I'm done, I call again.

It rings a few times, then a voice answers.

"Hello?"

"Frankie?"

"This is Frankie Sky. Who that?"

I smile. "This is Frankie, too. Francesca, Francesca Schnell, remember? From the pool?"

"Frankie Snell! Yes, I remember!" He giggles. "I dived for you, Frankie Snell!"

"You did. You need to be careful . . ." I stop because I can hear it, how much I sound like my mother. "First you need to learn to swim, I mean, that's all. Then you can dive in the water."

"I swimmed!" he says defiantly. "I swimmed and I dived!"

I can't help it and giggle, despite my nerves. "Okay, Frankie, you did. You dove and you swam. But maybe someone can help you work on your swimming a little."

"Frankie Snell come and teach me?"

Me, teach swimming? Now there's a cosmic joke if I ever heard one.

"Maybe not me, but I'll watch you, okay? Anyway, Frankie, is your mom there?"

"Yep, she here. She asleep." I glance at the clock. It's two in the afternoon.

"Asleep?"

"Yeah. On the couch."

"Is she sick?"

"I don't wake her," he says.

"Well good, don't wake her if she's sick."

"She not sick. She tired."

"Oh. Um, okay. Well, can you tell her I called?"

"When I'm done flying," he says.

"Okay, thanks." I start to hang up, then press the phone back to my ear. "Wait, Frankie, what? What did you say you are doing?"

"Frankie is flying," he says.

My stomach twists. I'm afraid to ask more, but I do. "Flying where? How are you flying, Frankie?"

"From my big tree in the backyard. Frankie can fly from there."

"No, Frankie, you hear me? You can't do that alone! Okay? Don't do that alone!" I'm too loud, frantic, like I'm yelling. He makes a whimpering sound on the other end. "Frankie, I'm not mad."

Quiet.

"Frankie?"

"Yep."

"I'm really not mad, I promise. I just don't want you to get hurt. And you can't practice flying alone. You need help for that kind of thing. Like diving. Those things need someone bigger to help. So, no climbing trees and no diving. Okay?"

"No flying," he says, "right?"

"Right," I say, relieved. "Okay, good."

"And no diving. And no climbing trees."

"Exactly! Perfect." I feel better, like maybe I've actually done something good. Because, seriously, where is this boy's mother? He seems constantly left on his own. I think of Mr. Habberstaad saying, *Do us all a favor . . . before that child gets himself killed.*

"Frankie, you still there?"

"Yep."

"Is your mom still sleeping?"

"Yep." I hear him moving, breathing on the other

end. Things rustling. Then he says, "Sometimes she sleeps very long."

"Really? Do you want me to come over?"

"Yep," he says, "want you to. Want Frankie Snell to come play."

I smile. "Okay, Frankie. I'll come over now. Do you know your address? Where you live?"

"Yep. Sycamore Street. Frankie Sky lives on Sycamore Street."

"Oh good! I know Sycamore. It's not too far from here."

"Nope. Not too far. Frankie Snell will come!"

I smile more. "What number, Frankie?"

"I lives at number two. Number two Sycamore Street, Hamlet Dunes, New York. Frankie Snell come here to play with me."

"Okay, I'm coming, Frankie. No flying till I get there, you promise?"

"No flying. I promise. No flying until you come."

Part II

▮▮ *eleven* ▮▮

As I'm about to knock on the Schylers' front door, it opens.

Frankie stands there in blue Batman underpants and a Superman T-shirt with a red towel wrapped around his shoulders like a cape. For a second I'm shaken because his face is more my brother's than I remember. But then he smiles and it makes me feel happy inside, as if a piece of Simon is right here in front of me.

I'm about to tell him he shouldn't open the door for strangers, but he says, "Is okay, Frankie, I seed you from the window." Then he pulls me in and quickly closes the door. Like he's afraid that, otherwise, I might leave.

Outside, the house is fancy and nice, like there's a crew of gardeners that landscape and take care of things, and inside, it's also nice, fancy-ish, but worn-down and messy, too, as if it's not been straightened in weeks. There's clothing everywhere, and towels and shoes. In laundry baskets. Strewn over the two large floral chairs and glossy banisters. All over the thickly carpeted floor. Not to mention toys and piles of magazines and such. *People. Entertainment Weekly.* And *Martha Stewart Living.*

Frankie pulls me to a couch across which Mrs. Schyler is sprawled, facedown, in a pair of very short jean shorts and a red polka dot halter top. One arm dangles off the side, a big, glittery ring sparkling from a finger. Her purse and the strappy red high-heeled shoes she had on the day I met her are next to the couch, as if she'd just come in—or was about to go out—when she realized she was too tired to make another move.

Frankie watches me study her. "See? I told you she was sleeping."

"You did." I pat his head and walk cautiously toward the sofa, but am stopped by a toy-sized Tonka-truck of a dog, black and white with pointy ears, that barrels at me from nowhere at full speed, yipping ferociously.

"No, Potato! Shhhhh! Stop! Dumb! I thoughted you were outside!" Frankie dives, nearly crushing the dog, losing his cape-towel in the process. The poor little thing lies captured, but wags his tail. Frankie scoops him up and stands with effort, the dog cradled awkwardly in his arms. "This is Potato," he says. "Go ahead and pet him. He won't bite you, really."

I scratch the dog between his ears, which he seems to like. "Potato's a good name. Did you pick it?" I ask quietly, even though noise clearly isn't waking Mrs. Schyler.

Frankie nods, squeezes the dog up to his face, and blows on its belly, making a raspberry sound. The animal yelps now and twists free, dropping to the floor and scampering up onto the couch where Mrs. Schyler

sleeps. He circles about ten times before settling between her legs. She stirs a little, but just barely. In front
of her on the coffee table I notice an empty wine bottle and half-filled (or half-empty) glass of pale yellow
liquid.

"Yep," Frankie says, tugging at me, "I said I did
named him with the really good name of Potato."

"It is good, Frankie," I say, laughing.

The dog puts his head down and closes his eyes.
Mrs. Schyler doesn't stir any further. Within seconds,
their breaths move in unison, a light snore coming from
either Mrs. Schyler or the dog.

"Well, they are both asleeped now," Frankie says.

He takes my hand and starts to pull me through the
room, past a baby grand piano and a long ornate end
table with carvings of cranes, or maybe herons. The
table is covered with framed photographs. I stop to look
at them.

In the largest photo, a handsome man in an army
uniform with lots of medals pinned to it holds a tiny,
blanket-wrapped baby I assume is Frankie. In another,
the same man in the same uniform, only fancier now
with a white cap and gloves, stands next to Mrs. Schyler
in a wedding gown. She looks happy and perfect, like
she belongs on the cover of a magazine.

"That is my daddy," Frankie says, "but he isn't here
anymore."

"No?" I put my hand on his head full of blond curls.
"What happened to him, Frankie?"

"He gotted killed in his truck in Iraq."

"Oh, that's so sad. I'm sorry."

"Is okay," he says. "He still loves me, but I don't get to seed him anymore."

"I get it, Frankie. I do." I kneel in front of him. "I have a brother who died, too. Now I don't get to see him, either."

He puts his hands on my cheeks and looks into my eyes. "Yeah, I knowed that already," he says. "Now can we go outside and fly?"

As he zooms through the kitchen, I feel light-headed. I need to ask what he meant, but he's moving too fast to answer my questions anyway.

"Frankie," I try as he slips out the back door that leads to a large deck with a sprawling backyard below, "what do you mean you know about Simon?"

"Who?" But then he whirls away and shouts, "Hey! Not again, Tato!" because the dog has rushed out through the closing screen door and darts between Frankie's legs, nearly knocking him to the ground.

"But you said—"

"I said stop, Potato! You stop!" And that's utterly hopeless, too, because the dog is already down the stairs and tearing across the grass like a maniac, Frankie racing behind him.

I stare, my brain trying to puzzle the pieces together. How could Frankie know about Simon? Nobody would tell a toddler a sad thing like that. Probably I'm just reading into things, so I try to shrug it off as I chase down the stairs after them.

The Schylers' yard is seriously huge. A rolling green hillside ends in a flat open stretch big enough to be a small baseball field. To one tree-lined side is a huge wooden jungle gym with bridges, a swing set, two slides, and a fort at the top with a blue and yellow canvas roof. Opposite that is a rose garden with trellises and pathways and a big pond with a waterfall rushing down. The kid could hurt himself any number of places here.

"There are big fat fishes inside that pond!" Frankie points out when I catch up, then takes my hand and pulls me right back up the hillside with him.

Here, at the top, a tire swing hangs from a giant old tree. Parked next to that is a kid-sized ride-on electric tractor, still with its key in the ignition. More injuries waiting to happen.

"Wow, you've got a lot of cool big-boy things here," I say, thinking of Mr. Habberstaad's words again.

"Yep." He lets go of my hand and races down the hillside, then back up, Potato charging after him, nearly tripping him with every step. At the top, panting, he climbs up on the tire swing and yells, "Push me, Frankie Snell!" and I do, Potato barking and jumping beneath him.

When he slows down a bit, I kick off my flip-flops, letting my toes sink into the cool, soft grass, and grab hold of two ropes of the swing. I walk backward, pulling it in a widening arc, then after several go-rounds let go. It swings out in dizzying circles over the hillside. Frankie squeals with delight, so when it slows, I do it again, letting it fly out in wider and wider rings. When I run out of steam and it finally slows to a near-halt, Frankie stands up and, using the ropes, pulls himself toward the branch above his head.

"Frankie, don't do that," I say.

"Is good," he says. "I does it all the time."

He works hard, straddling, pulling, twisting, and grunting, until he's hauled himself onto the branch, then stands on it, using the one above it for support. He looks down at me through the branches like Tarzan, a goofy, satisfied grin on his face.

"Seriously, Frankie, you're freaking me out. Get down."

"Is okay, really," he says. "I always do this up here."

"Really? You're like a monkey, you know that? So, how old are you, anyway?"

"Four. I just turned four the other week." My pulse quickens. Simon died in mid-June, right after his own fourth birthday. Which means Frankie is the same age as Simon was. "That is big, right?" he's asking. "Four is a really big age?"

I look at him peering down at me and try to keep my mind steady, instead of flitting to crazy places. "Yes, four is very big. But not big enough to fly, Frankie. You need to come down now. Please." I twist toward the house, to the Schyler's back door. "Hey, who takes care of you here, anyway? When your mom isn't feeling well, I mean?"

"She is feeling well," he says. "She is just sleepy and tired."

"Okay, who takes care of you when she's sleeping?"

"Frankie Snell does," he says, and smiles. I can't help it, I smile back at him. "And Grandpa Harris, too. Grandpa Harris takes care of me."

"Oh yeah? Does your grandpa live near here?"

He shrugs. "He comes to play with me, but lots of times he has work to do. And he buys me lots of toys. He buyed me my yellow tractor."

My eyes go to the tractor parked next to the tree. Those ride-on things are expensive. I wonder what else Frankie's grandpa paid for around here, especially since Mrs. Schyler doesn't seem to have much of a job.

"What about your grandma?" I ask.

"Don't gotted one of those."

"Oh, I'm sorry."

"Is okay. I don't need a grandma because I love Grandpa Harris lots and lots, even if he can't fix me, either." He lifts his feet so that he's hanging by only his hands.

"Frankie, do not do that!" I yell, my heart banging so frantically it hurts. He laughs but puts his feet down.

"Frankie is ready to fly now, Frankie Snell. You said you will teach me."

"Wait. Seriously, Frankie. I meant we would play. You can play-fly. You can't really fly, only pretend. You need to get down now. And, anyway, fix you from what?"

But he doesn't answer because he's let go of the branch, and his body is now hurtling through the air.

I stand helplessly transfixed as he sails, arms outstretched like a bird.

He stays airborne longer than I expect, and for one split second I have the ridiculous thought that maybe he can actually fly. But then he crashes to the ground and goes rolling down the hillside, finally stopping in a fetal position near the bottom.

"Frankie!" Potato and I chase after him, the dog's stubby tail wagging as if he thinks it's a game. When he reaches Frankie, he jumps on him, but Frankie doesn't move. Potato backs off, pawing gently at him, whimpering. Terror seizes my chest. How could I come here and let this happen? Potato nudges him with his nose, tail down, then looks at me as if to say, *I think you'd better do something.*

I kneel down next to him. His eyes are open. He makes them bigger and lets out a laugh. "Ow, that hurted," he says, trying to sit up, but Potato pounces on him, knocks him down again. "Stop it, Potato! Stop. It! Did you see how far I flied, Frankie Snell? Not pretend! Real! I flied really, really far!"

Despite myself, I laugh. Potato starts licking me now. Frankie, then me, then Frankie again.

"Ew, quit it, Potato. No licking!" Frankie shoves the dog away and stands, leaning into me for protection. He bends his arm up for inspection, and I can see now that his elbow is bleeding. Other than that, he looks like he's okay.

"Frankie, seriously, you scared me. It's not funny. You can't do stuff like that anymore. You could've gotten seriously hurt."

"Is funny, and Frankie Sky never gets hurt." He inspects the scrape some more and blows on it.

"Well, what's that, then?" I say. "You're bleeding. That seems kind of hurt to me. And it could have been worse. I'm not kidding." My voice is shaking now, the humor lost as the whole day catches up to me. I'm in way over my head. "You can't just dive into pools and fly out of trees like you're Superman. Do you understand? Not if you want me to come play with you. I mean it, Frankie. I'm serious. Okay?"

He looks at me, his lower lip quivering. "Okay," he says. "I want you to. I want you to stay and play. But you said you would teach me to fly."

"I know, Frankie, I know. I told you I'd help. But I meant from . . ." I turn and search around the yard. "Like, from the slide. Not from a freaking tree. That's too high up. And you can't really fly." I sound mad, and his eyes fill with tears, his whole mouth collapsing in a frown. I feel bad that I'm making him sad, but I'm not about to have him killed on my watch. "Besides," I say, trying to soften things, "I wasn't ready yet. You needed to give me a warning." I take his hand and start toward the house. "I'm glad you're okay, but you can't do that anymore. Come on now. We'll go inside and wash that off and find you a Band-Aid."

He's quiet as we trudge up the hillside, and I'm grateful for it. The kid is unnerving me. Maybe I should just go home. Maybe I bit off more than I can chew.

"Okay," he finally says when we've reached the steps

to the deck. "But I did told you. I said I was ready to fly, and I *can* fly, because Grandpa Harris tolded me so. He says Frankie Sky is an angel, so I don't need to worry about my boo-boo or dying or anything. And angels can fly, because angels always fly, so, see?"

I turn and stare at him. I have no idea anymore what he's talking about. "What boo-boo, Frankie? And why would you worry about . . . ?" But I stop. Because we've reached the back door, and when I open it, Mrs. Schyler is standing right in front of me in the kitchen.

At the sink, upright, washing dishes.

As if she's been there all along.

▖▘ *twelve* ▝▖

"Hello," she says, like it's no big surprise to see me. Still, I'm panicked wondering if she was watching, if she saw Frankie plummet from the tree. If she did, she doesn't let on. She's not concerned. She doesn't even turn to look at me.

She wears yellow rubber gloves in her short shorts and halter top and scrubs at a pan, normal as daylight, as if she weren't just comatose a mere half hour ago.

"Hello," I say. "I hope it's okay that I came here."

She turns and smiles now. Her face is so pretty with her blond curls pressed back in a headband. She looks younger than I remembered.

"It's Francesca, right?" she says. Even though she's smiling, I get butterflies. I've never just shown up in someone's house without permission before.

"Yes. I called, but then Frankie answered and . . ." I stop. What am I going to say? *But then Frankie answered and you were drunk and he told me he was trying to fly? So I came here to stop him, so he didn't break his neck while you were sleeping?* Besides, I was barely successful in thwarting that disaster, so what was the point, anyway? "Oh, and he kind of hurt his arm a little, I think." I nod at Frankie to show her, and he holds his elbow up. "He fell from the tree," I whisper.

She laughs a little, shuts off the faucet, pulls off a glove, and ruffles his hair. "Of course he did," she says.

"I flied, not fell," Frankie says. He twists his arm and inspects it. The bleeding has stopped. It's really not a bad scrape at all. "I barely gotted hurt," he adds.

"Right. What else is new?" Mrs. Schyler takes my arm and guides me toward the table. "Come, sit, sweetheart," she says. "I'm thrilled you came. Would you like anything? A grilled cheese? Some lemonade? You're a skinny thing, you know. Pretty like a flower. But skinny like a reed."

"No, thank you. I ate before I got here." I blush. No one has ever compared me to a flower before.

The table is the kind with a built-in bench on one side and chairs on the other. Frankie slides in on the bench side in front of the window, and I sit opposite him in a chair. Mrs. Schyler slips in next to Frankie, and Potato darts under the table and lies down by Frankie's feet. Mrs. Schyler touches Frankie's cheek, says, "Oops, I forgot a Band-Aid," and slips back out again. She disappears, returning a minute later with a Band-Aid with a Teenage Mutant Ninja Turtle on it.

"Don't like the turtle ones," Frankie says.

"I know," Mrs. Schyler sighs. "But I couldn't find a frog one, I told you that. It's only a Band-Aid. Just wear it."

"But the frogs make me better faster, right, Frankie?"

Mrs. Schyler looks at him, then me, bewildered.

"Francesca is my real name," I clarify, trying not to obsess on Frankie's frog thing, "but most people call me Frankie. It's a nickname for Francesca."

"Well, of course, I remember that now, but it's a bit confusing, isn't it? Would you mind if I stick with Francesca?"

"No, sure, that's fine."

"But Frankie is good because it's Frankie and Frankie!" Frankie says.

Mrs. Schyler laughs. "Well, then, welcome aboard, Frankie-Francesca. I assume this means you've taken me up on my offer. I'm sure a lovely girl like you is busy-busy in the summer, but . . . How old are you again?" She presses the turtle Band-Aid to Frankie's elbow, then looks at me, waiting for me to answer. Frankie immediately pulls the Band-Aid off. He frowns at it and sticks it under the table. I have to fight not to smile.

"Fifteen," I say, keeping my eyes glued to Mrs. Schyler. "Almost sixteen. I turn sixteen the first week of September."

"Well, of course you do, because almost-sixteen is the most perfect age for a girl. I almost remember it myself." She laughs again, but this time in a sad way. "Anyway, I'd like to have you as much as humanly possible. A mother's helper kind of a thing, you know? Have you done this before?" I open my mouth to answer, but she's not waiting for one. "It's been a rough time around here, and Frankie's grandpa has been bugging me to do this for ages. As you've seen, Frankie isn't the easiest child, and, well, I'm afraid I'm a bit permissive. It's very hard ... Anyway, he's a good boy, and it seemed like fate when he asked for you, so I figured I couldn't go wrong." She turns to Frankie. "You asked specifically for Francesca, didn't you, my little angel?"

Frankie nods, but he's busy tapping on Potato with his foot, somewhat un-angel-like. I push away the thoughts about fate that are trying to worm their way into my brain.

Mrs. Schyler continues, oblivious. "So, as you've seen, he can be a bit of a handful. I'm not going to lie. Will ten dollars an hour do?"

My resolve to leave and never return melts like a Popsicle on a hot summer day. Because, seriously? Ten dollars an hour is good money.

"Yes, ma'am," I say. "Sure, that'd be great."

Mrs. Schyler chuckles. "Goodness, Francesca, that *ma'am* makes me sound like I'm a hundred years old. I may be battered and broken, but I hope I'm not that old."

"No, no, not at all; you're beautiful," I stammer, but she holds up a hand.

"No worries. How about you just call me Brooke. Would that be all right?" I nod. "And I assume Frankie has shown you around." She pauses and turns to him. "Hey, now that I think of it, there may be some Kermit Band-Aids in the bathroom drawer. How about you go and check there? Do that for me, would you?"

Frankie pads off down the hall with Potato, and Mrs. Schyler pulls out the chair next to me and sits.

"I take it Frankie told you that there is no Mr. Schyler?" A flash of terrible sadness crosses her face, just for a moment, before she forces a smile again.

"Yes. He told me. I'm so, so sorry about that."

"Nothing for you to be sorry about. At any rate, that's pretty much all you need to know, at least for now." She thinks for a moment and laughs. "Well, there's plenty of other stuff you should probably know, but we can save that for another time. Is there anything we need to know about you?"

I freeze. How do I answer that? *Well, nothing except that I was responsible for my own brother's death. He drowned while I was supposed to be watching him. Like you're asking me to do with Frankie Sky.* I should get up and leave right now and never come back here again. What made me think I could be responsible for somebody's little boy?

Mrs. Schyler places her hand on my arm. "Children aren't responsible for themselves, Francesca, let alone anyone else. You know that already, don't you? For Pete's sake, eleven-year-olds are barely big enough to tie their own shoes. Now, almost sixteen, that's a different story. Almost-sixteen is a very responsible age. In any event, my Frankie likes you and trusts you, and that's all that matters to me."

My breath catches. Because it's clear that she's talking specifically about me and my brother. But how does she seem to have the details of what happened, because nobody knows about *that*? Well, except Lisette. I'd told her the ugly truth.

Sure, plenty of people know about Simon's death. It was plastered all over the local papers at the time. And, of course, there's Mom's morbid Foundation, so it's not like people don't know that my baby brother drowned. But one thing my parents had done, and had done well, was protect me from the world knowing that I was the one responsible. In that one way my mother had looked out for me and spared me the public shame.

She may hate me, but she doesn't want other people to.

I know I look surprised, but Mrs. Schyler doesn't offer any explanation. She just squeezes my arm as Frankie returns waving a new Band-Aid.

"Is Big Bird only, not Kermit," he says, ripping the wrapper off.

"Well, that's too bad. But we like Big Bird all right, yes?" Mrs. Schyler presses the new Band-Aid on, then walks back to the sink. She pulls the rubber gloves on and runs the water, as if to make it clear that this part of the conversation has been settled.

"No sense in keeping you anymore today," she says. "I've got a second wind and plenty to do around here. And Frankie can help me, won't you, Frankie?" She pulls a plastic step stool out from under the cabinet. "How about we start you officially on Monday, Francesca?

Is nine until three, Mondays, Wednesdays, and Fridays okay? At least to start. We'll see how it goes from there."

"Yes, sure," I say, standing. I nearly trip over Potato, who now blankets one of my feet. He rolls onto his back, tail wagging, his dog lips sliding back into a definite doggish smile.

thirteen

On the way home, I get a text from Lisette.

> Bradley says he totally believes in
> reincarnation. Don't tell my dad. :\ He says
> look up transmigration. Not typing more
> here. That's between u guys. (Ok, fine, he
> explained it & I still don't understand. ;P If u
> want more info he said call him.) p.s. WHY r u
> asking again?!

By the time I reach our house, my heart's pounding, though I'm not sure it's at the thought of calling Bradley (which I will obviously never ever bring myself to do) or at his thinking that reincarnation exists.

I kiss Simon's frog and run inside. Mom and Dad still aren't home, which is good, but they probably will be soon.

In Dad's study, I drag out the huge beige *Random House Dictionary of the English Language* that looks like it dates back to the Dark Ages. I turn bricks of pages from *B* to *G* to *L* to *R*, until I reach *S*, then *T*, then *TH*, and finally *TR*. The pages are thin, so it's hard to turn them without ripping, but, finally, there it is. Under *transmethylation* and *transmigrant*.

trans·mi·grate
(trans mi'grat, tranz -) *v.*, -grated, -grating
-v.i. **1.** to move or pass from one place to another
in order to settle there. **2.** to migrate from one
country to another. **3.** (of the soul) to be reborn
at death in another body; metempsychosis.

To be reborn at death in another body.

I push the book away, lie back on the floor, and stare
up at the faraway ceiling, my mind, for the millionth time
in just a few days, turned to a frenzied mush of questions. Simon died four years ago, right around the time
that Frankie was born. And Frankie looks like Simon.
I mean, his eyes and his hair match my little brother's
exactly. Not to mention they were both obsessed with
frogs. And Frankie said he *knew* that Simon had died.
How would *he* know that? Surely his mother wouldn't
have told him?

Could it really just be a coincidence that I found
myself at the Hamlet Dunes Country Club on the day of
Frankie's dive? Or was it some sort of weird kismet at
work that Mrs. Merrill lured me there? I mean, not that
she lured me, exactly.

Still, it wasn't like me to sneak into places I
didn't belong or tail people I didn't know. In fact, it
was the opposite of me. I was the hider, the fader, the

disappearer-into-the-woodwork. I was not the trespasser-into-places-I-don't-belong. Maybe whatever I thought was going on with my father was only intended to lead me to Frankie Sky.

The front door opens. Dad. I can tell from the heavy footsteps that it's him. Better him than my mother, but still. I sit up, close the dictionary, and heave it back up onto its shelf.

"Frankie? You home?"

"In here!" I jump up and fling myself into his desk chair and try to look casual. Dad stops in the doorway and gives me a quizzical look. He pales a little, and his eyes dart to his computer. *What is he worried I've seen?* Lucky for him, it's turned off.

He quickly smiles and says, "Whatcha doin' in here?" But it's too late to cover. I saw the guilty look on his face.

He walks over, stands behind me, and kisses the top of my head.

"Beans?"

"Yeah?"

"What are you doing in here? Did you need my help with something?" His voice stays cheerful, but edgy.

I stand up and pull Mrs. Schyler's note from my pocket, checking to make sure it's hers and not the one from Frankie Sky. I unfold it and hold it out to him.

"I got a mother's helper job today." It's not exactly an answer to his question, but no way I'm offering more information, or trying to explain that I think Simon's soul may have transmigrated into Frankie Sky. If I did, he would only give me that look, the one that says we all need to keep healing and moving on. The one he gives Mom when he's worried she's so fragile she'll collapse or shatter into a million broken pieces.

"You did?"

"Did what?"

"Get a job." He laughs. "You just said you got a job." He wraps his strong arm around my shoulders and squeezes. "You seem a little distracted there, kid."

He should talk. He's the one acting all weird lately.

"Oh. Right. Yeah. I did. For a woman named Mrs. Schyler. She hired me to watch her son, Frankie Sky. They live on Sycamore Street, so I can walk or bike there, no problem. I met her through Lisette," I add quickly, hoping to avoid questions I can't answer about what I was doing at the club.

"Frankie *Sky*? Are you sure that's a real name?"

"Oh, ha, yeah. Well, no. It's Schyler, really, but the kid says Sky. He's four. Schyler is hard for him, so he shortens it to Sky."

Simon is like the sky . . . But I force the thought away. I'm not dumb. I'm leaving out the lunatic details.

"Ah, cute." Dad nudges me out of his space and sits at his desk. "Okay, I've got to catch up on some work. Let me have some peace here." He turns his computer on, and, after a few seconds, his fingers start to move around the keyboard hunt-and-peck style. I stand at the front of his desk and watch him, but I can't read much from his face.

"Okay then." I back away, my eyes returning to the bookshelf where I left the dictionary sticking out at an odd angle. *Transmigrate. To be reborn at death in another body.* I close my eyes, feeling overwhelmed by all the hard questions. About Simon. About Frankie. About Dad.

I could go upstairs and call Bradley and talk to him about it. I bet he'd understand. And, oh, how I want to, but I'd have to ask Lisette for his number, and even though she told me to call him, I'd feel wrong about it. As if I'd ever have the courage to call.

But he said that I should. Okay, maybe not *should*, but *could*.

What if he *wants* me to call?

At the door I stop again and watch my father, and it hits me. I need to quit acting stupid, just like I need *him* to stop acting stupid. I need to stop thinking about Bradley and things I shouldn't want. Maybe he will, too, and then things can go back to normal.

"You know, we have sugar," I blurt.

"What?" His eyes dart up, annoyed, as if he doesn't know what I'm talking about. But I saw him flinch. I'm sure I saw him flinch.

"Sugar," I say, standing my ground. "You said you were borrowing some. But we have plenty. A whole box, actually, in the cereal cabinet."

He raises his eyebrows. I can't tell exactly what the look means, but I'm guessing it means I shouldn't keep pressing things.

"Huh. My bad, then," he says, nodding me out of his room. "I thought I looked, but I guess I didn't look too well. I'm on overload these days." He goes back to staring at whatever is on his computer.

I wait another second or two for him to change his mind and come clean to me, to promise me he won't do anything to hurt me or Mom or our family. But he just keeps looking at the screen.

◾▪ *fourteen* ▪◾

Saturday.

All morning long, snaps and bottle caps pop like gunshots, making me jump in my skin. Or maybe I'm just jumpy anyway.

I call Lisette early, hoping I might still have a fighting chance for her attention.

"Hey, Zette, wanna go to the beach with me?" I say when she answers. There's dead silence on the other end.

I don't blame her. My question surprises me, too.

I don't know what possesses me. I'm feeling a bit reckless, maybe. Lisette and I both know I haven't been to the ocean since Simon died. I never wanted to go back, and Lisette was good enough not to push me. Despite her own sun-worshipper status, she's always worked around me, choosing her beach days when I wasn't available.

But for some reason, the urge has come over me. I laugh self-consciously and wait for her answer, which is understandably limited.

"Um, Beans?"

"Yeah?"

"Nothing. It's just that . . ."

"What? It's nice out." I know I sound defensive, so I brighten my tone. "It just seems like a good day for the beach."

"Yeah, sure, okay, but . . . are you sure?"

"Yes, Zette, sure." I walk over and glance at myself in my closet mirror. "Well, pretty sure that I'm sure."

She laughs a little. "Ohh-kay then."

She waits, giving me time to change my mind, or maybe waiting for me to explain. But I can't explain why the urge has come over me. "What time?" I say, plowing forward.

"Noon?"

"Perfect. No plans with Bradley, then?" I quickly regret it. I'm not trying to make her feel bad, plus I know it just sounds like I'm jealous.

"No. He's away for the weekend with his family. At his cousins' at some lake. He says they always go there for the Fourth of July."

"Oh, bummer. Well, sucks for you, but works for me." I mean it, too. I miss Lisette, although part of me was maybe hoping that I'd get to see Bradley, too. Of course, the other part was terrified that I would. Anyway, except for the noise, I'd forgotten all about the holiday weekend. Or, at least the point. It's not like my family ever celebrates anymore. "I'm really glad you're around, Zette," I say, pulling my focus back to our sudden plans. "Do you think Alex can give us a ride?"

"Yeah. I think he was actually planning to go anyway, with a friend."

"Okay, cool. Call me back if he can't. Otherwise, see you here at noon."

"Okay," Lisette says, then there's silence again. Finally, "Beans, does your mother know?"

"I'm allowed to go to the beach, Lisette."

"I know you are, but, well, are you?" And, she's right. I'm sure that I'm actually not. Which is to say, my mother would go ballistic. Or weepy. Or weepy and ballistic, both.

"No. Probably not. I'll tell her we're going to the mall."

•　•　•

Downstairs, my mother and father are sitting at the kitchen table reading the paper, Dad with coffee and a bagel, Mom with her same old cup of tea.

"I'm going to the mall with Lisette. Alex will take us," I say.

Mom nods, but Dad looks up, concern on his face. "Is everything okay, Beans?"

"Yes, sure." I stare out the window, across to Mrs. Merrill's house. "How about with you?"

He raises an eyebrow at me, his eyes darting to Mom. He's right; I'm being a wise-ass. "Sure, with me. Beautiful Saturday out and I'm sitting here drinking coffee with your mom. What could be better? You going soon?"

"Yeah, noon."

"Well, keep in touch. I may make a pit stop into

the office for a bit this morning, some unfinished business with a closing. Been crazy at work, which is a good thing. But if I'm not here, your mother will be. So text if you're going to be late."

"I will," I say, my eyes laser-beamed to Mrs. Merrill's empty driveway. I don't say the other stuff I want to, about it being a Saturday and not a work day and all.

• • •

At noon, as promised, I hear Alex honking out front. I should feel worse for the lie, but I don't. We all seem to be lying around here. Plus, I'm happy to get out of the house, to get my mind off of things.

I take one last look in my mirror. *I need to do this. What kind of teenager doesn't go to the beach?* I make sure my bathing suit doesn't show under my clothes, then dash downstairs before Mom tries to talk to Lisette. I know Zette will cover for me, but I don't need her getting grilled by my mother. Not to mention, who knows what she might be wearing.

"I'm leaving. I'll check in later," I call, and pull the door quickly closed behind me.

Mr. Sutter's prized 1995 Chrysler LeBaron GTC convertible idles at the curb in the sunshine, Alex in the driver's seat, top down, summer music blaring from the stereo. A college friend is next to him, and Lisette is in the backseat. She's dressed in a bikini top, like we're going to the beach.

I stand frozen on our stoop.

I told her I'd go to the beach.

Lisette waves, and Alex hits the horn again for good measure. "Come on, Frankie, put a move on!" So there's nothing to do but walk forward.

"Hey, Frankie!"

I reach the car. Lisette wears cut-off shorts and a bikini top, no T-shirt. Her chest barely fits in the cups. Either she got bigger or it shrunk. Good thing my mother didn't see her. She must register my concern, because she slouches down low in the car.

"Hey," I say, standing there. I don't make any move to get in.

"Dude." Alex punches his friend in the arm. The guy realizes, opens the door, and jumps out to let me in. He's tan, tall, blond. A total surfer look. I'd bet anything he's from California.

I slide silently in next to Lisette, slip off my flip-flops, and slouch down like she is, feet up. Her toenails are a perfect watermelon red. Mine are pale pink. I wish I'd picked a braver color.

Alex says, "All set back there?" and takes off without waiting for an answer.

And just like that, after four dry years, I am headed to the beach and the ocean.

•　•　•

As we weave our way through town and eventually onto the expressway, I relax a little. Alex blasts the radio and sings at the top of his lungs, some old song from the seventies: *"Ooh, my little pretty one, my pretty one, when you gonna give me some time, Sharona? Ooh, you make my motor run, my motor run, Gun it coming off of the line, Sharona . . ."* Soon Lisette joins in, and the surfer dude drums on the dashboard, and the noise and the music and the wind are all so happy and loud and crazy that they finally start to drown out my nerves.

I put my head back and close my eyes as we fly down the highway. It feels overwhelming, but in a good way, to be here like this with Lisette. In this car full of friends, barefooted, with the top down and the music blaring, our bodies drenched in sunshine, the wind whipping our hair in our faces. I can't remember the last time I felt so weightless and carefree.

Then Alex signals and shifts to the right lane and eases our way off the exit ramp.

The smell of salt air fills my nose.

My breath grows rapid and shallow. A wave of nausea blankets me.

I can feel the blood drain from my face.

"You okay, Beans?" Lisette whispers. She looks at me with concern, as if to say, *What were you thinking?*

I don't know, Zette. I don't know what I was thinking.

She reaches out and squeezes my hand as the car crawls across the small bridge that traverses the inlet and leads to the beach where my baby brother died.

I try to focus on the music, the sunshine, the breeze, but everything's grown quieter and heavy. Alex takes a ticket from the toll machine, and the gate lifts.

The lot is crowded. Alex drives in and out of rows looking for spots. He finally finds one and maneuvers the car in. He puts the hardtop up.

Everything moves in slow motion.

I slip my flip-flops on, a huge lump caught somewhere in my throat. I fidget with my bathing suit straps and try not to cry. Lisette watches me, worried. Alex's friend opens his door, oblivious, steps out, leaving it gaping wide open for me.

Lisette squeezes me again. "You okay, Beans?" I nod. "We don't have to go if you don't want to."

"I'm okay," I say, but I have no idea if it's true.

Alex and his friend—Jared, he called him Jared— unload the trunk of towels, a small cooler, skimboards, then head for the dunes, lugging it all with them.

I step out, close the door, and lean up against the warm metal, let it support me. Lisette gets out the other side, closes her door. Watches me. The day is blazing hot. Heat rises from the pavement in lot B.

Is that where we parked that day?

Lisette stands next to me, quiet, not forcing. Waiting to see what I'll do.

I lift my eyes, stare at the dunes, at the steps that cross over them, and begin to propel myself forward.

● ● ●

"We go to the water, Beans!" Simon grasps my fingers. He keeps tripping in his new sandals. I practically drag him up the steps, keeping him from the grasses and weeds that poke through the sides because I know there's poison ivy there.

"Slow down, Pie Man! We've got to wait for Mom and Dad."

"No waiting, Beans! We makin' a castle. You said so!"

"The beach isn't going anywhere, Simon. If we don't wait up, Mom will get mad and yell. Do you want her to yell at us, Simon?"

But he doesn't listen. He just keeps running, tugging me impatiently with him.

• • •

"Beans, you okay?"

I blink and look up. I've stopped at the top of the wooden stairs that will take us over the dunes to the water. Lisette stands in front of me, eyebrows raised.

"Yeah, sure."

"Because I can just tell Alex . . . I can tell him you need to go home."

"No. Just walk."

I stare at my feet and think of this photograph I once saw of grains of sand magnified under a microscope, each grain its own tiny but perfect full-blown shell. I try to picture this now, how, under my feet, a whole miniature world exists — pink coral shaped like antlers, translucent raindrop hearts, amber spirals, each grain a complete miracle, too small for the naked eye to see.

"How about here, Beans?" I lift my eyes to where Lisette stands, watching me.

I've made it to the beach. She holds the blanket out.

The ocean that claimed my brother is only a few measly yards away.

• • •

"Hello? Anyone here?" More soft knocking, then the doorbell rings.

I stand on tippy toes. I can see the policeman through the small peephole, the deep, official blue of his uniform.

The door is closed, which is why he rings, and why I only see him through the peephole.

For days, the door was open, people flooding in and out, carrying foil-covered platters like worker ants. Lasagna, casseroles, cellophaned trays of sprinkle cookies shaped like half-moons with coagulated red jam inside.

Then it got quiet again, and Mom went back to her bedroom, groggy on some sort of medicine. And Dad went back to work because he had to, because "We're still alive here, and someone has to make a living," or at least that's what I heard him tell Mom the night before.

So now, when the doorbell rings, I'm the only one to answer it. I stare through the small circle at the officer.

He leans closer, which distorts his face through the glass like a fun house mirror. The bell dings again, but I can't open it.

I can't open it.

He's holding an envelope in his hand.

• • •

"Beans, can you grab the corner?" Lisette's voice jolts me back. She's struggling to lay out the blanket.

I pull the corner nearest me down flat, helping her to smooth things. My motions are distant, robotic. I'm here, but I don't feel like me.

Still, I am here, doing this thing, smoothing down our blanket at the ocean on a hot summer day. It's something. At least it's something.

Lisette wriggles out of her shorts and squints up at me where I stand, wooden. "You did it, Beans," she says, but her face is a question.

"I'm okay," I whisper, but she knows, waits patiently as I breathe in the salt air. After a minute or so, I feel better, like the tiniest bit of calm has washed over me.

I sit on the blanket next to her, willing my body to relax into the warm give of the sand. Lisette reaches over, rubs my shoulder, then tugs at the straps of my bikini top, the one that belongs to her old green bikini.

"Hey, this looks familiar. A little small, maybe. You think? You could really use a new one." I give her a look, like I know she's trying to cheer me up. "What?

You look great, Beans. You don't give yourself enough credit. I'm sure I have a sexier one you can have."

We lotion each other up and lie down. I close my eyes and feel the sun on my face, then turn my head to look at Lisette. She rolls on her side and smiles at me.

"So, what's up with you, anyway? You've been totally MIA. Don't make me beg for information."

"Me? You! You're always with Bradley." I stop because I know how jealous I sound. "And, really, nothing is going on. Well, not nothing, I guess, but nothing exciting." I roll on my side to face her. "Well, except I did get a job."

She sits up and stares at me. "A job, seriously? Doing what?"

"Mother's helper." I swallow through the dread that hits me when I say the words aloud. The irony's too obvious even for me. "Three days a week. Ten dollars an hour to start."

"Get out! That's amazing, Frankie. How did you swing that?"

And without knowing I'm going to, I tell her, let it all spill out about how I thought I saw Dad with Mrs. Merrill, and how I went to the club, and about Peter Pintero and Mr. Habberstaad. And, of course, about Frankie Sky, and how he looks like Simon, although I absolutely don't tell her the part where I think I was somehow destined to find him and how he may be my brother's reincarnation.

"Wow," she says when I finish. "You've been seriously holding out on me, Beans."

"Sorry. I haven't felt like talking about it much. And the stuff with my dad is way private. Besides, I'm probably crazy. I mean, there's no proof of anything. He hasn't been anywhere near the club as far as I can tell. I'm sure I just imagined it all."

"I know, but still . . ." She lies down again. "It had better be crazy, Beans, that's all I can say. Otherwise, oh brother, your poor mom . . ."

"You can say that again."

Lisette stretches a perfect leg in the air and points her toes like a ballerina, making her calf muscle flex. "But do you really think he would? He's the best. It doesn't sound much like your dad."

"I know. You're right." She is right. It doesn't sound like him. I feel better talking it all out with Lisette. I should have done it sooner.

"Anyway, enough about me and my stupid, morbid life." I lie down, too. "Tell me about you and Bradley."

She puts her leg down and stretches out the other one. Her legs are perfect, like everything else about her. "What's to tell? He's a guy." But her lips crack into a smile.

I feel a stitch in my heart, but ignore it, because I do want to know. If I can't have him, at least I can live vicariously, even if it kind of kills me to hear it. "Come on, Zette, details. I swear I won't be jealous."

She drops her leg. "Total lie," she says, because she knows me too well. "Besides, there's really, really nothing to tell."

"Do you kiss? I mean, tongue, everything?" I can't watch her anymore. I sit up and look out over the ocean. The sky is the brightest blue with puffs of white drifting by. "What else have you guys done?"

"Lie back down, Beans. You're blocking my sun."

"Lisette . . ."

"Yes, tongue. Of course, silly. A little bit more. But not that much. Promise. And, yes, he kisses good. Really, really good," she says. "Are you happy now?"

My chest aches with the worst kind of longing. "Wow, you're right," I say. "I'm completely, horribly jealous, with a big, fat, capital *J*." She laughs and pats my thigh, and I smile at her. "But I do want to know anyway."

She pulls me back down next to her and I stay there. I know there's only so much she's going to come right out and tell me, probably mostly because she feels guilty. And she's right. I want all of it so much. To be kissed by a boy. And touched. To feel whatever it is that Bradley makes Lisette feel. To be wanted. I want that more than anything.

I'm almost relieved when Alex and Jared come back up from the surf where they've been skimboarding and distract us by digging through the cooler for sodas. They plop down next to us, sandy and wet, and drink.

"So, how's the water?" Lisette snags the can from

Alex's hand and takes a huge swig before giving it back to him. He's good-natured about it; her brother adores her. "Not too bad," he says. "You girls going to come in?" Alex is cute. The strong, silent type. Good body, athletic. It's hard not to have a crush on him. If he weren't like a brother to me, I might—not that it would do me any good. Like Lisette, he could always have anyone he wanted. As he lifts his arm to his mouth to sip, his muscles tighten. My mind flashes to Bradley and my stomach drops. Jared glances at Lisette then away, trying not to let it register how hot he thinks she is. I see it, though, and Alex watches him, too. Not that it matters. Lisette wouldn't be interested. He doesn't so much as give me a once-over.

We make small talk, and when the guys are done with their sodas, they head back down to the water. Lisette stands, the obvious question plastered on her face: *Are you coming, Beans?* I've told myself I'm going to attempt this, to go in the water, or at least walk down and wade in the shallow surf. But now that the moment is here, I don't know if I can make my body obey.

Lisette pulls me up, pushes an errant strand of hair from my face, and loops it behind my ear. "Come on, girly," she says. "I have faith in you."

▪▫▪ *fifteen* ▪▫▪

As Lisette wades into the water, my legs turn leaden. I will them to push forward, but there's only so much I can do.

Lisette stops waist-deep and turns back. I nod her on, stepping sideways over the small swells that flop harmlessly in, leaving their foamy surf on the shore. Still, Lisette waits. "Go ahead!" I yell. "I'm not coming in!"

I dig my toes in the sand and fold my arms across my chest. Whatever I thought I could do, swimming in after Lisette I cannot. Truthfully, I can hardly bear it as she swims out, disappearing under each new wave, the water closing up, filling the void where her body just was, leaving nothing but empty horizon.

Each time, after a few breathtaking seconds, she resurfaces, shouting happily, and everything is okay. But first, my heart free-falls in panic mode.

● ● ●

"On shore . . . Yes, ma'am . . . down by the Neck, on the shore." The officer's voice drifts up to me where I sit at the top of the stairs.

He's talking about Simon's body.

I had run to get Mom, told her about the officer, and she had put on her bathrobe and come down to let him in. She was groggy, her hair a mess, but she didn't seem to care.

The officer was polite, apologized for interrupting, stood stiffly in the foyer.

There was a yellow envelope clutched in his hand. I knew the photograph was in there. We walked to the kitchen, and he put the envelope on the table. "You'd best have a seat, ma'am," he'd said.

"Francesca, go to your room."

Mom sat, and the officer sat, but I didn't want to go to my room. I wanted to crawl into Mom's lap and stay there with her. I wanted to see the photograph. I wanted to see Simon. To see proof he was there. Anything was better than going upstairs alone to imagine him chewed up by sea monsters and sharks.

If Dad had been home, he would have held me, but Mom didn't look at me anymore.

I'd climbed the stairs and sat, listening to the man's hushed voice, mumbles that floated up to me in broken, sorrowful bits.

"Yes, yesterday afternoon . . . No, no, right there, down on the Neck . . . One of my officers found the body."

Now the sound of Mom's choked tears and, "Not my baby . . . not my baby . . ."

I listen to her hiccups and wails until it finally turns

quiet again. The chairs scrape the floor, and I hear her thank him and close and lock the door.

. . .

"Francesca! Francesca!"

For a second I'm lost in the cold sweat of memories, but someone is calling me. I turn in the direction of the voice. The landscape has changed; I've wandered much farther than I realized.

Up near the dunes, Mrs. Schyler is waving enthusiastically. Next to her is Frankie Sky.

"I thought that was you!" she says as I veer up toward her. I feel off balance. The summer air seems to swim all around me.

I focus not on Mrs. Schyler, but on Frankie Sky, who drives a yellow Tonka truck in the sand.

"What are you guys doing here?" I drop to my knees next to Frankie.

"Beep, beep!" He backs the bulldozer onto my leg before plowing it forward to scoop more sand from a nice little hole he's got going.

"This right here is only our favorite spot in the whole wide world, right, Frankie? We practically live here in the summer, when we're not stuck at Grandpa Harris's stuffy old club."

"Right!" Frankie answers. "When we're not stuffed at the club."

Mrs. Schyler laughs. "Frankie sure loves the water.

Well, look at me telling you things you already know. That's half the reason we found you, isn't it?" She winks when she says this last part, making me wonder vaguely what the other half of the reason is. "I try to be a good mother, spend the days with him when I can . . . When I have the right kind of energy for the job." She looks at the water and sighs. "I used to have a lot more energy."

"She needs lots of energy because I am a water rat!" Frankie says proudly.

Mrs. Schyler looks at him. "You, my love, are a Tasmanian devil. Anyway, we were about to have a snack. Would you like to join us, Francesca?" She unzips a cooler and takes out a juice box and a bag of pretzels, revealing a narrow green bottle underneath. The label has a pretty drawing of a black swan. Her eyes dart to mine, then away.

She rips open the pretzel bag and several brown knots go flying onto the sand. "Is okay, right?" Frankie says quickly, his eyes searching his mother's to make sure. "Because we have much more pretzels than we need." Frankie pushes the truck through the sand, using the digger to scoop the fallen pieces. "In the summer, we come here lots of days," he says, "even before I was born. Lots and lots of days. Because I liked to come here even when I was still in Mommy's tummy. Then I would kick so hard to come out so I could meet my daddy and swim." He looks at Mrs. Schyler for approval.

"It's true. He loves that story." She pushes a pretzel closer to Frankie with her toe. He scoops it and drops it into the hole. "How, when my due date got close, I'd come here and walk and walk and walk, trying to make Frankie drop down."

"Really?" I ask, confused.

"Not literally drop down, but into the birth canal, you understand? I was huge by then, and a few days overdue, and he would go crazy the minute we reached the salt air. As if he could feel it from all the way inside here." She pats her stomach, and Frankie nods in agreement. "You could see him, like some strange alien, poking his elbows and knees out everywhere, big lumps protruding from my belly." She's smiling, but her voice turns sad. "Of course, his daddy was home on leave, and, boy, how my lumpy belly would keep him entertained."

Frankie drives his truck up onto my leg and parks it there. "Because they letted him come home to see me get born, right, Mama? Out on special distance station."

"Dispensation." Mrs. Schyler laughs. "Not *distance station*, Frankie. Anyway, yes, right."

"And so my daddy was here, and I liked how we all comed here to swim. Right on the day I was born! And both of you swimmed, and I was still in your belly, so I swimmed, too, so the water would help rush me out to my daddy before he had to go back to his work. And it did, right? Because that was the night I was born!" Frankie throws his arms in the air in a big finish.

Mrs. Schyler says, "I swear, Francesca, he always remembers the details. He must really love the whole idea," but I'm barely listening anymore, because I'm stuck on what Frankie said, about being on this beach, in this water, on the same exact day he was born. Which must have been right around the same time Simon died.

Was Frankie born the day that Simon died? Were they both in the water together?

Transmigrate. To be reborn at death in another body.

Did Simon's soul jump? Is his soul inside Frankie Sky?

Has Simon somehow come back to me?

I stand up, my whole body shaking, and mumble that I have to go, that I forgot that my friends were waiting and that I'll see them Monday morning. Then I start walking as fast as I can, away from all of it, back toward Lisette, where it's safe.

Except that nothing feels safe anymore.

◼◼ *sixteen* ◼◼

"Beans, where'd you go? You scared me half to death."

Lisette's combing her hair on the blanket, not looking all that scared. I drop down next to her. The walk back has calmed me a little, too, so at least my mind isn't spiraling out of control.

I couldn't have been gone that long. Lisette's hair is still wet from the ocean, and Alex and Jared are still skimboarding in the surf.

She rakes the comb through the salt-encrusted knots. I take it from her and work at the hard-to-reach spots in back.

"Sorry," I say, trying to decide what information to impart. "I just went for a walk and lost track. Went farther than I meant to."

I don't know why I don't tell her about Mrs. Schyler and Frankie Sky. It's right there on my tongue, but then I keep it curled up instead. Maybe I just don't want her to think I'm too weird—or worse, that I'm losing it, like my mother.

Lisette takes the comb from me and puts some shine conditioner in her hair. We sit for a while in silence, watching Alex and Jared crash in on their boards at the shore.

"So what do you think of Alex's bubblehead friend?" Lisette asks finally, nodding toward the surf.

"He's okay." I scrape at the sand with a shell. "I'm not really one to say."

"Cut it out, Beans," she says. "And, by the way, my boyfriend says you're cute, so you don't have to just take my word for it."

I lift my eyes, surprised, and open my mouth to ask, but she says, "What? I keep telling you that, Frankie, you just won't believe me." She squeezes my bare arm, and I gently move it away, hoping she doesn't feel the goose bumps that appeared at the thought of what Bradley said.

For a few minutes, I don't say anything or ask anything else. Because at this moment, everything feels normal between us. I soak it all in and let it wash over me, along with what Bradley said, while the sun bakes down warm and happy and cooks all the harder questions away.

• • •

By late afternoon, we're starving and decide to drive to a local seafood shack to get some burgers and fried clams, agreeing we'll head back to the beach after to see if we can catch some early fireworks. The Fourth isn't until tomorrow, but there's usually stuff going off all weekend.

I call Mom to tell her we're having dinner at the mall

and going to a movie with Alex and his friend after. She doesn't question me, even though I don't know the last time I went out like this for hours on end. Maybe she trusts Lisette and Alex, or maybe these are the freedoms that come with being almost sixteen.

Or maybe she doesn't care where I am.

"Where's Dad?" I ask, mostly as an afterthought as she's about to hang up the phone.

"Not sure." She pauses as if she's just now considered it herself. "He went out to run errands a few hours ago. I guess he hasn't come back yet." It's Saturday evening, and Dad's out running errands? My mind goes to Mrs. Merrill's driveway. I wonder if her car is parked there.

"Okay, then," I say. "Have a good night. I love you."

"Okay, Francesca." The phone clicks, and she's gone.

● ● ●

By the time we get back to the beach, the sky is a deep plum and the air has begun to erupt with the whiz and pop of early fireworks. Alex drops us at the steps to the dunes, says he and Jared will be back in a few, and returns twenty minutes later with two shopping bags full of soda, cookies, and a six-pack of beer.

Alex is almost legal and usually pretty responsible, and there's only the one six-pack, so I don't really worry about it. What surprises me, though, is that he takes the first one out, pops the cap off, takes a swig, and then holds it out to Lisette.

"You know the deal, two sips and that's all. Dad would kill me if he found out."

"Aye, aye, Captain." She salutes him and takes a long sip, then hands the bottle to me. I stare for a second, then close my fingers around it. It's freezing cold in my hands. I have never had a sip of alcohol in my life and didn't know Lisette had, either. I give her a look like she's gone mad, but she nods to let me know I should go ahead and try. I take a sip and force it down. It tastes awful, like shoe leather with lime, and I wince as its cold trail winds its way down my throat. Lisette laughs and takes the bottle back.

"Look at you, Beans! You're a pro now." She takes a second sip and another really long third. Alex gives her a stern look, and she says, "Okay, okay, last one, I swear," making bug eyes at him as she takes one last swig. She hands the bottle back to me, almost empty, and Alex gives up and opens himself another.

This time, I take a slow, careful sip, then finish what's left.

"Not bad, right?" Lisette asks, getting up. She walks back toward the bags, and I smile, giddy and rosy-cheeked, because already, after those few sips, a nice heady warmth has washed over me. "Oh my God, you rock, Alex!" she shouts, heading back toward us. For a second, I'm worried she has another beer, but then I see two narrow boxes in her hand. "Where on earth did you get these?"

"I have my sources," Alex says.

She turns and waves them at me. Old-fashioned sparkler sticks. Lisette and I both love sparklers, although I haven't touched one in years. I have so many memories of being in Lisette's backyard, twirling with sparklers like they're mini batons, and writing our names in script in the air, the sparks trailing their neon glow in the darkness.

Lisette drops to her knees, lights two, and hands one to me. The tip flames and sputters and sends electric-white bits flying everywhere.

"Careful, come on!" she says, breathless. "Our names in double-script, remember?" And of course I do, so we wave them like that, in tall, wild curlicues going in opposite directions from the middle out. She spells out *Lisette Annabelle Sutter* and I write *Francesca Mia Schnell* magically across the black sky. "God, I love these things," she says, dropping to pull out two more. We run to the water's edge with them, white light fairies dispersing in the air behind us. When they're nearly out, we stand and watch the red-orange ends burn down.

"What does it feel like, Zette, seriously," I ask, letting the last little ember singe the tips of my fingers, "to kiss a guy that way?"

She looks out over the water, her face illuminated by moonlight, and holds her burnt-out sparkler in front of her.

"Like this, Beans. It feels just like this. All electric and sparkly. Like your entire heart is on fire. And when it's over, you can't wait to do it again." And though I promised not to be, I'm filled with envy. "Soon enough, it will be you, too, I just know it," she says. "Hey, I have an idea! Come on!"

She pulls me up the beach to our stash. "This time, let's write our wishes in the air. Anything you want. The name of who you love, or want to kiss, or it doesn't even have to be about a boy. Anything you want to come true, okay?"

I'm still light-headed and agreeable, whether from the beer or the day in the sun, I don't know, but I happily go along. Maybe because there's a part of me that's actually starting to believe in things I didn't before, at least in some minuscule, incalculable way. I mean, I'm standing here on the beach, at the ocean, and that alone feels like a magical thing.

With the first stick I write, *Give me answers about Simon and Frankie,* but decide that's stupid and morbid and melodramatic, so I write, *Let a cute guy ask me out.* After that, I write, *Let my dad NOT be in love with Mrs. Merrill* and with the next one, *Let me look like Lisette,* three whole times before the sparkler burns all the way down. And with my last stick, my head abuzz with beer and sea air and sparklers, I scribble the outline of a huge heart and write, *Let me kiss Bradley Stephenson before summer is over.*

I stop spinning. My face prickles hot and panicked

in the dark. I scribble my burnt-out sparkler over where I can almost still see the words linger. I turn to Lisette, horrified, but she's oblivious, dashing off her own sparkler wishes in the air.

When her last one dies out, she says, "Not yet, Beans, okay? I'm so not ready to go," so we sit side by side again, watching the waves lap up on the dark shore.

Lisette rests her head on my shoulder, and I stare off, feeling quiet and tired as the effects of the beer wear away. In the distance, an occasional firework explodes and rains down in a shimmer of green, red, and purple. Beyond us, the ocean is gentle and calm, defying me to believe that it took my baby brother.

Finally, I tap Lisette's arm. "We'd better go," I say. We hunt down Alex and Jared, gather our stuff, and head back to the car. On the way over the dunes, Lisette leans into me and says, "So, Beans, what did you sparkler-wish for?" And for the third or fourth time in a few short days, I lie.

▪️▪️ *seventeen* ▪️▪️

Monday morning, eight forty-five. I drag my old bike from the back of the garage and bike the short distance to Frankie's house. I lean it against the garage, walk up the steps, and ring the bell. I try to stay calm and focused, but I'm nervous, plus, all I keep thinking about is asking Frankie Sky when his birthday is.

Potato barks and there are rapid footsteps, then Mrs. Schyler's voice, muffled, as she yanks open the door. She's dressed in a black cap-sleeved dress, half-zipped, with white roses printed on it. She has one black pump on her foot, the other in her hand, and a black straw hat on her head. Her cell phone is pressed to her ear, and the dog is scooped under her arm like a pile of laundry.

"Oh, hey, Mrs. Schyler, am I early?"

"No, no, not at all, and it's Brooke, remember? No, you're not early, I'm running late. So sorry." She closes the door behind me, lets Potato down, and slips the other shoe on her foot. "I'm so very glad that you're here. You have no idea." She rushes toward the kitchen, still talking, but to me now, I think, not to whoever was on the phone a second ago.

"A dear friend of my father's has died unexpectedly. And, of course, I've only just heard about it this morning. My father, Frankie's Grandpa Harris, is always trying to spare me things. At any rate . . ." But she's lost her thoughts, rifling inside kitchen cabinets.

I look around for Frankie, but he's not here. Maybe he's still sleeping.

"Anyway, I've known the man all my life, and his poor wife, and well, he was like an uncle to me. It's too, too sad, and I simply cannot have my father go alone. Trust me, people can drop on you left and right like flies, and you still never get used to it. He's pretty broken up, as you can imagine." She stops at the sink and pulls out a bottle of Advil. "Sit, sweetie," she says.

I nod and sit at the table in the same chair I sat in the other day. Potato darts under and curls up at my feet. Mrs. Schyler pops a few pills, puts the bottle back, then pulls out an amber prescription bottle and taps out some pills onto the counter. I look away as she swallows them down. I feel like somehow I'm intruding.

"Headache," she says, sighing. "So, now, where was I? Oh yes, good, I've nearly got everything together."

She grabs a large box of Cheerios that's open on the counter and dumps some into a plastic snack baggie. Several pieces go skittering to the floor. I get up to clean them, but Potato beats me to it. "Good doggie," Mrs. Schyler says, kicking a few toward him with the tip of her shoe. She tosses the baggie into a canvas beach bag that also sits on the counter. A pair of shorts, a T-shirt, and blue water wings with yellow inflation tabs are piled alongside that.

"Anyway, it's supposed to be a scorcher today, and I'll probably be gone for several hours. So I figured I'd drop you and Frankie at the club. Is that all right, Francesca? Better than being stuck here at home, yes? You do have a suit with you?"

I nod and tug at the bikini straps under my T-shirt to show her, but she doesn't turn around.

"At least you'll have access to the pool there, although be sure not to let Frankie dive, will you? But, goodness, listen to me. Telling you things you already know." She finally turns and looks at me. "Good Lord, why is that child so completely convinced he can swim?"

She says it like she thinks I might have an answer. Images of souls, like translucent, stretched-out angels, float up through my brain, clouding any logical response. But Mrs. Schyler isn't waiting for one anyway; she's already dashed from the room.

Several minutes pass before she returns. "Goodness, some days . . ." she says, practically dragging Frankie behind her. He's working at the ties on his swim trunks. "We couldn't find the right ones, with the right frogs." She rolls her eyes at me, lets go of Frankie, and starts scooping the stuff from the counter into the canvas bag.

"Needed *these* frogs," Frankie says, "because they are the bestest ones!" He looks at me and flips a shy wave.

Mrs. Schyler winks now. "He wanted to look perfect for you."

I can't help but smile. "Hi, Frankie Sky," I say.

"Hi, Frankie Snell," he giggles.

I reach over to help Mrs. Schyler. "No, no, I've got it," she says, tossing the water wings in and sliding the bag onto her shoulder. A small pink pill, unstuck from the bag's bottom, drops to the floor. I pick it up and hold it out to her.

Mrs. Schyler looks at it in my palm and drops the bag back on the counter. "Oh shoot, I nearly forgot. Frankie, come. Right now."

She grabs the pill from my hand, applesauce from the fridge, and a spoon from a drawer and buries the pill in the sauce. Frankie stays back, but Mrs. Schyler says, "Now, sweetheart, we really don't have time." He walks forward, mouth open, and allows her to feed it to him. She tosses the spoon in the sink. "Good, let's go," she says, returning the applesauce to the fridge.

"Is he sick?" I ask, following them through the living room.

"Potato, stay!" She uses a foot to keep him back as Frankie and I squeeze out the front door. "What, dear?" she asks, struggling to open the car door.

I help to load stuff and buckle Frankie into his booster seat. Mrs. Schyler backs out of the driveway and pulls into the street. I wait for her to answer my question now, but she's focused on the road as she maneuvers us toward the club.

"Is Frankie sick, Mrs. Schyler?" I finally ask again.

"I mean, if he's sick, I think I should know." She turns and looks at me, confused. "The pink pill," I clarify.

"Oh no. Not sick, not at all. Well, not exactly. The pill is purely prophylactic. For protection, that is. Frankie was born with a condition. Well, we think he was . . . It's called an atrial septal defect."

"A what defect?" I think of Frankie that day, standing in the tree, saying *even my grandpa can't fix me,* and suddenly I'm not sure I really want more information.

"A hole in his heart," she says, pulling into the club parking lot. "But I promise you, it sounds way worse than it is."

◼◼ *eighteen* ◼◼

Mrs. Schyler chatters happily, rushing us through the lobby of the club, but I can't focus. I mean, how can having a hole in your heart sound worse than it is?

"I'm sorry to leave you on your own like this your very first day, but I know you'll be fine. And, of course, Henry—well, that's Mr. Habberstaad—is my father's good friend. Did Frankie mention that? So don't let his cranky self fool you. You have any trouble, you go to him. He's just a mushy old teddy bear inside." She winks at me and keeps walking.

The club's lobby is at the other end from Mr. Habberstaad's office. There are red leather couches and chandeliers, a few big-screen TVs scattered around the walls, all showing the same golf game, and there's a pro shop across the way. I know I've been here before, but it feels fuzzy and different, like in a dream. Then again, everything feels like that from the time before my brother died.

Mrs. Schyler points out the bathrooms, the members-only dining hall, and a large library with another big television and fancy board game tables in case it rains. Frankie heads toward the TV, but Mrs. Schyler yanks him back. "Not now, Frankie, we're going outside to the pool! Where was I? Oh yes, Mr. Forrester, my father, has a tab here. So when you're hungry, you and Frankie can simply head to the dining room and eat, then sign for it at the end. Just write the number 4285 on the check. Well, trust me, Frankie knows how to do it. Plus, you're officially on my member guest list here, so you should have no problems at all."

We've reached the hallway that runs past Mr. Habberstaad's office and out through the back door to the pool. "Oh, and if Frankie gets bored, there's a wonderful playground just across the street. You know it?" I nod. "Yes, of course. So feel free to take him there." She glances around as if to see if she's forgetting something. "Well, then, I'm sure you have it all under control." She kneels in front of Frankie and holds his shoulders. "Now listen to me, Frankie, you be good, you promise?" She kisses his cheek and stands, then rushes back down the hall.

I look at the closed door to Mr. Habberstaad's office, where I was summoned just a few days ago, wondering what I have gotten myself into.

Well, at least this time I'm not trespassing.

"Let's go to the pool, Frankie Snell," Frankie says, not seeming to mind that his mother has gone. He grabs my hand and pushes his whole body against the door.

"You can just call me Frankie," I say, helping him to open it. "You don't have to keep saying my last name."

"Two Frankies is too confusing," he says. "We can't both be Frankies, right?"

"Well, if you want, you can call me Beans." I say it without thinking, and the minute I have, I'm sorry. That's all I need is Frankie calling me Beans around here, especially with Peter Pintero listening.

I'm about to retract it, but Frankie looks up at me, his eyes wide and smiling. "Really? Beans is your nother name? Because I like it so much!" So there's no way I can take it back now.

"Okay, fine, but only you, Frankie." I squat to his level and hold my fingers to my lips. "It's a private name. So don't go telling other people."

"Why?"

"Because it's special. Only my dad calls me Beans. Well, and also my friend Lisette."

"And me!" he says delightedly.

"Yeah, sure," I say. "And you."

• • •

The pool is quiet after the holiday weekend. Only a handful of people fill the lounge chairs. But, of course, it's still early.

I look around quickly, wondering if Mrs. Merrill is here, but I didn't see her car in the lot, and the back section of the pool where she usually sits is empty. I tell myself I should stop worrying about it anyway, since even if Dad is fooling around with her, he's clearly not doing it here.

I follow Frankie toward the pool, where he stakes out two chairs up front. *Great.* My eyes dart to the lifeguard chair. Peter Pintero is staring at me.

I give a little wave, slightly pleased that he's probably wondering how the heck I got in here through the main entrance. Then again, I guess it's clear that I'm here with Frankie Sky. Still, it feels like a victory, so I smile a bit to myself. Peter nods back at me, but doesn't give anything away.

I drop the heavy canvas bag near my chair, slip off my shorts and my T-shirt, and adjust my bikini while Frankie runs off to get towels. He has to stand on tippy toes to reach the counter where the towels are folded and he knocks a few down, so I rush over to help him gather them.

"Good work, Frankie," I say when we've returned and laid them out on our chairs. I lie back and let the sun's warmth soak into me.

"Let's go, Beans!" Frankie tugs my arm.

"Shhh." I open an eye at him, but can't make out his features against the bright sun. "You can't just yell *Beans* out like that, I told you. It's a private name, remember? And anyway, Frankie, we just got here. Let's warm up for a bit."

"Don't wanna warm, Beans. Wanna swim! You said you will teach me."

Shoot. Not exactly. My eyes shift to Peter again. I guess I could try. There's a lifeguard here, at least, and I knew how to before. "Okay, fine, Frankie. Give me a second."

I sit up and dig through the bag for the water wings that Mrs. Schyler packed. One of them has slid down to the bottom, and by the time I fish it out, Frankie is running toward the pool.

"Hey, mister!" I yell. "Get back here now! You need to put on the wings."

"I don't like wings!" he calls, charging for the deep end. I run after him, shouting, and grab his arm hard.

"You'd better not touch that pool unless I'm with you, do you hear me? Don't you dare touch that water alone!" My body shakes, and I know it comes out harsher than I mean. Frankie's lip quivers. I let go of his arm. "Don't cry, Frankie," I say, kneeling to eye level. "You just need to put on your water wings. And stay in the shallow end. I'm not the best swimmer, and I don't want you ever to get hurt."

"Frankie won't get hurt. And those are not wings. Wings are to fly. Those are tighty things that pinch me when you blow them on."

I laugh because, well, because he's ridiculous, but also because, technically, he makes a point. They're not wings. I have no idea why they call them that. He laughs, too, and wraps his hands around my neck, bringing his face right up to mine. "I is funny?" he says, breathing his Cheerio breath up my nose.

I move him back a little so we can see straight into each other's eyes, so he can see how serious I am. "Yes, you are funny, but you still need to wear the floaty things."

He shakes his head. "Frankie Sky knows how to swim. I tolded you that already, so please can we go in now?"

"Okay," I say, "but no wings means we stay on the steps." I'm a little relieved to have an excuse not to go in.

He pouts a little, but takes my hand and pulls me toward the shallow end. I leave the water wings deflated by our chairs, take a deep breath, and wade in with him onto the first step.

The water is cool and crisp, a perfect sparkling teal. The red-and-white peppermint inner tube bobs along the opposite edge. My eyes keep darting up to Peter, but he's got his head tipped back like he's sleeping.

Frankie tugs me and we wade down a second step. I fight the dizziness that washes over me and keep my grasp on Frankie, who I can feel is trying to break free.

"Let go, Beans, I can stand here by myself." And I do let go, because he's pulling me in farther than I'm ready to go.

"Frankie . . ."

He stops on the second to last step, the waterline up to his chin. He turns around slowly and smiles at me. "Hurry, Beans, what is taking you?"

"Come up one more step where you can stand better, and I'll tell you." I reach out and he shakes his head, but then catches the look on my face and takes my hand. "You want to have a contest, Frankie? See who can hold their breath the longest? We'll put our faces in and count. You can go first, then I will. That's important to do, to work on our breath, before we keep learning to swim."

"Yep, I do," he says.

"Okay then, stand right here with me. You put your face in and I'll count until you come up again."

He takes a giant breath and puffs his cheeks out and ducks his face under. He pops back up, huffing and puffing, about two seconds later.

"Five!" I say anyway. "Pretty good, Frankie."

"Now it's your turn, Beans!" He grabs the railing and swings from it, his feet off the steps but in water. My heart lurches. I glance up. Peter is paying absolutely no attention.

"Okay, but while I go you have to hold on *and* put your feet down." He drops them, and with my heart still racing, I hold my breath and force my face under.

Everything grows quiet. I can hear Frankie's voice in the distance. "Four, five, six . . ."

I slowly open my eyes.

Everything is liquid and blue. And, like riding a bike, it suddenly all comes back to me. How to hold my nose closed from the inside and just let myself be submerged. As if everything underwater settles down.

I move my head from side to side and watch strands of my hair sway like brown seaweed. The sunlight filters down through the surface in rays, and particles drift through them like silvery glitter. Beyond me, Frankie's chubby legs dance on the steps as he counts.

"Eleven and twelve and thirteen . . . !"

When he reaches twenty, I come up even though I don't need to, because I don't want Frankie to feel bad.

"Twenty!" he yells. "You gotted twenty, Beans!" He's got this huge grin on his face, which fills me completely with happiness. "My turn again!" he says, then barely takes time for a breath and goes under. I count super fast this time, making it to fifteen before he comes up panting.

We play this game for what feels like another fifty rounds before I notice that Mrs. Merrill has arrived. She sits in her usual chair, talking on her cell phone in the corner. I glance at the giant white clock on the clubhouse. It's almost eleven thirty already.

"Come on, Frankie. Enough water. Let's dry off and maybe get some lunch and hit the playground."

"Okay," he says. "Lunch, yep. And then we can go on the merry-go-round."

"Yep," I say, the way he does. "Then we can go on the merry-go-round. But first dry off and get lunch."

I try to stall things a bit so I can keep an eye on Mrs. Merrill. Which isn't too hard, since Frankie doesn't want to get dressed until the sun dries every drop of water off his body. Finally, I help him peel off his swim trunks and switch to his shorts and sneakers. As we're about to go inside, I sit back down and tell Frankie we need to wait. Because at eleven forty-five, like clockwork, Mrs. Merrill stands up and heads toward her cabana. I watch discreetly as she taps past us, disappearing behind the white-shuttered door.

"Come on, Beans. We're hungry. Let's go get lunch."

"Hold on, Frankie. I've got to stay here for one more minute."

"Why?"

"Because I'm watching someone."

"Why?"

"Because I need to."

"Okay."

He sits down next to me and looks in the direction I'm looking. "Where is the person?"

"She went in her cabana."

"Oh. Where is her banana?"

I laugh. "Not *ba*nana, *ca*bana. Those doors, over there." I nod with my chin.

"Oh, yep, right," he says, and slips his hand in mine and squeezes.

One minute passes, then another, then it must be close to ten. Frankie gets antsy, kicks his feet against the chair, plays with the seafoam green vinyl bands stretched across them. I can't say I blame him. There's nothing to see. How long am I going to sit here once again, waiting for Mrs. Merrill to emerge?

"Never mind," I say. "We can go. Come on."

"Okay." He takes my hand and pulls me toward the club entrance.

In the dining room, the waiter comes to take our order right away. Frankie says, "Hi, mister. We are Forrester, 4285. Please put it on our tab."

The waiter laughs and says, "You got it, Frankie."

He brings a bread basket and pours us water, and Frankie orders mac and cheese with apple juice while I get a burger with fries.

"You're good, Frankie," I say when the waiter leaves. "How do you know how to do all this stuff?"

"I am special," he says. "My Grandpa Harris tolded me that."

All of a sudden, I remember the pink pill and the hole in Frankie's heart.

"Special how, Frankie?"

"Because I have a boo-boo in my heart." He shrugs. "But it only hurted me once, so we don't need to worry. Also, because I knowed how to fly, because Grandpa Harris says I is an angel and magic."

"You can't really fly, Frankie." I don't mean to sound mad, but I know I do. I'm not sure why. The conversation is making me anxious.

Frankie touches my hand with his fingers and gives me a serious look. "Yes, I can, Beans."

I look hard at him. "Frankie, do you think that maybe your grandpa just meant that one day, when you're really, really old and you die, that maybe *then* you'll be an angel and fly up to heaven, but not now?"

"No. Not then. *Now,* Beans. Because Grandpa said if Frankie got dead from the heart booboo, then it's okay, because Daddy is in heaven and Frankie is an angel and will fly up there. Because angels have wings and can fly. Well, also, birds can fly." I roll my eyes, but Frankie says, "Is true, Beans, angels and birds can fly. Oh, and airplanes."

"Fine, Frankie, I know. Whatever." And thankfully, the waiter brings our food, because I don't want to talk about this anymore.

Frankie tucks his napkin in his shirt and forks a mouthful of macaroni up to his mouth, then stops and blows. "Can't eat it yet 'cause it's hot," he says. I nod. "And Beans is wrong. Frankie can fly, and that is true, so no more talk about that."

His eyes are teary now, so I feel bad. "Okay, sorry, Frankie. I was only asking. I was trying to make sure you're safe and understand."

He blows hard on his fork again, and most of the macaroni falls back in the bowl. He takes the ketchup and squeezes it into the bowl, then stirs until it turns the cheese sauce the color of lava. When he's done, he looks up at me. "Also, Frankie Sky can swim, too. Fly *and* swim. Both of those things, Beans."

"No, you can't, Frankie. Not yet. So quit saying it. Okay?" I pick up my burger and put it back down. "But you will soon. I bet you'll learn fast how to swim."

"Can too, Beans," he says.

"Cannot, Frankie," I say. "And seriously, do you have to say *Beans* every single sentence? It's kind of like a secret name, remember?"

"Yes, I remember, Beans."

After that, we eat in silence. Periodically, he glances up and smiles and squeezes macaroni through his teeth at me. Which is gross, but also funny, and eventually it makes me laugh again. When the waiter comes, I sign the check *4285* like Mrs. Schyler told me to, which feels weird, like I think I'm royalty or something. Then we leave the dining room on the lobby side to head toward the playground.

Halfway through the lobby, Frankie stops. "Have to go to the potty, Beans." He turns back and beelines toward the door with the word *Gents* on it.

"Do you want me to go with you, Frankie?" I ask.

He shakes his head. "Nope, is just for boys."

"Do you want to go in mine instead, so I can go with you? You're allowed."

"No. I can go alone. I always do it when Mommy is here." So I push the door open and let him through.

"Take your time, okay?" I call as he disappears inside. "I'll wait for you out here."

I walk to the big picture window in the hall that looks out over the pool. Peter Pintero is climbing down from the lifeguard stand. Maybe he's coming in to get lunch. As he walks past the window, he sees me, but barely nods, just keeps walking past toward the back door.

My eyes shift to Mrs. Merrill's cabana, second from the end. Cabana #2. The white shuttered door is closed. I'm about to walk away when I see something else, the one thing I couldn't see from where I was sitting at the pool. From this angle, I can see around the backs of the cabanas, and I can see there are doors on both sides. Front and back doors.

And then everything becomes clear. Mrs. Merrill isn't staying inside her cabana. She's leaving the club from the back. No wonder I keep losing her!

I race to the front of the club and out the main entrance to the parking lot. Because if Mrs. Merrill is leaving, where is she leaving to? *And who is she leaving with?*

But I'm wrong. She hasn't left. Her black Mercedes is right there. Right in the front where it always is.

Then something else occurs to me, something worse, something horrible, and I take a few more steps out toward the lot. My eyes scan it frantically and I almost miss it, way back, in the row nearest the street. Dad's car. Dad's car is in the lot.

I tell myself to breathe, to calm down.

Maybe it's *like* his car, but not his?

I take a few cautious steps to the edge of the curb, but at that moment, the car—my dad's Jeep—backs out and speeds away, and I can't tell from here who's inside.

The parking lot is still.

I stare at the empty spot where it was, trying to fight back tears. I have to stop kidding myself. I know my dad's car when I see it.

So, then, what if it was?

I try to wrap my frazzled brain around the possibilities, when I'm bumped from behind, stumble, and nearly fall flat off the curb.

"Oh goodness! Excuse us! Eliza, you *have* to watch where you're going."

A mom and her child walk past. "It's okay," I say absentmindedly, then snap back as I realize that I'm busy worrying out here, and I've left Frankie Sky inside.

I run back inside the club, my eyes darting around the lobby, but he's not there. Or in the pro shop, or the game room. I run down the hall to the bathroom. It hasn't been that long. He must still be in there.

I bang on the door. No answer. I push it open a bit.

"Frankie? You in there?"

No answer.

"Frankie!"

"Lose something?" I whirl around. It's Peter Pintero at my shoulder. I fight the panic that's erupted; I try to fight back more tears.

"Can you just see if Frankie is in there? He was going to the bathroom."

"Sure," he says. "Relax," and disappears inside.

I wait for what seems like an eternity, a million horrible thoughts about pedophiles and kidnappers banging through my brain, before Peter reappears shaking his head. "Nope, empty," he says, and instantly, I know where Frankie is. The same place Peter is not!

I run down the hall and tear out the back door, my

heart threatening to rip a hole through my chest. I pray he won't be in there.

I stop short at the edge of the pool, still somehow dumbfounded that he is.

Everything stops.

The sky.

The air.

The world.

Frankie Sky is in there.

Sinking to the bottom like a stone.

▪▪ *nineteen* ▪▪

For a split second I stand unmoving, confused, the sun beating down, the smell of the ocean, the salt air, permeating my nose. It's as if I'm not here, but back there, four years ago, watching my own body freeze. But this time I tell myself to knock it off, that I can stand here lost and reminiscing and watch Frankie drown, or I can get my butt in the pool and try to help him.

I kick off my flip-flops, take one deep breath, and dive, not having any idea if I even remember how to swim. I hit the water, my body shocked, but my brain focused on one thing: not letting Frankie Sky drown.

I kick like mad. My shorts feel heavy and my T-shirt twists uncomfortably around my arms. It only takes a few seconds to get to where Frankie is, but as I reach down, already he's sinking lower, slipping out of reach. He looks up at me, eyes open, blond hair swirling, legs and arms moving to push upward. He still has his shorts and shoes on. They must add to his weight, because he's not making any progress.

I kick harder and stretch my arms, but I can't make it to him, and I can't stay under any longer. I need to go up and get some air.

I resurface, gasping for breath, then push myself under again.

Either I'm moving down faster, or Frankie is rising up now, because he's closer to me, his arms and legs pushing outward, scooping water and fanning it away. As if he's doing the breast stroke. I reach for him, but my fingers just miss, and I have to come up for air again.

I gasp—one, two huge breaths this time so I can stay down longer—and kick back toward him, but now he breaks through the surface. I kick after him, relieved to see his head lift, momentarily, out of the water.

He goes back under, and I flail after him, but this time he pops right up again, his legs and arms moving in unison. Rhythmically, in perfect, froglike motions.

He's *swimming*.

I copy him, relaxing a little. After several strokes, it comes naturally, from memory.

Because I'm bigger and stronger than he is, I could pass him, but I don't. I slow my pace, stay behind him, and watch, still winded from fear, as he moves steadily toward the steps of the shallow end.

When he reaches them, he stands and waits until I catch up, my chest heaving, my brain still having trouble fully comprehending.

Behind him, Peter Pintero stands in the sunlight, hands on his whistle, face looking mildly amused.

"You could have come in and helped," I snap, wanting to be angry at someone. "Isn't that your job?"

"I was coming, I swear. But then it looked like you had it under control."

I don't answer. I can't deal with Peter right now. I need to deal with Frankie. He needs to be scolded. He needs to listen to me.

I turn to him. He's smiling, huge.

"We is wet," he says, laughing. "Even our clothes is all wet!"

"Frankie, I swear to you, it's not funny . . ." But I don't finish, because he's so happy and proud that I can't help but laugh also.

Part III

▪▪ *twenty* ▪▪

When Mrs. Schyler picks us up, Frankie tells her that I taught him how to swim. By then, the sun has dried our clothes, and Frankie is smart enough to leave out the rest of the shady details.

"How wonderful!" Mrs. Schyler says, but her voice doesn't sound like she means it.

She's still in her black-and-white dress, her hat gone, her hair pushed back in a headband. She looks like she's been sleeping. When I slide into the passenger seat, I see that she wears slippers on her feet.

I wonder vaguely if it's even legal to drive in house slippers, but then, who am I to talk? I nearly let Frankie drown because I was too busy playing Nancy Drew.

The more that I think about it now, the stupider it all seems—worrying about Dad and Mrs. Merrill. I can't be distracted anymore. I have to concentrate on Frankie. I have more important things to do.

I tell myself, that's the last of it. That I'm letting things go with Mrs. Merrill. Because even if I were to catch them at something, at anything, what would I actually do?

I have bigger problems just keeping Frankie safe.

If the kid is going to kill himself, it's not going to happen on my watch. Provided he doesn't give me a heart attack first.

Speaking of which, I need some answers about Frankie's heart.

"Mrs. Schyler?" I say as she turns onto Sycamore Street and parks in her driveway.

"Brooke, sweetie, really, it's Brooke." She unbuckles, slips out, and ducks down to look at me through the open door. "Francesca, would you mind terribly hanging around another hour or so? I have a splitting headache from the funeral and would very much like to lie down."

She doesn't wait for an answer, or even get Frankie out of the back, so I guess she assumes my answer is yes. I watch as she shuffles up the stairs in her pretty black-and-white dress with the roses and her fuzzy pink bedroom slippers.

"Backyard, Beans?" Frankie smiles. "You push me, but I tired, so I promise you I not gonna fly."

• • •

On Wednesday, Mrs. Schyler greets me in a hot pink dress with white paisley patterns and a pair of bright teal, open-toed shoes. Potato barks at her feet, but his tail wags ferociously when he sees me.

"Frankie, now, let's go!" She rushes off toward the kitchen.

As I follow, she rattles off the details of our day:

She's got a charity luncheon, something for wounded soldiers. She forgot all about it until the last minute, or would have given me more warning. She'll drop us at the club again; she hopes I won't mind. And she'll pay me on Friday for the week.

"Come here, Francesca, sit," she says, motioning to the table. I watch her at the sink as she takes out the Advil and the other two bottles of pills. The yellow pill she swallows, the pink one she puts on the counter.

"Frankie!" she yells again, then, "Potato! Go on. Go and get Frankie, would you?" But the dog just curls up under the table and looks at her.

"Mrs. Schy—Brooke," I blurt, uncomfortably, "what is the pink pill for again?"

She nods apologetically, as if she realizes she never answered my question. "Oh, yes, sorry. To prevent fluid buildup. Because of the hole in Frankie's heart."

"What kind of hole?"

In my mind, I try to picture the blue-and-red plastic heart model our science teacher, Mr. Antonucci, used to have on his desk, the kind you could take apart in sections like a gory 3-D puzzle. I try to picture it with a giant hole in the center and imagine what that might mean for Frankie Sky.

"Well, that's a good question. We've never been quite exactly sure." She sits down next to me and places her hand over mine. "Not to worry, sweetheart. You've seen him. He's a happy, healthy, energetic little boy." She laughs, but I'm not sure she sounds convincing.

"Then how did you find it?"

She gets up now, walks to the window, and looks out over the sprawling backyard.

"He had an episode. Just once. A few days after we brought him home. Charles—that's his father—had just gone back to Iraq. He was only given a few days' dispensation, and Frankie arrived late, so he had just one day with him, with us, after Frankie was born."

I watch Mrs. Schyler as she speaks. Even though she's so curvy from the front, from the back she's narrow and thin. In some ways, she reminds me of my mother.

"Anyway, it was the middle of the night, later than that actually, like four thirty in the morning, and Frankie starts to cough from his crib. Loud enough to wake me, though every little thing in those days did. So I go to the crib, and by now he's coughing and crying, but it's an odd cry, choked, like he's struggling for breath." She shakes her head and wraps her arms across her chest. "I call 911, but don't want to stand there and wait. His color is odd, and we're not far from Northside General, and I figure there are no cars on the road.

"So I throw him in the car seat—by now he's purplish and wheezing, really, really struggling—and I'm terrified, so I fly there. The whole trip must have taken three minutes. And the whole time—it seems crazy now—but I'm praying, I'm praying out loud." She turns and looks at me. "I'm not a very religious person, you understand? My father is God-fearing, but my mother was an atheist, and she was the one who ruled the roost, so I never really learned how to pray."

I nod because I understand.

"But I do. For some reason, I pray. So I'm driving and I'm praying, to whatever I can think of, which in the end is the most frivolous, ridiculous thing."

"What thing?" I croak the words out, caught up in the story.

Her eyes flash to mine. "Oh, it's so silly, Francesca, really! In my grandmother's house on the tub—this was my father's mother—was this ugly little plastic statue of a saint. I used to play with it in the tub when she bathed me there. So, of all things, his name comes to me at that moment. Saint Florian. Some obscure little patron saint of Lord knows what.

"So that's who I pray to. After all those years. Some ugly plastic saint on my grandmother's tub." She laughs.

"Oh."

"Anyway, my child is choking, and I'm praying to Saint Florian, Patron saint of drowning, that's what it was, I remember now. Drowning, because of the tub. Of course, I only learned this later, looked it up at some point because, well, I guess because it seemed to work and I was still scared, and I think I wanted to thank him." She shakes her head. "I know it's silly, but I was curious about his true derivation. Saint Florian. Patron saint of battles and harvests and drowning. That was it. It was such an odd combination."

I swallow hard, my mind spinning. Because what are the chances that a prayer to *that* saint — the patron saint of drowning — kept Frankie Sky from dying from a hole in his heart?

"Francesca . . . ?" She sits down next to me.

"Tell me," I say, my voice shaking. "Tell me what happened with Frankie after that."

She touches my hand. "I assumed it was clear. By the time we reached the emergency room, his breath had returned to normal and he was cooing happily. Not pale, not coughing, not gasping. It was a bit embarrassing, actually."

"And then?"

"Well, at that point, I felt downright silly — a hysterical new mom and all that. It was hard without Charles . . . I figured he had probably just choked on his own saliva in his sleep. I had half a mind to turn around and take him home."

"But you didn't?"

"No. I was already there. And he was only a few days old. They said I should have him checked out. Better safe than sorry."

"And that's when they found the hole?"

"Yes, on an echo test and EKG." Mrs. Schyler stands and walks to the fridge, her eyes darting to the clock over the stove. "Goodness, look at the time. I really must pull us together."

She grabs the applesauce from the fridge, yells for Frankie again, and buries the pill in a spoonful. "The hole was between the two upper chambers, difficult to get to. The doctors were dumbfounded, because such a large opening should have affected him at birth. He should have been weak, lethargic. There should have been other symptoms. But there hadn't been. Which made them doubt the results. We took him home just fine, and then . . ." Her voice trails off. She takes the amber prescription bottle down from the sink, uncaps it, drops out another pill. "Well, it was as if it just appeared. They said they'd never seen that happen before."

"So what did you do?"

"As I said, by then, he was fine, so I didn't know what to do. One of the specialists wanted to operate, but that was risky, so we weren't sure."

"But how could you just leave it there?" It comes out like an accusation, and I blush.

"We didn't just leave it, sweetheart. We thought long and hard on it, Frankie's grandpa Harris and me. By then, Charles was gone . . . so much had happened by then, so we decided to wait a bit, since he wasn't showing any more symptoms. Two weeks later, he was still fine, and when we scanned him again, there was almost no sign of abnormal activity. Little evidence of a tear on EKG. As if the hole had come that night, and then disappeared. As if . . . Well, never mind. That's a whole other story, and we really do have to go." She turns toward the hallway. "Where is that child? Come, I bet you haven't even seen his room."

I follow her out of the kitchen and down a long

hallway, my head swimming with questions. Potato practically trips me as I walk, following way too close underfoot.

As we reach the end of the hall, I can't help myself and say, "But aren't you worried? What do I do if . . . I mean, what if it happens again?"

She turns around and holds a finger to her lips and whispers, "We can't just sit around worrying, now can we? And it hasn't happened since. So, knock wood, Francesca, the child seems perfectly fine, doesn't he? And he takes the medication, so there's that. But, just in case, I did something silly." She giggles, almost embarrassedly. "Wait till you see. I went out and bought a statue of Saint Florian. I had to search high and low for one, but I found it and I put it next to his crib. It's been in his room ever since." She shrugs and turns the knob to Frankie's closed bedroom door. "Maybe my grandmother knew something."

She opens the door, and Potato rushes in and jumps up onto Frankie's bed. "Frankie," she says, "you know you're not supposed to close the door."

The room is big and messy, but meticulously decorated in deep blues, greens, yellows, and oranges. Frogs are everywhere, tree frogs and bullfrogs and tropical frogs, painted on walls, printed across borders, stuffed on his bed and on chairs. It takes my breath away.

"Frankie?" Mrs. Schyler says. He's nowhere to be seen.

She rolls her eyes and nods at the dog, who jumps

down from the bed and runs to the far corner, to a small fort made from blankets and sheets pulled over the top of some chairs. Potato stands nose to blanket, tail wagging.

"Frankie, I said we need to go! I told you an hour ago to get ready."

The blankets rustle.

"Frankie!"

Potato dashes under now, taking the blanket with him, unveiling Frankie crunched in a ball, like Toto unveiling the Wizard. Frankie shoves him away. "Hey, dumb Tato! No fair!" He starts to pull the blanket back over himself, but stops when he sees me. He stands up. "What taked you so long, Beans?"

"I've been here, Frankie," I say.

"Beans?" Mrs. Schyler raises her eyebrows.

Now I roll my eyes. "A nickname my dad gave me."

Frankie walks over and sits on his bed, and Potato jumps back up with him. He pats the dog's head. Mrs. Schyler walks to a laundry basket in the corner and retrieves some clothes.

"Would you mind getting him dressed, Francesca?" She hands me the pile and glances at her watch. "I really need to get you kids off to the club."

I nod and she wanders out. I sit on the bed next to Frankie.

And that's when I see it, the little ivory statue of Saint Florian. He's ugly, wears a long flowing robe and a pointed hat, and holds a bucket and a flag with a cross on it. *The patron saint of harvests, fires, and drowning.*

My heart nearly stops, because I've seen him before. A bigger version, the first and only time that I went there.

On my mother's desk. At the Drowning Foundation.

Next to a photograph of Simon.

■■ *twenty-one* ■■

On the way to the club, Mrs. Schyler seems distracted
and frazzled. It's as if she has two different sides; one
second she's chatty and reassuring, the next she's a
flighty, disastrous mess. Maybe it wears on her, dealing
with Frankie all on her own.

Speaking of which. He taps on the back of my seat
with his foot. "You promised, remember? First let us go
to the playground, right, Beans?"

I twist around and give him a look. After all, it was
his fault we never made it to the playground the other
day. He's the one who went diving into the pool. He's the
one who scared me half to death.

His eyes meet mine. He smiles angelically, like
Simon used to.

Mrs. Schyler glances at him in the rearview mirror.
"Now listen good, Frankie. You'd better be behaving
yourself."

●　　●　　●

I tell Frankie we need to put our stuff down first, so
we bring our bags to the pool and Frankie gets towels

and lays them on the same chairs as Monday to stake them out. The pool area is empty, not even Peter Pintero yet. It's nearly ten a.m. I wonder if he's late.

I also wonder if Mrs. Merrill will be coming today, then remember my new resolve about having undistracted focus, so I make a mental note to cut it out with the worrying about sneaky Mrs. Merrill. I need to do what I'm being paid for, which is keep an eye on Frankie Sky. Which is not exactly easy, to say the least.

As soon as we reach the playground, Frankie breaks free and makes a beeline for the merry-go-round. Not the ride-on-a-horse kind, but the platform-with-the-handles-you-pull-as-you-run-then-jump-on-once-it's-spinning kind.

Frankie climbs on, grabs the handles, and yells, "Turn it, Beans, please!" He leans way back, face tilted to the sky.

I grab a handle and start to run. It takes me a few laps to get it moving decently, and several more to get it going at a good speed.

"Faster!" he yells, head back, eyes closed, his tongue stuck out in the air.

"What are you doing, Frankie?"

"Am tasting the wind, Beans! It is cold and minty like this!"

"Hah, Frankie!"

I let go and stare at him as he whips past me in circles, his blond curls like Simon's, blowing free in the wind. *Simon.* Is Frankie Sky part of him? Or is that totally crazy? I sit on the ground and close my eyes against the dizzying circles that spin in front of me and inside my head.

When the merry-go-round stops, Frankie looks down at me, disappointed. "Hey, Beans. Can you please do it again?"

"Okay, Frankie, sorry."

I stand and start to run again, this time in the opposite direction. Frankie says, "You, too, Beans, you come be with me when it's fasty fast, because that will be lots of fun!"

I shake thoughts of Simon away and work to gain speed, faster and faster until I'm running like mad, then jump on next to him and throw my own head back in the wind. I stick my tongue out like he did.

"Is it good, Beans?" he asks.

"Yes, Frankie. It's really, really good."

▪▪ *twenty-two* ▪▪

"Hey, Frankie, that you?"

I startle and look to my right. I've been lost in thought, staring blankly across at Mrs. Merrill's house.

Bradley Stephenson approaches, stands at the curb—my curb—a hand cupped to his eyes, squinting at me. My heart pounds so hard, I'm sure he can hear it from there.

"Me? Yeah."

He walks across the lawn—my lawn—smiling at me.

"Thought so. Cool. I didn't know you lived here."

"All my life."

He sits on the stoop. *My stoop. Next to me.* I try to tamp down the fire that's spreading up my neck to my cheeks. "What are you doing here?"

"Heading to Zette's," he says, but I know where he lives, and my street is out of his way from there.

Stop it, Francesca! Maybe he wasn't coming from there.

"Oh, right, sure," I say.

"So, how's your summer going? I heard you got a job." He smells good, like soap and guy things, which isn't helping to steady my nerves.

"Yeah. Mother's helper. For a boy who lives over on Sycamore Street." I try to get words out, say something smart, but it's hard to think through my pulse beating crazily in my brain. "And the money is good, so that's cool. How about you? Keeping busy?"

Keeping busy? Dumb. Idiotic. I'm a moron.

"Yeah. I just got back from my cousins'. They have a really nice house in Pennsylvania. It's on a lake. We did the whole barbecue/fireworks thing. And fished and stuff, you know."

"Oh, right, Zette told me."

He looks at me, and I quickly look away.

"Oh, and get this," he says. "So every morning we'd go out and swim in the lake. And there was this big nest near the lake. I mean, really big." He stretches his arms out to show me, and his hand touches my arm. Electric currents zip through me. "Sorry," he says, moving it away. "Anyway, my little cousin says that a brown pelican is living there, and I tell him he's wrong, because I kind of know this stuff, and I know pelicans only live in Florida and tropical places. But then I'm swimming, and the next thing you know, this huge brown bird goes flying over. Clearly, it's a pelican, with that big bucket beak and everything. Like this." He scoops his hand under his chin and laughs. "It was crazy, Frankie, I'm telling you."

I don't know what to say. I almost can't breathe sitting next to him. I want to say something deep and smart and meaningful, and then my mind goes to Lisette's text, and I realize I should ask him about reincarnation.

I'm about to, but he shrugs and stands, suddenly looking embarrassed. "I don't know why I told you that story," he says. "You're probably thinking I'm weird. Lisette would. But, anyway, I guess you had to be there."

I want to jump up and tell him he's not weird, not weird at all, and that I totally get it, so not to go, because if anyone understands, I do. I understand completely. But my words are stuck, and, anyway, he's already walking away.

"Good seeing you," he says, turning back once as he heads across the grass.

My heart crushes. I had so much more I wanted to say.

"Yeah," I say instead.

I watch him walk in the direction of Lisette's house, wanting to kick myself for being so stupid, then kick myself again for caring. What does it matter what I say, or don't say, to Bradley Stephenson? What does it matter if he thinks I'm a moron? He's Lisette's boyfriend, not mine.

But why did he come over? Is it so impossible that he could like me?

I watch until he's gone from view, then look up at the blue sky above the tree line and imagine how pretty it would be to see a pelican soaring through the leaves. How awesome it would be to be a bird and just be able to fly away.

My eyes light on the giant old tree on our front lawn. When I was little, Dad would swing me around in front of it, upside down by my feet. I would put my arms out and close my eyes and pretend I was a bold, beautiful hawk flying across the sky.

Even though it was fun, it was terrifying, too, because what if he let go and my body went sailing through the air and I crashed, headfirst, into its enormous trunk? As Dad would laugh and spin, I'd feel the blood rush to my face, making my cheeks full and my sinuses press down hard. But I'd never tell him to stop, because I wanted to be brave for him.

I think of Frankie earlier, head tipped back, tongue out, gleeful on the merry-go-round. Making me go up there and spin with him. Making me dive in and swim. Maybe Frankie will force me to be brave again.

Then again, I wasn't very brave with Bradley just now. I didn't even ask him the one thing I wanted to know. Maybe if I wasn't acting so dumb, hoping for mixed signals where there are none, I could have asked him about reincarnation.

Why do I get like that around him? Why do I like him so much? I look across at Mrs. Merrill's house. *Ugh, is that what's going on for Dad?*

I lie back on the cool stoop and close my eyes against all the unanswerable questions.

Maybe I should just go across the street and talk to her.

What if I pound on her door and tell her to just leave my dad alone? What if I confront her? But I won't, because it's not me. I don't do those kinds of things. Plus, my father would never speak to me again, and I need him. He's the only good thing that I have.

Well, Dad and Frankie. Frankie, who's almost like having my brother.

I kiss my fingers and stretch my arm out to place the kiss on Simon's frog. "Tell me, Simon, what do you think?" I ask out loud. "Do I need to try to stop whatever's going on over there?"

As the words leave my mouth, the earth shakes, vibrates under me, a sure sign, but then it's only my cell phone buzzing from inside my pocket.

I pull it out, disappointed, and hold it in the air above me. Texts from Lisette:

> So, any news on the you-know-who front?
> p.s. Text me, seriously. I want to know what's going on.
> p.p.s. Plans this weekend, maybe?

I look at the time. Bradley will be at Lisette's any minute. I wonder if he'll mention he was here.

I sit up and pull one of Mom's metallic gazing balls into my hands from where it's buried in the thick tangle of summer stems and blossoms and hold it in my lap like a crystal ball. It distorts my face like a fun-house mirror. I wish it would give me some answers.

Like what Frankie Sky has to do with my brother.

What if Simon did transmigrate? What if Frankie holds a piece of Simon's soul?

I lower my face closer and closer, until my eyes glaze over and my features stretch out and disappear. It starts to give me a headache, so I close them altogether and rest my cheek against the ball.

If some piece of Simon—no, Simon's very soul— still lives in Frankie Sky, then could I forgive myself, even a little, for letting my baby brother drown?

◼▮ *twenty-three* ▮◼

"I seed you from the window, Beans."

Frankie stands in the back of Mrs. Schyler's open hatchback, watching me as I walk up the driveway. He's dressed in swim trunks and a T-shirt, a life vest already buckled around him. As I approach, he holds a foot in the air to show me. "I gotted new water shoes, Beans."

"You can walk on water, then, huh?"

"No." He frowns. "That is not how they work."

"I know. I was joking, dude."

"Yep. I knowed that," he says.

He jumps out of the car, grabs my hand, and pulls me toward the house. "We're going to the beach today. Mommy, too. Even Tato is coming!"

"Ah." I stare up at the house. Butterflies flit in my stomach, though whether at the thought of the beach again or the thought of spending an entire day with Mrs. Schyler, I'm not sure.

"Is to celebrate my swimming! But I still have to keep my vest on."

"Good idea," I say absentmindedly.

We pass through the empty living room and into the kitchen, but I don't see Mrs. Schyler. The counter is littered with stuff—coffee cups, cereal boxes, the canvas beach bag, some of Frankie's clothes, and an open cooler, the same one they had at the beach last week. Frankie stops in the center of the room and starts fussing with the buckles on his life vest. "Need it off, Beans."

"Here, let me help you, Frankie. Where's your mom, anyway?"

"She was here, but then she gotted tired and said to wake her when Beans got here."

"Oh, okay." I undo the last buckle and he slips out and tosses it on the chair.

"Don't eat it, Tato." He shakes a finger in the dog's direction. "Beans, I need to go potty now."

I leave him in the bathroom and continue down the hall toward his room. At Mrs. Schyler's bedroom, I stop. Her door is open, and she's sprawled across the bed, facedown, in jean shorts and a halter top, a pair of flip-flops near the bed. Not exactly in beach mode.

I take a few cautious steps in, around laundry baskets and other things strewn about the floor. "Mrs. Schyler, do you want to get up?" I whisper, but her breath is heavy; it's clear there's no way she's waking up right now.

I turn to her nightstand and read the labels on a few of the prescription bottles lined up there. *Diazepam. Imitrex. Prozac.* I pick up the last one, Prozac. It's an antidepressant my mother takes, too.

"Mrs. Schyler?" I try again, but she doesn't move.

I tiptoe over to the bookshelves in the corner and let

my eyes scroll across them. There are all sorts of novels, steamy-looking romances with titles like *Hearts Afire, Lana's Secret, Lana's Revenge,* and *The Dream Held in Your Eyes.* There's a whole shelf of self-help books. There must be twenty by Deepak Chopra. I take a step closer, my eyes skimming the titles: *The Happiness Prescription; Reinventing the Body, Resurrecting the Soul.* I pull that one down and flip it open.

Breakthrough #1: Your Physical Body Is a Fiction.

I close the book. Whatever that means, it terrifies me.

I slip the book back in its place and look down the line of other titles. *The Story of Saints; A Child's Book of Saints; The Reincarnation of Soul: The Fallacy of Death.* I glance at Mrs. Schyler, but she's still breathing deeply, so I grab that last one and turn to the back cover, my eyes frantically reading the words.

Throughout history, religious scholars have agreed upon the existence of the soul, but differed on what happens to the soul after death. Is the soul inextricably linked to the physical body ceasing upon death? Or rather, is it an autonomous entity surviving a body's physical demise? In this volume, Dr. Nelson provides strong evidence that the soul is migratory and transferable in nature, and survives death, as we commonly understand that term . . .

There's a noise at the door, and I quickly slip the book back on the shelf, but it's just Potato, tail wagging, Frankie's life vest clutched in his mouth.

Behind him, Frankie comes running. "Dumb dog,"

he yells, "put that thing down! I tolded you no before!"
He stops at the door when he sees me. "Hey, Beans."

"Hey, Frankie," I say, finger to my lips. "I think your
mom needs to sleep more."

• • •

Mrs. Schyler wakes up around noon, and we get to
the beach by one.

The day is perfect and clear. We park in lot C, head
over the dunes, and set up our blanket several yards from
the shore. Mrs. Schyler pulls Frankie over and slathers
him with sunblock, then buckles him into his life vest.

I stare down the beach toward where I hung out with
Lisette just last week. We haven't talked much since
then. Probably because I've been busy with Frankie
and, as I know, Bradley is back from his cousins'. So
she's probably busy with him.

*If only I had talked more the other day. If only he'd
stop by again.*

"Francesca, do you need lotion?" Mrs. Schyler taps
me with the bottle.

"Oh, right, thanks."

"Here. Let me help you." She hands Frankie a pail
and shovel, and Frankie moves down the beach a little
to dig. "Francesca will be right there," she tells him.

I kneel, my back to her, and hold up my hair. She
rubs the lotion gently over my back and shoulders the
way my mother used to do.

"Thank you for letting me sleep this morning," she says.

I think of her earlier, facedown on her bed like my mother used to be so often in the months after Simon died. Her room dark, her shades drawn, as day after day passed by.

Has Mrs. Schyler been doing this since Mr. Schyler died?

But somehow, Mrs. Schyler seems different from my mother. Like she has those same dark moments my mother does, but around them she's cheerful and light. As opposed to my mother, who seems like she has no memory of how to be light.

"I intended to have the whole day here. I'm sorry we got such a late start." She takes my hair from my hands and releases it loosely around my shoulders. "Come, turn. I guess you can do the rest." She hands the bottle to me and smiles in this friendly way that makes me feel warm inside. I lotion my legs, chest, and face and hand the bottle back to her.

"There, that's better." She stretches out on the blanket while I keep an eye on Frankie. "Some days, Francesca," she says, touching my arm, "I'm really so okay. Others, I'm literally too tired to move. Do you ever have that feeling, where your mind wants to be in motion but your body feels like it's buried in quicksand?"

I nod.

"Frankie's father and I, we were high school sweethearts. We started dating when I was fifteen. That's your age, if you can imagine." I close my eyes and Bradley flashes by, so, yes, I can imagine. "Anyway, I don't know that I'd recommend that path to everyone, but for us, we were happy. Truly. I never dated another boy after Charlie, and I didn't want to. I know that must sound crazy to you, but I loved him from the minute I set eyes on him."

"It doesn't sound crazy," I say. "It must be hard for you."

"It has been, though I'm so very lucky to have Frankie. Anyway, it's the weirdest thing, but last night I got a call from an old army buddy of Charlie's. He's a good guy, a real nice guy. He and Charlie were in basic training together. He lives up in Cape Cod, and he calls once in a while to check up on me. But last night he mentioned me visiting. He was flirtatious, and fishing very sweetly, but still. Well, somehow, it just sent me spiraling. He was Charlie's friend. Wouldn't that be some sort of betrayal? Plus, there's Frankie, and you know what a handful he is. And, well, listen to me burdening you."

I press my toes in the sand, wishing I were wiser and knew the right thing to say. "I should probably go play with Frankie," I say instead.

"Did Frankie tell you how his father died, Francesca?"

"Yes, he did. I'm sorry."

"Well, I never told Frankie this—of course I didn't, how could I? He's way too young to understand. But when Charlie died, it was that very same night, nearly down to the minute, that Frankie stopped breathing. The night in his crib . . . the night the hole was found."

Her eyes meet mine. Mine fill with tears.

"It was only six days after Frankie was born. Not even a week. I could never understand how God could do that. Take my baby's father away before he even got a chance to know him. But the weird part was that it was as if Frankie knew something happened to Charlie, too. It was as if he felt it, experienced it firsthand, in the innermost depths of his heart."

Tears slip down my cheeks. Mrs. Schyler reaches over and brushes them away with her thumbs. "I believe that's what happened, Francesca. I swear I do. I believe that when we love someone, we experience their pain as our own. And there are so many things we just don't know or understand." I nod. "I bet you do, too. Of course you do. Okay, go on, sweetie, don't be sad. You go on and play with Frankie."

"Okay." I walk toward Frankie, thinking about all those books Mrs. Schyler has, how she must want answers, something that makes logical sense. Or proof that the stuff that doesn't make logical sense can possibly be true.

I stop, turn, and walk back to her. "Mrs. Schy— Brooke?" I say.

She cups her hands to her eyes and sits up. "Yes?"

"I don't know why exactly, but I think you should go. You should call that nice man back, Mr. Schyler's friend, and go see him."

• • •

Early the next week, I receive a cryptic text from Lisette.

Double date! Saturday! Mystery man (trust
me). Beach and movie. Alex will drive. Tell ur
mom mall. Home by 11, promise.

Mostly I want to say no, that if I can't have Bradley, I don't want anyone. But I know that's melodramatic and wrong, and, besides, I need to take the advice I gave to Mrs. Schyler.

I call Lisette back — at least let me find out who it is — but no one answers. I text, Are you kidding? Tell who! and wait, but I don't get any response.

At dinner, I mention to Mom and Dad that I may be going out with Lisette on Saturday.

"You've been busy lately, getting out a bit more. I like to see that," Dad says. He gives Mom a look, like she should chime in with some support, but she keeps her eyes averted. He smiles at me, and, as always, there's something so apologetic about it. Like he knows that I know that my own mother hates me, and he feels pretty bad about it.

Suddenly, I want to tell Dad everything. About how I've been swimming again, first with Frankie at the pool, and then even in the ocean. Not very deep, but still. I waded in with him, nearly up to my waist. I want to tell him that Mrs. Schyler thinks that I am useful, and trustworthy, and good. I want to tell him that this

Saturday, Lisette and I are going on a double date, and that maybe, just maybe, some guy as great as Bradley Stephenson will kiss me.

I want to tell him about how Frankie Sky reminds me of Simon in every single happy way there is. That, yes, sure, he makes me miss Simon, too, but most of all, he makes me feel like Simon is near me again.

With all my might, I want to blurt these things out loud, not only to Dad, but to Mom. And I want them to be happy and sad and surprised and concerned, and for us to all hash things out, in a real discussion, with tears and laughing and arguing and making up, like other normal families do.

But I don't. I don't say a word. Because we are not a normal family, and probably never will be again.

∎∎ *twenty-four* ∎∎

Up in my room, I try Lisette again, but no answer. I text her instead and tell her to please stop torturing me and tell me the name of my mystery date.

I lie around for a while trying to think of what to do next, but my mind is preoccupied with all the same questions about reincarnation and Frankie's connection to Simon. Like, what Mrs. Schyler meant that day in her kitchen when she wondered aloud to me why Frankie was convinced that he could swim.

This thought jars something in my brain. I run to my closet and dig way in the back for my box of old school projects and reports. There are piles of stuff: construction-paper drawings, dumb poems mounted on oak tag, composition notebooks filled with ridiculous short stories about friends and animals and sea life. I scoop it all out until I come to what I'm looking for: a paper I wrote the year before Simon died.

Wolfgang Amadeus Mozart; The Musician
and the Man, by Francesca M. Schnell

It was Mr. Brenner's class, some silly ten-year-old's research paper. It meant nothing to me back then.

<u>Biographical Background</u>: Wolfgang Amadeus Mozart was born in 1756. His father was Leopold Mozart. His mother was Anna Maria Pertl Mozart. He was born in Salzburg, which is now Austria. He was a classical composer who composed over six hundred works during his career, and is one of the most well-known of all the famous composers. He started composing at the age of five.

I remember that when Mr. Brenner had given the class our list of choices, I had picked Amadeus because my mom had been watching a movie about him. I had no idea he was actually the same person as Mozart until I read the book from the library on him.

But I'm looking for something else. I flip pages of my kid-like print until I see it, under its own heading, in the middle of a page:

<u>Was Mozart A Prodigy or Something More?</u> By the time he was five, Mozart had already written a piano concerto, a sonata, and several minuets. His compositions were not simple, and they were technically accurate. How could he know how to do this?

Because Mozart was so young, people

called him a prodigy. But could that alone really explain how amazing he was?

By the age of eleven, Mozart had completed a full-length opera. People began to think it was more than genetics or good DNA. Maybe Mozart had been reincarnated with the soul of a great composer. Maybe only that could explain how he played so well.

Good Lord, why is that child so completely convinced he can swim?

Had Simon's soul swum into Frankie Sky? Did the ocean have something to do with it?

Mrs. Schyler had been in the ocean with Frankie on the day he was born. Frankie hadn't been born until later that night, but if that was the same day Simon died, maybe Simon's soul transferred then and there, and that's why Frankie thought he could swim. Maybe Simon couldn't swim yet, but his soul could, and did. Maybe his soul swam into Frankie Sky.

I toss the report into the box and shove it all back into my closet. At my desk, I flip on my computer and type in the term *transmigration,* then click on the Wikipedia entry, which directs me with an arrow back to *Reincarnation:*

The word "reincarnation" derives from Latin, literally meaning "entering the flesh again." The Greek equivalent *metempsychosis* (υετευψύ χωσίς) roughly corresponds to the common English phrase "transmigration of the soul" and also usually connotes reincarnation after death, as either <u>human</u> or <u>animal</u>, though emphasizing the continuity of the soul, not the flesh.

I scroll down, passing information on Buddhism, Jainism, and Hinduism, until I get to the names of famous philosophers I've at least heard of or learned about in school.

In *Phaedo,* Plato makes his teacher <u>Socrates</u>, prior to his death, state: "I am confident that there truly is such a thing as living again, and that the living spring from the dead."

I ex out the screen and walk quietly down the hall and open the door to Simon's room. I switch on the light and walk over and sit on Simon's bed.

Fisher Frog tips over when I do, yellow-green legs poking up in the air. Mom's gift to Simon from me when he was born. I'd forgotten all about him. He was Simon's favorite, a soft, plush terry, with his white shirt and black jacket and shoes. When he got bigger he named him after Jeremy Fisher from the Beatrix Potter books.

I pick him up and hug him to my chest. He still smells of Simon, of powder and peaches, the smell of his baby shampoo. Is it just in my head, or is it possible for things to hold his scent for so long?

On the nightstand is the little table lamp with the frog engineer. I flip the toggle and the train starts up, clicking its circle around the base. It startles me. I didn't expect it to work after all this time, as if I believed that all the parts of Simon's world stopped the very same moment that he did.

I switch it off again and stare at the glider chair across the room, with its tweedy flecks of ice-cream colors. Mom had nursed Simon there for what seemed like forever. I remember feeling jealous, whining for her to finish, to stop paying so much attention to him.

"Five minutes, Francesca. He's just a baby. You and I will have plenty of time." The memory of her words makes my heart tighten.

Beyond the glider is a bookshelf still filled with Simon's books, many of which had been mine before his. I put Fisher Frog down on his pillow, walk to the shelf, and run my fingers along them—*The Tale of Peter Rabbit, The Tale of Mr. Jeremy Fisher, Where the Wild Things Are, In the Night Kitchen, Sylvester and the Magic Pebble*—until I find the one I want.

I slip it out and study the cover. *Frog and Toad Are Friends*. Two frogs, one yellowish, one green, sit in the mushrooms and leaves, the yellow one reading a book to the green one. I never knew which one was Frog and which was Toad, but Simon did, and he'd correct me when I mixed them up.

I open to the table of contents:
SPRING
THE STORY
A LOST BUTTON

A SWIM

THE LETTER

The titles flood back like the names of favorite toys.

I close the book and pull two others in the series, *Frog and Toad All Year* and *Frog and Toad Together*, then run my finger along the shelves. There is no dust. In fact, every inch of the room is perfectly clean. I think of my mother coming in here every week to vacuum and wipe off all of Simon's old things, and it makes me sad. It makes me feel sorry for her. Who is she keeping it clean for? It's not as if Simon is coming back. I wish she'd raze the room, empty his things, turn it into something new and cheerful and productive.

I run my finger along the shelf again, wishing it were thick with dust, that I could write *Francesca Schnell Was Here* in gray-white fuzz so that she'd find it the next time she came in here to clean.

I write it anyway, invisible letters that slip across the pristine wood.

I turn to leave, the three books in hand, but my mother is there, staring at me through the crack in the door.

"Francesca?" She pushes the door open. The look on her face is wild, furious. As if I've betrayed her.

My eyes dart to Simon's bed, where I left Fisher Frog lying faceup on his pillow. I was going to fix him before I left. Leave everything the way I found it.

But my hands, they still cling to his books. *Frog and Toad.*

"What?"

I hear it in my tone, in that one word, how it is laden with attitude and anger. I want to suck it back, but I can't. It's already out there in the air.

One defiant little word, *What?*

She glares, her eyes filled with disbelief, then tears. Why is she so angry at me? Have I done something so wrong? I mean, back then, yes, I did everything wrong. I left my baby brother unattended. But here, now? I have done nothing wrong. And yet, I will never be forgiven.

"Francesca. Why are you in here?"

Why should I not be?

Have I trespassed? Am I a criminal? A thief? Isn't this my house, too?

He was also my brother.

But, of course, I have no rights here anymore. I am— and will always be—the person who let Simon drown.

"Francesca, I'm speaking to you."

I set my contaminated feet upon Simon's sacred ground.

"I don't know why I came in," I whisper. "I just needed to. I wasn't doing anything, I promise. Just being here with . . ." My eyes go to Fisher Frog, then to my hands. I'm holding out the books. "I wanted to bring some to read to Frankie Sky."

"Who?" She shifts. Her anger crackles. Every move is stilted with the effort to contain herself. To not lash out at me like she wants to.

"Frankie Schyler. The boy I watch?" Does she not

hear one single thing that I say? Does she not pay me one iota of notice? "He likes frogs, so I wanted to read them to him. I promise I'll return them." My voice shakes. I want to get past her and leave.

"Don't," she says. "Put them back. All of them. I need them to stay there like they were." She blocks the door, her arms wrapped to her chest, against me.

"Seriously? I can't . . ." But I don't finish. It's not worth it. It doesn't matter. There's nothing to argue about anymore.

I walk back to the shelf and slip the books in their places, each spine perfectly flush, as they were. My eyes dart to the spot where I wrote my name, but of course I can't see anything there.

I turn back to her. "Done. See?"

"Thank you," she says.

She walks to the bed and takes Fisher Frog and props him at the end where he was, then looks around to see what else I've moved out of place. When she's satisfied, she ushers me out the door. But she doesn't need to worry. I'm gone.

◼◼ *twenty-five* ◼◼

Friday morning and it's raining. I pray tomorrow will be sunny. I'm excited, if terrified, for my big double date with Lisette.

We've been exchanging texts, but all she will say is Trust me, or When have I steered u wrong? And I do, and she hasn't, so I stop pestering her.

Still, I run through the names of all the guys I can think of who are on the baseball team with Bradley. The truth is I don't know most of them. Bradley has one friend I've met who's kind of cute. Michael Peach. I could probably be happy with him. Nice smile, dark hair, dimples.

"You taste like Peach," I will say after we kiss.

"And now you do," he will answer, leaning back in to taste me some more . . .

I look over my choice of outfit again, the one I think I've settled on. A three-tiered black-and-white polka-dot miniskirt and white hoodie over a green burnout T-shirt and my green no-lace Converse sneakers. I hold the skirt up against me in the mirror and twirl, checking both sides. Bradley's face keeps popping into my head.

I try to replace him with Michael Peach, but my brain isn't having that at all.

I flop down on my bed and imagine us together here, Bradley beside me, our fingers linked, just talking about baseball and pelicans and things. But Lisette's mad face keeps horning in, her gorgeous, blond, Barbie-doll locks blocking him from my view.

I give up and think about Frankie Sky instead. I'd better get dressed and get over there. So what if my boyfriend is a four-year-old? At least he loves me back.

I laugh at the thought, but the truth is I already love Frankie Sky, I do. And I'm grateful for whatever weird, crazy karma brought me to him.

• • •

Downstairs, evidence of Mom still sits on the counter: half-eaten toast, a teacup with the paper tag dangling. I toss the toast in the garbage, rinse the plate and cup, and put them in the dishwasher.

I wander down the hall to Dad's study. He's at his computer, dressed for work in khaki pants, a sports coat, and a tie. When I knock, he looks up, his eyes shooting back to the screen. Does he look guilty? Hard to say.

"Hang on a sec, Beans." His fingers move fast across the keyboard.

"What are you doing?"

"This?" He looks up, then back down to finish whatever he's typing. "Nothing much. Just some prep work for a big closing next week." He shuts the computer and walks over to me, smiling. "You still here, then, eh? You need a ride to work? I'm on my way."

Relief. He's going in to his office, then.

"Sure," I say. "I've just got to get my things."

As I run upstairs, I hear him singing some dumb old song about San Jose. Well, good then. Whatever. As long as he's going to work.

In my room, I grab my backpack and a bathing suit in case it clears up and head back to the stairs. On the landing, I change my mind, double back, and walk to Simon's room.

I open the door, go to his bookshelf, and take down the three books about Frog and Toad. I press the other books together to close the gap and slip the ones I took into my bag. On the way out, I grab Fisher Frog and quickly shut the door behind me.

I run back to my room and sit Fisher Frog on the bottom of my bed, then toss a blanket over him, and close my door as I leave.

• • •

It's been weeks since I've been in Dad's car. He got a new one a year ago, unlike my mother, whose is still the same one from Before.

As always his car is neat, but today it seems neater.

It smells like leather and rug shampoo and air freshener. There's one of those cardboard pine trees swinging from the rearview mirror.

My head swims with accusatory questions: *Why is your car so clean? Why do you have an air freshener? What are you hiding in here?* I feel like the Spanish Inquisition. Maybe I should just ask him straight out: *So are you or are you not having an affair with Mrs. Merrill?*

Of course I won't, and I don't, but part of me relishes the look I'd get if I could. But then, I'd upset him, and I don't want to alienate my father. Who would I have left?

I reach into my backpack and pat the Frog and Toad books. I'm excited to read them with Frankie, someone who wants to be with me. So be it if I've resorted to stealing things from my own home.

I turn up the music — Dad's got some lame oldies station on — and scope around for evidence. I pop open the glove box and close it, pop it open and close it, like I'm fidgeting rather than snooping. Each time, I let it gape open just a few seconds longer, but nothing seems out of the ordinary in there. I slip my fingers into the door pocket, then pretend to drop something and lean down to peek under my seat. I pull the lid to the console between the seats up, but don't see anything of note in there.

Of course I have no idea what I'm looking for. Tissues with lipstick, maybe? A lost earring? As I'm about to close the console, I see Dad's eyes shift ever so slightly. The movement is small, but I catch it, and there's something suspicious about it.

"What do you need, Frankie?"

"Nothing. Why?"

"Because you're rummaging. Like a squirrel looking for nuts or something."

I laugh because he's funny. "I thought maybe you'd have a mint," I say, because I know I saw some in there.

"Oh look, you do."

I pull out the tin of Altoids, snap the lid open, and place one on my tongue. It burns there, way too strong for this early hour of the morning. I want to spit it out, but need to kill time, so I take another few out and slip them in my pocket, my eyes darting back to the console. To the spot beneath where the tin sat.

Something glints there. A small silver key against the black bottom.

I start to put the tin back, but Dad says, "Just keep them, Frankie," and bangs the console shut with his elbow.

He's mad. Does he know I saw it?

"Thanks, you sure?"

"Yes. I have more. Is there anything else you need?"

I shake my head, my mind swimming. "Good then." He turns onto Sycamore, I point out the house, and he pulls over at the curb. "Have a good day, Francesca." He calls me Francesca, a warning, and pulls away before I've barely stepped out of the car.

After Dad drives away, I sit on the Schylers' front stoop under the overhang. I'm early and don't want to wake anyone.

I stare through the raindrops at the house across the street and wonder whose key that was in Dad's car. Is it possible it's just some random and meaningless key? Lots of people have random keys that go to nothing, right? Keys that went to something once, but don't now. Or maybe it goes to Dad's office.

At nine o'clock, I stand and ring the bell. Frankie answers in two seconds flat. Potato slips between his feet.

"Hey, Beans. I was waiting and waiting, but you just stayed there sitting."

He's in shorty pajamas with airplanes on them, just like a pair Simon used to have. It makes my heart skip, but then everything these days does. I mean, all little kids have pajamas with airplanes on them.

"If you saw me, Frankie, why didn't you open the door?"

"I seed you from the window," he says, as if that explains anything, closes the door, and pulls me toward his bedroom. Potato follows. As we pass Mrs. Schyler's room, he puts his fingers to his lips and whispers loudly, "Shush, she is sleeping, so we have to be quiet in my room." We sit on his bed, and Potato jumps up and curls in a ball on his pillow.

I haven't been in his bedroom since the day Mrs. Schyler showed me the statue of Saint Florian. Now I pick it up and hold it in my hand. It's lighter than I expected because it looks like real stone, but, really, it's just cheap old plastic.

I study the man's funny hat with the feather and his robe with all the folds and the flag with a cross on the front. Around the base, etched in fake gold, are the words *Non vel ocean mos somniculous nostrum animus.* Latin, I'm guessing. I have no idea what it means.

I pull out my cell phone and type in the words so I can look them up later, though I'm not sure why I'd want to know. Maybe all this endless sleuthing is finally getting to my brain.

"Frankie," I blurt, "when *exactly* is your birthday?"

"June," Frankie says. "When Grandpa gotted me the tractor."

Simon died on June fourteenth.

"But which day, Frankie? Do you know which day you were born?"

He nods and holds up his pointer fingers on each hand, side by side. Either a two or an eleven.

"The second, Frankie, or the eleventh?" I ask, impatient. "Is your birthday June eleventh?" I feel oddly relieved, but then he shakes his head, looks at his right hand, and pops three more fingers up on that hand. One on the left. Four on the right. Fourteen.

"That is the right way," he says, nodding.

"Fourteen? June fourteenth, Frankie?"

"Yep, June fourteenth. That is Frankie Sky's birthday."

I try to steady the room from spinning out from under

me. I need to keep focused, to get more answers, or I'm going to drive myself crazy.

"Frankie," I say, trying to keep my voice from shaking, "do you *know* Simon?" The words, out in the air, feel dangerous.

"Yep, sure I do, Beans. I knowed Simon."

Tears fill my eyes. I don't know what to do, how to feel. Everything's gone swirling in my brain. Maybe this is what I knew from the first second I met Frankie, but just couldn't let myself believe.

He stands in front of me, tugs on my knee. I try to see his face, not Simon's, but it's impossible. His face is the same as my brother's.

"Do you want me to show you how, Beans?"

"Yes, Frankie," I breathe. "I want you to show me how."

"Okay. Is easy."

He lets go of my knee and walks across his room to his bookshelves. What does he have? What kind of proof of my brother's existence will he bring and place in my hands?

He stands on a plastic step stool in front of his bookcase and rummages. It takes forever till he finally jumps down. "Here, Beans," he says, placing an old DVD in my lap.

I stare in disbelief at the case. *Alvin and the Chipmunks*, it says.

"See, this one." He points to the chipmunk wearing a red sweater with an *A* on it. "This one is Alvin, and he is the most famous one. And this is Theodore. And this one, here, is Simon. I like Simon. He is smart. He is my favorite one."

My eyes, fill with happy or sad tears, I'm not sure. But I start laughing, too, because how can I help it? Because sometimes it's all you can do.

twenty-six

Somehow, Saturday gets here. Way too early, I put on my pre-chosen outfit and my green Converse sneakers, pin my hair back in barrettes, put a little eye shadow and lip gloss on, and study myself in the mirror. I look as good as I ever will.

Mom and Dad are in the living room on the couch, engaged in some sort of serious conversation. They shut up the minute they see me. Dad gives me a fatherly once-over.

"Hey, Beans, you're headed out, then?"

"Yes. The mall, remember? And a movie, maybe. With Lisette and her boyfriend and his friend."

Dad raises his eyebrows. "Well, that sounds awfully like a date. Good for you! You look beautiful. So, perhaps it actually is?" He winks.

I roll my eyes at him. "Just friends. Like I said."

"Well, have fun anyway. But check in. And be home by eleven."

"I will."

"No later than that," Mom says.

When the horn honks, Dad cuts me off at the door and heads out first, so I'm already feeling self-conscious.

I trail behind, my eyes searching frantically for my date. The top is down, Alex is driving, Bradley's in the passenger seat. My heart starts up at the sight of him. In the back is Lisette. Lisette and my mystery date. I stop in my tracks.

My heart sinks.

My mystery date is Peter Pintero.

Not Michael Peach.

Not even close to Bradley Stephenson.

I want to turn back, go inside, but I force my legs to walk forward, fighting the tears that want to come. It's not like he's a bad guy or anything. He's just not who I was hoping for.

Bradley smiles as I approach. "Hey, Frankie, good to see you."

"Hey." I keep my head down so as not to give away my crashing heart.

From the backseat, Peter parrots him. "Yeah, hey, Frankie, good to see you." He laughs like it's a joke or something, but if it is, I'm not in on it. Still, I need to smile and suck it up and not ruin the day for Lisette. She was trying to do a good deed. And it doesn't have to be a date if I don't want it to be.

Bradley opens the door and gets out, holding the seat forward for me. I slip past him into the back, my arm tingling where it brushes him. Next to me, Peter smiles dumbly, punches my arm all friendly, like the stupidest sort of hello.

Dad stands at the driver's side talking with Alex. My

parents have known the Sutters forever. I stare down at the floor wondering if Lisette realizes that I know Peter from the club. She must, but if she did, wouldn't she think to ask me if I liked him? It's not like I've mentioned him at all.

Then again, I've been close-lipped about everything lately, so I know it's my fault, not hers. I still feel blindsided, though. I begged her to tell me who my date was. If she had, I could have said no.

"Okay, kids, not too late. And try to have fun." Dad winks at me and pats the car in permission for us to go, then starts back toward the house. The smell of suntan lotion fills my nose. Has it only been two weeks since I went to the beach with Lisette? It feels like a century ago.

"So, fancy meeting you here, huh, Schnell?" Peter cracks up like it's hilarious. Whatever. It's not like there are guys lining up for me.

"Hey, Frankie!" Lisette leans forward, and Peter's eyes dart down her shirt. I want to tell him to put his tongue back in, but it's not like I even care. "No hello for your BFF?" She reaches across and squeezes my bare thigh, a trace of alarm on her face.

I try not to look her in the eyes, because I'm afraid if I do she'll see how disappointed I am.

"Okay, everyone set, then?" Alex asks, turning the radio to blasting and taking off in the direction of the beach.

●　　●　　●

Between the music and the wind, there's not much chance to talk. Fine by me; I don't have much to say. Lisette sings, and Bradley alternates air guitar and dashboard drums in the front. I can feel Peter watching me, so I just keep my eyes straight ahead.

Out of the corner of my eye, I check out Lisette. Her outfit is similar to mine: little black micromini with a pink T-shirt. Not that it would matter what she wore. Her bikini straps show through, which makes me realize I should have worn one, too. I guess I wasn't thinking about swimming.

When we reach the beach, Alex drops us at the steps. "What time, guys?" he asks, and Lisette says, "Not sure if we'll skip the movie or not. I'll text you later, around six, okay?" Alex salutes her and speeds off.

Lisette slips her hand in Bradley's and the two walk ahead of us, laughing and kissing as they head up the steps and across the walkway that crosses the dunes. Peter hangs back with me. I can barely get my legs to move. I pray he doesn't try to take my hand.

"So, Schnell, a little weird seeing you like this, huh?"

"Yeah, a little."

"It was Brad's idea. When I told him you work at the club, he was like, let's all hang out. Since you and Lisette are best friends."

"Yeah," I say. "Best. But I didn't realize you and Bradley were friends."

"We don't hang out all that much, but Coach holds

a few summer practices, and since we're on the team together . . ." He bends and picks up a rock in the sand and chucks it. "Though, not in the same league. He'll play for college, for sure; he's that good. Me, I mostly sit. At least I made varsity." He shrugs. "I'm a better swimmer. Went eight and two in 'fly this season. Pretty good."

I feel a little bad for him now. I guess that's why I didn't realize he was on the team.

"So, what about you? How's the job with the Schyler kid?"

"Frankie? It's good. He's funny."

"You seem good at it." My ears turn hot at the compliment.

We walk up the narrow steps to the dunes. I stay pressed against the railing, careful not to brush against him, which is dumb. I don't know what's wrong with me. Peter's actually nice. I'm the one being a jerk here.

"His mother seems a little nuts," he's saying, "and she drinks, which is why the kid's always running amok. But, of course, she's friends with Mr. H, or they probably would have banned her long ago."

"Really? She's nice," I snap. "I feel bad for her."

He shrugs. "She's hot, that's for sure. Anyway, you must be doing okay, because the kid hasn't drowned yet." I flush bright red and look away. "Shoot. I'm really sorry, Frankie. I didn't mean it like *that*. I just meant I've had to fish him out of the pool more times than you can count . . ." He stops and jams his hands into his pockets. "And, well, about your brother, I really didn't mean that drowning thing like that."

I look past him, down to the water where Lisette stands in the surf with Bradley. I wonder how much she's told Bradley about Simon, and what he's told Peter in turn. There are things she promised to keep private. But she wouldn't. I know she wouldn't tell him it was my fault.

"It's okay," I say, walking again. "Let's just catch up to those guys."

We stop short of them, where they stand with their backs to us in the surf, dark silhouettes haloed in golden sunlight. Bradley has his arm around Lisette's shoulder, the water sparkling beyond them. They look like cheesy models on a Hallmark anniversary card.

Bradley turns around and sees us and nods.

"Hey," Lisette says, turning, too, "you guys good?"

No! I want to say, *I am not good. I am very, very bad. I can't even begin to believe you'd think I'd like Peter Pintero. He's a total insensitive dork. And, by the way, what did you tell Bradley about my brother?* But instead, I say, "Yeah, sure, fine," although I can tell I don't sound too convincing.

"Dude, the water's kind of rough," Bradley says. "You guys want to walk down to the inlet instead?"

I'd forgotten all about the inlet about a half mile down the beach, a narrow strip of water that runs perpendicular to the ocean along the dunes. When the tide isn't too low, there's a tide pool that collects at the entrance, and you can wade in and find all sorts of cool things in there. We used to go down there with Simon.

As we walk, my heart aches for Simon, though in my mind I've started confusing him with Frankie Sky. I stay quiet as Lisette, Bradley, and Peter gossip about the usual stuff—who's dating who, which teachers suck, and what they've been doing so far this summer. In his defense, Peter tells some pretty funny stories about the club and lifeguarding, and some hilarious ones about Mr. Habberstaad. Apparently, his enormous distaste for the paper umbrellas is a well-known fact around the club.

Peter includes me in the stories, too, making it sound like I actually have a social life, saying things like, "Right, Frankie? You know, the weird dude who works in the pro shop, who looks like Mr. Magoo?" which makes me feel somewhat connected and good.

We reach the inlet. The water is thigh-high and crystal clear. Lisette strips off her T-shirt and skirt and tosses them in the sand. I don't have a bathing suit on, so I just slip off my Converse sneakers and wade in.

The tide pool brims with sea life. Horseshoe crabs, minnows, even a few harmless moon jellies. Still, Lisette is squeamish and wants to get out. She suggests we go in the ocean instead. "At least we can swim there," she says, wading out gingerly. "Something's going to bite me in here." I remind her that the same sea life is around her in the ocean as is here. "Yeah, but I don't *step* on it in there." She shudders, making her way back out. "I'm telling you, Frankie, there are freaking crabs all over the bottom!"

Peter, who hasn't taken his eyes off her bikini'd body, says, "I'm game!" and follows her out like a puppy.

I wait for Bradley to go with them, but he stays here, in the inlet. In fact, he's not even watching Lisette. He's bent over, swishing his hands through the water. "Man, look at this one. It's enormous," he says, hauling a horseshoe crab out by its tail.

"Come on, guys!" Lisette says, then looks back at me and cringes apologetically. She doesn't know that I've been in there, in the ocean, swimming with Frankie Sky.

"It's okay, I forgot a suit, anyway," I say. "I'll hang here. You guys go ahead without me."

Peter doesn't seem to care either way. He whips off his shirt and follows Lisette toward the surf. When she gets there, she turns and yells, "Hey, Brad, aren't you coming in with us?" I'm wondering the same thing, my heart beating fast, as he sloshes up next to me.

"I'll be in soon!" he yells back.

I stare down, away, to anywhere but next to me.

"So, it's just us, then," he says.

I don't answer because I'm finding it impossible to breathe.

twenty-seven

"Aren't you going in?"

Bradley looks at me, and I look at him, and there's this weird, awkward moment where our eyes lock.

"Nah. I'm going to hang back here and explore for a while. You want to come with me?"

Yes! "Won't Lisette mind?"

He shrugs. "I doubt it."

I look down the beach after her, wondering what I should do. But Bradley is right. She's already swimming out into the waves.

We move to the edge of the inlet where it's easier to slog along. My heart is having serious palpitations, which makes it hard for me to think.

Why did Bradley stay back? Does he feel sorry for me?

"Man, look at that!" He points up to where a large bird swoops overhead and disappears into the dunes. "You know what that was?" I shake my head, pretty sure it wasn't a pelican. "That was a great blue heron! They don't even live here; they build their rookeries on Gardiners Island, but they come here to feed."

"Rookeries?"

"Yeah, nests. They have these huge nests they call rookeries. But not over here. Is it okay if we head in that direction?" He points away from the ocean toward the dunes.

"Yeah, sure," I say, barely managing two words.

As we walk, Bradley points out plants and animals, amazing things I never knew existed here. Not just horseshoe crabs, but minuscule bugs that skim the very top of the water. He makes Long Island sound like some sort of exotic paradise. He points out eel grass (which grows in meadows and can grow up to four feet tall), eastern oysters (their pearls are pretty, but not worth much), and orange-billed winter cormorants (his favorite birds, even if they're common, because they all stand facing in one direction, their beaks making goofy expressions). He tells me how when bluefish feed in a frenzy, it appears as if the water's surface is boiling. He shows me how clamshells have rings that tell you their age, the same way a tree trunk does. As he talks and points and digs, his eyes sparkle, and it gets harder and harder to remind myself that he's Lisette's boyfriend rather than mine.

Every few minutes, he wades deeper into the inlet to scoop up another handful of life-filled silt and sand.

"See this?" he asks, pushing at a little white speck. "Yeah?"

"It's a mole crab. They're so small, you can't tell which side is their head and which is their butt. So you have to watch how they walk. Because they walk backward, so, see, if I touch him like this, he goes that way, so his head is over here."

I try to watch as he pokes at it, but I'm lost in his lips and the sound of his words.

"How do you know all this stuff?" I finally manage.

"AP Biology. Mr. Barrett. Plus, I went to this camp in Florida one year. I thought I wanted to be a marine biologist."

"You did?"

"Yeah."

"But you don't anymore?"

He shrugs. "I don't know. I just think all this ocean stuff is cool."

"Oh."

"What do you like?" he asks.

"I don't know," I say, and for the first time in a long time, I realize how very true this is. I'm starting eleventh grade and I haven't even thought about it. As if I have no permission to really want or care about anything. I guess I should start thinking about it soon. "I like the water," I suddenly whisper. "And swimming. And I love my job with Frankie Sky." Tears spring to my eyes when I say this, and I turn my head so he won't see.

He looks off across the inlet politely, letting me collect myself. "That's so cool that you do," he says finally. "So, are you thinking about your brother?"

"Yes," I say, "I guess I am." I stop, but it's not because I don't want to tell him more about Simon. In fact, it surprises me how much I want to be open with him.

"That must've been hard," Bradley says, sloshing forward again. "My mom lost her brother, too, when she was, like, eight years old. He was only five, so it's kind of like the same as what happened to you." I nod, overwhelmed by his telling me this. I wonder if Lisette knows. "He died in a car crash. Her father was driving. My grandfather. My mother wasn't in the car. She still remembers him to this day."

"Yeah, I don't think you ever forget," I say.

He stops again and looks at me. My stomach churns, in a good way. "That was dumb of me," he says. "I didn't mean it like that, like you'd forget him. What I meant is she still misses him, like a lot, like every single day. And she's forty-three, so I know it must be really, really hard."

I look down at the water.

"Anyway." He bumps my shoulder with his, nudging me to walk again. "I didn't mean to be morbid. I can find you more mole crabs." I laugh, and he smiles this cute sideways smile he has. After a while, he says, "Hey, you want to sit down for a minute?"

I look back toward the ocean for Peter and Lisette, but we've walked so far, it's hard to make out much from here except a few big boats dotting the horizon.

"How far out do you think those guys are?"

"No idea."

"How come you didn't go with them?"

"Me? I don't know." He steers us up toward the dunes. "I guess I'd rather be doing this."

The sand toward the dunes is warmer and feels good on my toes. I try to walk a few paces ahead of him to keep our shoulders from touching. Because I want them to be touching so badly.

My mind races through everything—from his invitation to the movie and Lisette telling me he thinks I'm pretty, to the other day on my front stoop—but I can't form a solid, reasonable thought.

"Hey, hold up. Check this out!" He kicks at something in the sand, then leans down and fishes it out. "Wow, cool. Here, for you." He places a flat, white disk in my hand.

I blink at it. It's a sand dollar.

I feel light-headed at the sight of it and at the swirling sense that everything lately is unexplainable, bigger and more powerful than I am.

"What?" he says. "What's wrong?"

"It's just that these things, they're rare, and . . . Well, never mind. It's stupid."

"Tell me."

"You want to know?"

"I do if you want me to." My heart goes tumbling when he says that.

"It's just that, when I was little, I was kind of obsessed with shells. I collected them. Nautilus shells, jingles, scallops, everything. But I didn't have one of these. And I really wanted one, so I was always hunting for them. And, well, it's what I was looking for the day my brother died." My voice cracks, but I manage to keep back the tears. I've never told anyone that part, about the sand dollar, not even Lisette. I don't know why I'm telling Bradley now.

"Wow," he says, "that's pretty crazy." I nod and swallow, closing my fingers around the perfect circle in my hand. "So, do you want to sit for a second?"

"Yes, okay. I think I do," I say.

He drops down in the sand, and I sit next to him, my knees folded up, my arms wrapped around them. I open my palm and look at the sand dollar again. No doubt it is magical.

"Are you okay, Frankie?"

"What do you mean?"

"You seem so sad."

"I'm not sad." My heart starts up again with all the things I want to say. "Not now, anyway. It's just that this summer, so far, it's been the weirdest thing. Ever since it started."

"Weird how?"

"Well, you said you believe in reincarnation, right?"

A look crosses his face, confusion then recognition, like he remembers Lisette was asking for me. "I do," he says. "I believe in lots of stuff like that. But definitely in karma and reincarnation."

"How come?"

"Why not? I mean, take a computer. You plug it in, and there's electricity in the wires, in the walls, so it runs. When you unplug it, the computer doesn't run anymore, but the electricity is still there, right? It doesn't just disappear. So I guess I think of our bodies like that, full of energy and information. And when we die, that has to go somewhere. So I think it does. It travels into another person's body."

"Do you mean like a soul?"

He shrugs. "I guess. Why are you asking me, Frankie?"

I look him in the eyes, and it kills me how deeply he looks back at me. Like he really cares what I'm thinking.

"I don't know, exactly. Well, kind of I do. Promise you won't think I'm crazy." He nods. "Okay, this kid I'm watching . . ." I stop because my breath goes away. Because he's resting his knee against mine.

"Yeah?"

Like, actually touching mine.

"It's just that this kid, he looks exactly like my brother. And his birthday — it's the same day my brother died." I pause and take a deep breath. "Which wouldn't be that weird, except he was here, at this same beach, the day my brother died."

"Wow."

I nod, because I don't know what else to say, because I don't even know what I'm saying anymore, and I don't really care, either, as long as I'm talking about it with Bradley.

I stare out over the inlet, trying to ignore what his knee is doing to my stomach — oh, and his hand, which is also on my leg now — and figure out how I got sucked into this vortex. This horrible, wonderful, amazingly dizzying vortex.

My sparkler wish flashes through my mind.

"Like the Christmas Island crabs," Bradley is saying. "Did you ever hear of them?"

"The what?" I blush. I can barely think, let alone follow the conversation.

"The red crab migrations." He sits up straighter and pulls his knee away from mine. I try to focus on what he's saying, but my brain has fled a million miles away.

"No. I'm sorry, the what?"

He laughs. "The Christmas Island red crabs." He draws a circle in the sand and puts legs on it. Then pincher claws.

"No, why?"

"Well, Christmas Island is this place in Australia. I don't know why it's called that, so don't ask. But it's covered in these bright red crabs. Like millions and millions of them."

"Millions?"

"Yeah. I swear. Anyway, they're land crabs, but they need to lay their eggs in salt water. Don't ask me why about that, either. They just do. So every year they migrate from the land to the ocean to lay their eggs. Then, as soon as they're done, they head right back to land again." I nod, but my head feels buzzed, like the night at the beach with Lisette. "Anyway, it takes days for these crabs to make the trip, and there are so many of them it's crazy, like a red carpet moving sideways across the roads. You should see it, Frankie."

"I'd like to." I want to say more, but can't muster

anything because I'm dizzy from the combination of his story and the way he says my name, but also from the fact that his hand is on my leg again, and his thumb is rubbing my thigh. I do everything in my power to keep it from trembling.

"Yeah, it's cool. But the point was, you were asking about karma." *I was? I don't remember what I was asking.* "Because it takes them forever to do all of this, and there are so many crabs that they have to close the roads, so the cars can't use them for days. Except they can't close all of them, so the crabs that pick the wrong roads get crushed to bits, hundreds of thousands of them. So how can you explain that? I mean, except by having bad karma?"

I have no idea because your finger is moving on my leg.

"Frankie?"

"Yeah? Sorry."

"Sorry for what?"

God, I don't know! Sorry that the crabs get crushed. Sorry that there's such a thing as bad karma. Sorry that I'm sitting here with you, because whatever's about to happen, I know I won't be able to stop myself. Because even though I want to be sorry, I'm not. I'm sorry I'm not sorry! I'm the opposite of sorry.

"Frankie?"

"Yes?"

And then there are no more words, because Bradley Stephenson's lips are on mine, and he's kissing me, his warm tongue nudging its way in and swirling around with mine. And Lisette is right, because the whole world goes spinning, and the air bursts with sparkler bits, silver-white wishes erupting like light through a dark sky.

Exactly the way I imagined.

And then he stops. "Shoot," he says. "Shoot." He looks down.

I look down, too. I don't know what to say.

Neither of us says anything.

Finally, he says, "It's getting late. We should probably get back to Pete and Lisette."

I push myself up, but I'm off balance. I start to walk the wrong way, but then realize and turn the right way. I walk fast, my arms wrapped around me. The sand feels cold now, and I wish I had my shoes. My sneakers are back at the tide pool.

The tide pool, which seems like hours ago.

God, what if Peter and Lisette are looking for us?

Bradley speeds up behind me, the sand crunching under him. "Frankie . . ."

He catches my arm, but I yank it away. "It's no big deal, don't worry about it . . ." he says. But I just focus on the sound of the sand. "Frankie, wait. Talk to me!"

I want to cover my ears, block him out, block it all out—everything except the part where his hands are on me and we're kissing.

• • •

When we reach the tide pool, it's empty, quiet. The sun is starting to dip, but Lisette and Peter aren't in sight. Their stuff is still there, though, on the edge of the inlet, so I guess they haven't come out yet.

I turn to Bradley, my arms still wrapped tight to my chest.

"We can never do that again, period. Okay?" I can barely make the words come out, and in my heart, I mean them less than anything I've ever spoken. I wish I could unsay them, throw myself into his arms like in one of those cheesy romances that Mrs. Schyler has on her shelf, but Lisette doesn't deserve that. And I don't deserve it. *It's no big deal,* he had said.

"Right," he says. "I got it." He shoves his hands in his pockets, veers away from me toward the edge of the tide pool.

I sit in the damp sand next to my sneakers and stare out at the ocean, to where I think I see them, Peter and Lisette, two dark spots swimming in.

■ twenty-eight ■

At least Bradley's right. As far as Lisette goes, every-thing seems okay.

She seems oblivious to anything wrong, rambles on about some friend of Peter's cousin who was out on the water on a Sunfish. Where they've been hanging for the past hour. *While I was kissing her boyfriend.*

"You should have come!" Lisette says, pulling at a corner of Peter's towel to dry herself. "It was pretty awe-some." Peter hands her the whole towel, then helps to wrap it around her.

For a split second, I find myself praying that Lisette and Peter have fallen in love out there in the water, on that Sunfish, and that she'll break up with Bradley for-ever. Then he'll proclaim his love for me, and everyone will live happily ever after.

"So, hey," Lisette says, leaning her still-wet body against Bradley's. "Did you guys have fun?" When she moves away, you can see dark splotches across his T-shirt where she's marked him.

"Yeah. We just walked," Bradley says.

"Do you want to stay longer, or should I call Alex so we can make the movie?"

I stay silent. I don't really want to do either. I only want to be with Bradley again.

"Up to you," Peter says.

"Movie," Bradley says quickly.

"Is that okay with you, Frankie?"

"Yeah, sure, it's all okay," I mumble.

"Movie it is, then," Lisette says, texting Alex as we start the long walk back to the parking lot.

• • •

The movie's some comedy-thriller spoof with zombies and werewolves and dead people popping up everywhere. I can't pay attention to save my life, because all I can think about is Bradley.

Periodically, I glance over. He sits on the end, his fingers entwined with Lisette's. Next to me is Peter. He smells like sweat and suntan lotion and popcorn. It's better than being next to Lisette.

Even from here, I feel like the guy in that Edgar Allan Poe short story about the murderer who buries the old man with the telltale heart. The old man's heart beats so loud from under the floorboards, he's sure it will give him away. I'm surprised she can't hear mine ratting me out from here. If she finds out, she'll hate me, and she'll have every reason to.

And yet. I glance over at Bradley again, and my heart just crushes some more.

I stare down at my lap and try to think of something

happy instead. I close my eyes and picture Frankie Sky and me on the steps of the pool at the club.

In my mind, he smiles at me, and I take his hand, and we wade into the water and swim.

●　●　●

I shut the bathroom door, turn on the shower, and let it run.

The water is cool. I can't stand it hot. I like the feel of the cool water on my skin.

It's September. Two months since Simon died. The days are so different than they used to be.

I went back to school this month, and that's different, too. I can tell that everyone feels sorry for me.

I double-check that the door is locked, strip off my clothes, and lean over the cool porcelain ledge to stopper the drain and let the bathtub fill.

I'm not supposed to take a bath, just a shower. I'm not allowed to fill the tub.

I'm supposed to hate water, but I don't.

I leave the shower running as I slip into the filling tub. I do this all the time now, so she won't know.

The water envelops and soothes me. Sometimes I slide all the way under, lie faceup, eyes open, and pretend that I'm drowned. I do this now, let my hair float outward, let my lips loosen, let the water seep in.

Drowning doesn't scare me. If I drown, I will be with Simon.

After a minute, I turn onto my belly and swish my hair back and forth, side to side. I am alive again, a beautiful mermaid now, with gills and a tail. I live in this ocean and am happy and have friends here. We'll explore and explore together until we find the portal at the bottom, the one that will take me to my brother.

• • •

I don't know how I made my legs walk from the beach to the car, or my body ride in the car next to Peter to the movies, nor how I got from the parking lot into the cool, dark relief of the theater. Now, once again, I make them stand and carry me out of the theater into the dark July night, where, thank goodness, Alex is already waiting.

In the car, there's chatter about the movie, about Bradley taking his road test next month, about the beach, and baseball, and Lisette and me trying to sign up for yearbook committee next spring. I participate as little as possible, without really taking in most of what is said.

Eventually, I close my eyes and lean my head back against the seat, thankful that the night is warm and Alex has the top down. I just need to keep breathing until we get home.

When we reach my street, I say, "Thanks, guys," and wait for Alex to pull up to the curb.

As I start to get out, Peter grabs my sleeve. "Oh

man, now I know! It's been bugging me all afternoon." I yank away. I have no idea what he's talking about.

"Your dad! When he came out earlier, I thought I knew him from somewhere." I nod as if I care and slip out of the car. "The club," Peter blabs on. "I've totally seen your father at the club."

I nearly fall out of the car. "I doubt it," I snap as Lisette leans forward with alarm. I try to calm my tone. "We used to belong, but not for a long, long time. But maybe he went golfing or something. Anyway, good night."

Lisette nods at me, letting me know it sounds legit and that Peter can't possibly hear my panic, the voice screaming accusations in my head.

I stand on my lawn and watch the car disappear down our street, feeling completely sick to my stomach. About what Peter said, about Bradley and me, about what I've done to Lisette. She's only ever been a good friend, and I'm a terrible one. She doesn't deserve to be cheated on.

I reach the spill of bright yellow light from the front stoop, and realize all the downstairs lights are off. Only my parents' bedroom light is on. They must already be in bed. Without thinking, I veer across our driveway to my father's car.

My heart pounds like crazy, but part of me doesn't care if he catches me. Let him be mad. Let him tell *me* I'm being deceitful!

Praying it's not locked, I pull the handle on the

driver's side door. It opens and the interior light switches on. I lean in, lift the console lid, and feel around for the small silver key. It takes less than a second. It's still there under a fresh box of Altoids. If it were so secret, wouldn't he have moved it? Maybe it's not Mrs. Merrill's key. Maybe it goes to his office.

Still, there's only one way to find out. I close the lid and slip out, shutting the car door as quietly as I'm able, and walk back to the stoop and sit.

Across the street, Mrs. Merrill's house is dark. Am I really going to do this? Be guilty of breaking and entering? But it's not a crime if I just try it in the lock and leave. It's not like I'm going inside.

I flip the key in my hand, and it glints in the moonlight like magic. But whose magic? What may be magic for my father will be the end of any happiness for me.

I think of Bradley, the day he "just stopped by" on the way to Lisette's, and then today, wading with me through the inlet. How badly I wanted to kiss him! How badly I want to kiss him again right now. Why can't I be anywhere with Bradley instead of sitting here worrying about my dad?

I want that life, the one where I'm someone's girl-friend, where I get to feel happy and loved. I want to be her, someone other than the girl with the dead brother and the unhappy mother and the possibly cheating dad.

Is that what's going on with my father? Is that how he feels, too? Does he need to escape his life? My mother? Does he need to escape Simon's death?

Tears trickle down my face, because what if he does? And what if, to escape Simon, Dad needs to escape me, too?

A light behind me flashes on, and the door opens. I squeeze the key tight in my fist.

"Beans?" Dad says.

"Yeah?" I wipe the tears.

"You okay?"

"Yeah," I say. "I was just sitting here with Simon's frog."

"I'll join you." The wicker chair on the porch creaks as he sits down. "So, did you have a good time?"

I shrug, then shake my head.

I want to do more. I want to tell him what happened with Bradley and all the stuff going on with Lisette. But even more than that, I'm suddenly overwhelmed with the desire to tell him about Frankie Sky. Because maybe if he could meet Frankie and see what I see — see that he's somehow connected to Simon, or at least see that it's possible — maybe that would make everything different, and we could all let go and try to be happy again.

A light flickers across the street at Mrs. Merrill's, and I hear him shift in his chair. And that's all I need to know to realize it won't matter at all. It won't matter what I try to say, or show him, or share, if he's already left us in his head.

I slip the key in my pocket. I have to know. Either way, to prepare myself, I really have to know.

"Sorry it wasn't better," he says. "It's a pretty night at least, huh? Cloudy, though, no stars. I guess that means rain for tomorrow."

"Yeah," I say. "I guess." I kiss my free hand and place it on Simon's frog. Then I stand up and kiss my father's cheek. "I'm tired now. I'm going to bed."

• • •

I lie on my bed and reach for the key in my pocket, but pull out the sand dollar instead.

It wasn't a dream, then. Part of me was thinking it was all in my head.

I slip the sand dollar back in my pocket and retrieve the silver key, holding it in the air above me. It doesn't look like a house key, exactly. It's smaller. Maybe it goes to her back door. At any rate, there's only one way to know. And, if it kills me, I'm going to find out.

If my universe is crashing in, I'm going down with answers.

Part IV

▪▫▪ *twenty-nine* ▪▫▪

Dad is a weather forecaster, because in the morning, it's pouring like crazy. The kind of rain that falls in sheets, nearly impossible to see through.

Mom and Dad are both in the kitchen when I get downstairs. It's Sunday, so even the Foundation is closed. Mom's reading the paper and, thankfully, asks me no questions. In fact, she doesn't even look up at me.

Dad, on the other hand, who is fiddling with his cell phone, keeps giving me weird looks, though what kind of weird, I'm not sure. Maybe he knows I took the key.

If you're so worried, I want to say, *why didn't you just get rid of it?*

I try to make use of myself, find something to do, but it's hard to think about much besides Bradley. And with all the rain, there's really nowhere for me to go.

Of course, Lisette calls and texts, like, ten times asking if I'm okay and apologizing about Peter. I didn't think . . . it was Bradley's idea. I am so, so sorry! or Beans, call me back. No more mystery dates, I promise. And: Seriously, Beans, please call me, in yet another. Every time my cell phone buzzes and her name pops up, I fill to bursting with guilt.

It's fine. No problem, just busy with Frankie, I finally respond, hoping she won't realize that it's Sunday.

For hours, I lie on my carpet and stare at the ceiling like a lovesick fool, a thing I never thought I would be. Then again, I'm a lot of things I don't recognize these days.

Eventually, I get up and go to my desk, slide open the thin, secret pencil drawer under my computer, and stare at the key where I hid it. It's on a single ring, no markings, nothing to identify it except a tiny six-digit serial number.

My cell phone buzzes again. I close the drawer and grab it. Btw, can you believe what Peter said about your dad being at the club? What is UP with him, Beans? Do you think you should say something?

I hit delete and pull up the note I typed myself from Frankie's house the other day, the words from the base of Saint Florian.

Non vel ocean mos somniculous nostrum animus.

If I can't solve Mrs. Merrill or Bradley, maybe I can find some answers about Frankie Sky.

I type *Saint Florian* into the search bar, click on the first website that looks decent—Catholic Saints Through History—and scroll down and read.

Saint Florian was an officer of the Roman army in Noricum, a Celtic kingdom of Austria. He died in the days of Diocletian.

I seriously have not one clue what that means.

Though venerated, Florian suffered at the hands of his faith. When the Roman regime sought to eradicate Christianity,

Florian confessed his faith and was beaten, burned, and scourged. He survived all of these torments through his unyielding faith, but was finally thrown into the river Enns, a millstone tied around his neck. His body was found by a pious woman, but it was too late to save him.

Saint Florian holds patronage of firemen and chimney-sweeps and is believed to protect against bad harvests, battles, fire, flood, and storms. He is also the patron saint of those in danger from water, floods, and drowning.

Patronage of firemen and chimney-sweeps? Some of the information seems plain weird, and the rest, contradictory. How can Saint Florian protect from drowning when he died in the water? How does he save others if he couldn't save himself?

I open another screen and type *Latin to English translation* into the search bar. I click on the first site and type the saying from the base of the statue, one word at a time, into the text bar: *Non. Vel. Ocean. Mos. Somniculous. Nostrum. Animus.*

As each word comes up, my eyes bounce from the Latin to the English, picking through choices, more and more frantically by the end.

non
non : not.

---

vel
vel : or, (adv.) even.

---

ocean: ocean.

---

mos
M:
mos : will.

---

somniculous
somniculous : sleepily, sleep, drowsily, drowse.

---

nostrum
noster nostra nostrum : our, ours.

---

animus
animus : courage, vivacity, bravery, will, spirit, soul."

My heart beats wildly. I know it says *drowse*, but it's so close to *drown*, and both sort of mean to put to sleep. I read through again to make sure I'm not seeing things, and when I know I'm not, I shut down my computer, grab my cell, and race downstairs.

Not even the ocean will drown our soul!

I need to see Frankie Sky.

I fly past Mom in the kitchen. "I'm going to Frankie's!" I yell.

"Francesca!"

"What?"

"It's pouring outside."

I turn around. *Not even the ocean will drown our soul.* "It's okay," I say. "Seriously. I don't mind the water."

As soon as I say it, I realize my mistake. I can see it flash in her eyes. She stares at me hard, her face red with fury.

"God, what?" I glare back. "All I meant is the rain-water. The stupid, harmless rainwater. When will you stop it, Mom? Why do you always have to go there?" I slam the door before either of us can say any more.

• • •

I run to Frankie's through the downpour, happy to get drenched, to have the rain slip down my shirt, splash up my shins, slosh between my toes in my flip-flops. I want to be soaked to the bone. I don't care how hard it pours, I just need to see Frankie Sky.

Not even the ocean will drown our soul.

I know in my heart—have always known—that he is somehow connected to Simon.

When I reach his house, I bang on the door, wondering if they'll mind me just showing up on a Sunday. Soaking wet, for that matter.

Frankie opens the door, Potato squeezing through his legs.

"You are really wet, Beans."

"I know, Frankie. I know. I just wanted to see you. You answered the door fast!"

"I seed you from the window," he says.

I laugh. "I know you did."

Mrs. Schyler isn't home. Frankie's Grandpa Harris is. I recognize him from the photographs. He sits on the living room sofa, a kid's book in his hand. *Frog and Toad Together.* The other two books are on the cushion next to him.

"So, you must be the infamous Beans," he says, taking off his glasses as he stands. He puts out his hand. "I'm Mr. Forrester, Frankie's grandfather."

He's a handsome man, tall with white hair. I can see the resemblance to Mrs. Schyler.

"Yes," I say, "Frankie talks a ton about you."

"Oh, Lordy," Mr. Forrester says. "I can only imagine."

I laugh. I'm not surprised that I like him.

Frankie returns dragging a big beach towel, which he hands me, then walks over and leans against his grandfather.

"Grandpa Harris was reading the story. The one about Frog and Toad. Finish the story, Grandpa. Beans likes it, too, so she can listen."

Mr. Forrester raises his eyebrows in question.

"Yes, sure," I say. "I've got nowhere to go."

"Well then, we were just reading 'Cookies,' that was it, wasn't it? 'Cookies' and 'The Lost Button.' Those two stories, over and over again." He chuckles and winks privately at me. "For the past two hours, now, if you can believe that."

He sits and puts his reading glasses back on, as if those two story titles mean nothing. But they don't. Because they were Simon's favorites, too.

"Sit, Beans," Frankie orders. He takes my hand and pulls me down cross-legged next to him in front of Mr. Forrester, then slides closer so our knees touch and slips his hand in mine. His skin feels warm, and for a second, I think of Bradley, and my heart wrenches.

Mr. Forrester opens the book and says, "Where were we, now? Oh yes. Here. The cookies. Frog can't resist all those cookies."

He starts to read, but Frankie says, "Hold on, Grandpa. I need to remember Beans to the story." He turns to me. "Toad made the cookies and Frog loves them so much, so they keep eating and eating and eating them. But now they will get fat, so they need to stop. But Toad can't stop, so Frog, he is trying to help him." He nods, satisfied. "Okay, go ahead, Grandpa."

Mr. Forrester adjusts his glasses. "'We must stop eating!' cried Toad as he ate another. 'Yes,' said Frog, reaching for a cookie, 'we need willpower.' 'What is willpower?' asked Toad. 'Willpower is trying hard not to do something that you really want to do,' said Frog."

Mr. Forrester stops and raises an eyebrow at Frankie.

"'You mean like trying not to eat all of these cookies?' asked Toad," Frankie says enthusiastically, just the way Simon used to.

Mr. Forrester laughs and keeps reading, and Frankie chimes in, but now I'm not thinking about Frankie or Simon anymore, because I'm thinking about Bradley, and how I am like Frog and want to kiss him, and how Bradley is just like those cookies.

• • •

When the book is over and the rain lets up, I tell Frankie I should probably go.

"My daughter should be home soon," Mr. Forrester says, as if he's inviting me to stay.

"She is visiting someone," Frankie says. "She is visiting Joey. He is my daddy's old friend."

"Oh," I say, smiling, because maybe, just maybe, I actually did something good.

"Is okay," Frankie says, walking me to the door, "because yesterday and today was Grandpa Harris Day, and also I got to seed you."

I kneel down in front of him and hug him as tightly as I can. "I know, Frankie. I know. I was lucky to see you, too."

He hugs me back, then stops and puts his face to mine.

"Frankie Sky loves Frankie Beans," he says. "Bigger than the whole wide ocean."

██ *thirty* ██

I lie on my bed thinking about everything that's happened in the last few weeks. There are too many coincidences. There's the sparkler wish, and Saint Florian, and whatever with Dad led me to the country club in the first place. And Bradley finding that sand dollar. So I can't help feeling that they're not really coincidences, but something bigger and magical at work.

I pick up the sand dollar from my nightstand and run my thumb over its smooth, round surface. *A deliciously tempting cookie.* Why did Bradley find a sand dollar, of all things?

I put it aside and reach for my computer. I type *brown pelican* into the search bar, hoping to prove to myself that it's all just nonsense, that what I shared with Bradley means nothing. Maybe then I can let it all go.

Louisiana's state bird . . . Louisiana's state bird — the brown pelican — appears on state seal, flag, and state quarter . . .

Pelican, brown, Wikipedia . . . The largely marine brown and Peruvian pelicans, formerly considered . . . The symbol of the Irish Blood Transfusion Service . . .

Meet the Oil-covered Pelicans, symbols of the BP Oil spill/80 beats . . ."

My eyes move as I scroll, the whole time my brain mocking me. *See? Meaningless! Stop making excuses, Francesca. Pelicans are pelicans. It was just a stupid story. Bradley is a cookie, and you MAY NOT HAVE ANY MORE COOKIES!* Yet I can't stop scrolling down the screen.

Oil Spill Hits Gulf Coast Habitats . . . Conservationists see Louisiana's brown pelican as symbol of wildlife risk . . .
Why Did Louisiana Adopt the Pelican as Its State Bird? . . . The bird has been Louisiana's symbol since the arrival of early European settlers . . .

Just as I'm about to be sensible and quit, I see it there, a few more search results below:

Brown Pelican Resurrection/downsouthlifemagazine.com . . . people have associated the pelican with themes of sacrifice and rebirth . . .

I click on the link. It takes me to a photo of the soaring bird, and underneath:

Pelican Spirit guide: the Pelican is a symbol of rebirth, resurrection, forgiveness.
When a Pelican crosses your path:
• Forgive yourself

• Let go of things you can't change, be they mental, material, or emotional.

I ex out of the screens, my breath rapid and shallow, my mind racing, and stare at my desktop, a photograph of Lisette and me from last New Year's Eve. We were at her house, a party her brother was having. We have glow sticks and noisemakers, and there are bits of confetti in our hair. And I can see it now clearly, how happy Lisette is, and how sad I am, even when I think that I'm celebrating.

I stare at the girl on the screen. At me. I'm not Lisette, not blond and curvy and carefree. But I'm not bad; maybe I'm even pretty. But my eyes are so very sad.

When a pelican crosses your path, forgive yourself.

Oh, how I wish that I could. But I can't, because I know. I know only one single thing:

It was easy. I was supposed to be watching.

Not shell-hunting.

Not getting grapes.

Not walking away.

I was supposed to be watching Simon.

That's all I had to do.

thirty-one

Monday after lunch, Frankie and I head to the playground.

We're swinging on the swings when I see Bradley Stephenson walk in. Right there in front of me, strolling through the gate to the playground. My heart does loop-de-loops like one of those old-fashioned acrobat squeeze toys.

I drag my feet in the dirt to slow down. If only I could get my heart to do the same. He walks over, hands jammed in his pockets, a sheepish smile on his face.

"Hey," he says. "Peter told me you come over here from the club sometimes."

Peter? What could he have said to Peter? Why would he say he was looking for me? Speaking of which, why *is* he here looking for me?

"Who is this, Beans?" Frankie slows his swing next to mine. I've forgotten he's even there. I turn and give him a look because he called me Beans. He never remembers it's private.

Bradley raises an eyebrow as if he's waiting for me to answer.

"Just a friend, Frankie," I say. "What's up?" It

comes out casual, which is good. Way more nonchalant than I feel. I try to gauge his face. Is he mad? Maybe he came here to tell me to stay away, to stop throwing myself at him.

Did I throw myself at him?

"I just wanted to apologize. For the other day, you know. It was my fault." He looks at Frankie. "Could we go and talk for a minute?"

Go where?

"No. I've got to watch Frankie," I say.

"It'll just take a second. Please?"

I look at the sandbox. "Frankie, can you play in the sandbox for a minute? If you dig the roads and make hills, we'll get sticks after to make houses and bridges, like the other day?"

"Yep, I remember," he says.

He heads to the sandbox and starts digging. I look at Bradley. "He's not usually so agreeable," I say.

We walk a few feet to a large tree that shades the far edge of the sandbox, and Bradley leans against it. We can talk here, half-hidden, but I can still see Frankie at the other end okay. My hands sweat and my heart beats like crazy again. I've moved too close, and take a step backward, but he catches my wrist. "Wait, stay here, Frankie," he says.

I can feel the current from his hand to my wrist, warm and buzzing and good.

Frog, I say in my head, *do not eat the cookies! Absolutely, positively no cookies.*

"So, listen, Frankie . . ."

It kills me when he says my name.

"Yeah?"

He laughs self-consciously. "I'm not sure, actually. It's just that—well, first, I wanted to tell you that I'm sorry. You were upset Saturday, and I really didn't mean to do that. I'm not like that at all. But I like you, too. I want you to know that. I mean, I really, really like you. So, I wasn't just using you, I swear."

Does he mean it? How can he? He's with Lisette. How can he possibly like me instead?

"But anyway," he says, "I know it was wrong. And I promise it won't happen again."

"Oh." My mind screams ten different responses, none of which is the right thing to say. "Well, good, thanks," I finally choose.

"Okay, then. I should probably go."

"Okay."

He lets go of my wrist and starts to walk away, then stops and heads back again. "Oh, crap, I brought you something. I almost forgot." He reaches in his pocket, pulls out a red crab claw, and holds it out to me. It's real, not plastic. "It's from Christmas Island," he says.

I take it and reach out to touch his arm, only to thank him, I think, and the next thing I know—I really don't know how—his arms are around me and his lips are on top of mine.

Cookies, and cookies, and cookies, and cookies, and cookies.

When I finally manage to stop us, I'm breathless and light-headed.

"Oh geez, I swear . . ." he says, but I'm as much to blame as he is.

"What is wrong with us?" I whisper. "You're Lisette's boyfriend. She's my best friend. This has seriously got to stop."

"I know," he says. I squeeze the claw in my hand and pray that he never leaves. "Can I give you one more kiss good-bye?"

I don't say yes, but I don't say no, either, so he leans in and we kiss some more, and the whole time my mind is screaming, *No cookies!* but I just keep eating all the crumbs.

●   ●   ●

When I get home from the club, Mom and Dad are still out, and the driveway across the street is empty. Maybe I'm still high from my encounter with Bradley, or maybe I've just gone crazy, but I run up to my room and grab the key, head back across the street, and slip into Mrs. Merrill's backyard.

I pass the row of purple hydrangea, climb the few steps up her deck, and stand at her back door.

Now I'm a liar, a cheat, and a criminal.

The key goes a quarter of the way in and stops. I pull it out and flip it upside down. It doesn't go in at all this way. I flip it back and try again.

The key definitely doesn't fit.

Fine. Great. So it isn't Mrs. Merrill's key. Now I can add *stupid* to the growing list of bad things that I am.

I yank it from where it's wedged in the lock and turn to leave, but I can't, because Mrs. Merrill is standing in my way.

"Francesca? Is there something I can help you with here?"

I try to process what to do, to say. It startles me that she even knows my name. And then I do the only thing I can do. I burst into a great big, heaping mess of tears.

Mrs. Merrill sits me down on the steps. "Now, now," she says, patting my back gently, but she's impatient, too, annoyed. I can tell that she's waiting for me to explain. But I can't. I can't get any words out through the tears.

Maybe it's panic, or maybe it's all the pressure of the past weeks that comes crashing in on me right here and now, but try as I might, I cannot stop myself from crying. It's like everything's gone crazy inside me, and this girl—the one who bribes her way into country clubs uninvited, who kisses her best friend's boyfriend and likes it, and who sneaks into her neighbor's backyard to break into her house—I swear she isn't me. I don't know who I am.

Or maybe I do and I just can't take the truth: that I'm no longer just the girl who let her baby brother die. I'm moving on, even if it means moving on to being someone bold and fearless and wrong, who sneaks into places and steals other people's boyfriends. And if I'm perfectly honest with myself, I'd rather be that. Let me lie and thieve and screw up until I rot away in hell, but just don't let me be no one, nothing, except that other girl. Because that other girl, the sad-eyed one staring back from the photograph on my computer, I don't want to be her anymore.

My body shakes with sobs, and all the while Mrs. Merrill keeps her arm around me, and shushes me. "There, there, dear." When I finally quiet down, she says, "It's okay, Francesca. I'm sure it's okay. Why don't you tell me what's going on?"

I lift my head from where I've leaned it on her shoulder and look up at her. "I'm so sorry," I whisper. There are tear marks on her pretty white top.

"No worries. Do you want to tell me what happened?"

And maybe it's something in the way her voice is so soothing, or the fact that she hasn't called the cops yet to have me arrested, or maybe it's really that I think Dad must know her and trust her — and, worse, like her enough to be doing whatever it is that he's doing (or not doing) with her — but I tell her. I tell her every little thing that has happened to me these past weeks, like some crazy floodgate has opened, letting my life rush out in a gushing, unstoppable waterfall.

I tell this woman who is probably stealing my father away details I wouldn't share with my parents or even Lisette. About how Simon drowned, and how Mom blames me and hates me, and always has, and always will. About meeting Frankie Sky, who looks so much like Simon, maybe *is* Simon, or at least maybe holds Simon's soul. And about Mrs. Schyler, how she drinks and takes pills, but only because she's sad and alone, because her husband died. About how hard it is to have a best friend who's so very beautiful when I'm so plain, and how I kissed her boyfriend, and now I keep on kissing him, even though we both know it's wrong.

Because what kind of crazy miracle is it for a guy like Bradley Stephenson to like me in the first place, when he can have anyone he wants, including Lisette? And how I think I may even be in love with him because we have some weird, special, cosmic connection, and so it crushes me, because I know I need to stop and that, sand dollars and pelicans aside, I simply can't be with him again.

It all comes out in random, jumbled spurts, some of which start me up crying again. At points, Mrs. Merrill laughs a sweet, sympathetic laugh, or says something simple like "I get that" or "I remember feeling that way, too, I promise you, I do." But mostly she just listens and strokes my hair until I'm done.

When I think I'm all cried out, I sit there for I don't know how long. And just when I think I've embarrassed myself enough—can't embarrass myself any more—I blurt out about her and Dad, in words that turn accusatory and cruel.

"And the reason I was even at the club, before Frankie and all that, was because I saw you—I saw you with my dad in your house. You have no right! You have no right to be messing with my father! And don't tell me it wasn't him, and don't tell me it was for sugar, because you were wearing a robe . . . and we *had* sugar, a whole freaking box of it, at home. So don't even try, because you're a liar, and he's lying, and I want you to stay away from him."

I burst into a fresh cascade of tears. I want to hit her. I want to hate her. I want to scratch the key across her pretty car. Even as I let her pat my arm.

I turn to go, but she reaches out and grabs my wrist, not hard, but in a pleading way. Her eyes search mine, but she stays quiet for a painfully long time.

Finally, she whispers, "I thought that was you I kept seeing at the club."

I glare at her, filled with this weird mix of fury and wanting to like her. Maybe because her face looks softer and older in this light, and more sad, like she is also fighting back tears.

"Well, I know it was wrong to follow you, but I had to. I had to be sure. Because honestly, Mrs. Merrill, if Dad loves you and not Mom anymore, he'll leave her, and then . . ." But I'm choked up again, can't finish the words.

She rubs my shoulder and looks out over her yard. "Now, now, Francesca, that's not going to happen. You don't need to worry about that."

I hear what she says and register it, for everything it is and that it isn't. Because she doesn't deny what I've said or contradict me. She doesn't say she isn't having an affair with Dad. She doesn't say he hasn't been to the club and that there's nothing going on between them.

She doesn't tell me I'm ridiculous, and that everything I thought was all in my head.

She doesn't say what I hoped she'd say most of all: that she's married, and Dad is married, so nothing is, or ever could be, going on. She simply says not to worry. And I hear the omissions loud and clear.

▮▮ *thirty-two* ▮▮

Despite all the drama, for a day or two things seem more normal. I work for Mrs. Schyler—full-time now, practically—and try to keep my mind off Bradley. I avoid Lisette, too, and she seems too busy to care. I hope Mrs. Merrill doesn't tell my dad about what I said, but Dad doesn't say anything to me, so I guess she's keeping it to herself.

As always, being with Frankie Sky helps. He keeps me busy and always knows how to make me laugh.

Take now, for example, in the chair next to me at the swimming pool. He's wearing a ridiculous pair of cobalt blue aviator sunglasses.

"Nice glasses," I say.

"Mom broughted them back for me from Cape Cod."

"Well, they look good on you."

"The guard guy is watching you," he says.

I glance up, and he's right. Peter stares at me from his lifeguard chair. He does that all the time now, since the day of the beach debacle. And, worse, since Bradley's visit to the playground.

I want to tell him to quit it and mind his own stupid business, but instead I nod at him, and he looks away. *People are seriously weird.*

I look back at Frankie and shrug.

"You is blue, Beans," he says. "Blue, blue, blue."

"Not when I'm with you, Frankie."

He frowns and moves the sunglasses off and on his eyes. "No, Beans is blue. Really. I can see her."

"I know, Frankie. I was making a joke. Blue means the color, but it also means sad. And I'm never sad when I'm with you."

He pushes the glasses down again and makes a funny face at me. I giggle, and he smiles back.

"Beans is blue, but not blue, right?"

"Right," I say, leaning across to push the glasses up the bridge of his nose.

The sunglasses are a gift from Mrs. Schyler's new boyfriend, the friend of Mr. Schyler's from the army who lives in Cape Cod. I'm glad I encouraged her. Mrs. Schyler seems like a different person already. More relaxed and less tired than before. Plus, the busier she is, the more hours she needs me for Frankie. And Frankie's the one thing that makes me completely happy.

"Hey, you want to go to the playground, Frankie?"

"No," he says, "not now."

"You want to swim?"

"Okay, sure."

I help Frankie swap out his blue sunglasses for green goggles. We wade into the shallow end together, holding hands, taking the steps slowly because the air is hot and the water feels especially cold. Frankie shivers a little and doesn't go splashing off like a wild man like he usually does, but instead hangs by me on the steps.

Finally he ducks under, and I watch him swim back and forth across the width of the pool. After a few laps, I glance toward the back of the pool area for Mrs. Merrill. Her chair is empty. No big surprise there, I suppose. She'll probably never set foot here again.

Frankie crosses back to me again, his little arms and legs moving in perfect froglike motions. I wade down the last step and take off after him when he turns, catching up so we swim side by side. It's a wonder to me that I stayed out of the water for so many years. And a bigger wonder that I've made it back in. Underwater is the one place where everything feels light and hopeful and okay.

When we get out for lunch, the sun is high and the sky is a perfect, cloudless blue. We dry off and put our clothes on and head inside to the dining room.

It's not until afterward, as we step out the back door to the pool, that I notice a lock on Mrs. Merrill's cabana door. *Of course!* Now I remember seeing her pull a key for it from her bag that very first day I was here. That weird small key goes to this door.

"Beans?" Frankie pulls on me. "What's wrong?"

I look at his worried face, and suddenly it's more important to make him happy than to fret about what it means that Dad has the key to some cabana. Besides, what does it matter if Dad runs off with Mrs. Merrill? Will anything actually change? It's not like Mom seems happier because Dad comes home every day. How could I blame him if he left?

"Nothing, Frankie," I say, steering him toward our chairs. "Everything is okay." And, miraculously, at least for the moment, it is.

● ● ●

The next afternoon, I sit on the stoop and pull out my cell phone. It was buzzing all day at the club. Probably another text from Lisette. She keeps sending them, just a few words, a smiley face, or a "hey." I've barely paid attention. Let her think I'm still mad about Peter instead of feeling guilty because of Bradley.

I scroll through:

> Beans, everything okay? U barely answer my calls. :(
> Hey. Seriously. Am starting 2 worry about u.
> Pls call. Is all ok with ur Dad?
> BEEAAANNNSSS!!!! >:(
> Hey, Bradley says he saw you! Pretty funny.
> :)

Pretty funny? Is that her interpretation, or is that what he told her? Is that all he thought that it was? I tell myself he had to say something lame to cover, but still, my heart breaks a little anyway.

K, r u mad at me? >:(I'm sorry about Peter.
Will u ever forgive me? I want 2 c u before
I go to Bible Camp. Leaving tomorrow. Did
u forget? Days & days of nothing but the
outdoorsy woods. Are u seriously not gonna
say good-bye?

Bible Camp! I'd almost forgotten. Every year, Lisette and her brothers go with their parents for two weeks at the end of each July for a retreat. The camp's in Maine, and Pastor Sutter is one of the main counselors. Kids come from all over the country. Now that they're older, Lisette and her brothers help run things. Lisette's gone every summer as far back as I can remember. The camp is by a lake, rustic, with wooden bunks and outhouses, and not a piece of electronic equipment allowed. Unless you sneak it in, which Lisette always does.

Lisette would mind it more, but it's coed, at least, which usually means a chance to scope out new boys. Of course, this summer she won't need that since she already has the most amazing boyfriend in the world.

Which is when the full impact hits me: She's leaving Bradley for two weeks, too. I could have him all to myself if I wanted.

But I don't want that, right? Because that would be totally wrong.

I delete her texts and send one back. Sorry. Been busy with Frankie. If I don't see u before u go, have a great time! Lame, I know, but it's the best I can manage right now.

I hit send, rub a kiss on Simon's frog, and head inside before I get any more crazy ideas about Bradley or do anything else stupid to get myself in trouble.

Except that the minute I reach my room and see my green sneakers on my bed, I know that it's already too late.

▪▪ *thirty-three* ▪▪

Not only are my sneakers on my bed, but Fisher Frog is gone.

A folded piece of Mom's stationery sticks up out of one sneaker. I'm sure I don't want to know what it says. I know it can't be good, since the other sneaker is turned on its side, leaving a pile of sand released onto my bedspread.

I pull out the note and unfold it, my hands shaking.

You left these downstairs for days. I thought I'd be nice and clean up for you. Of course, unless the Hamlet Dunes Mall is now covered in sand, you'll need to explain where you were last Saturday night. It clearly wasn't the mall.

—Mom

I read her words again, growing angrier as I try to sort out the real reason why she's mad. Because we both know it's not because I left my sneakers out by the kitchen door, or even because I lied to her about where I went. She's mad because she knows I went to the beach.

And if that's the reason, forget it. I don't give a crap what she says. I'm done hiding from the water; I'm done standing safely on shore.

Just because she chooses to spend the rest of her life in a dark basement of drowning, misery, and doom doesn't mean everyone else around here has to. Simon is dead, for God's sake. Simon is dead. Does she really want us to all die with him?

I throw the note into the wastebasket and take my sneakers and pound them out over the wastebasket, too. I watch the sand spill, wishing I could click the heels together like Dorothy and make myself disappear. Wake up from some nightmare like she did to find myself elsewhere. Anywhere but this stupid, broken house.

I slip the sneakers onto my feet, happy to still feel some grains press beneath my toes—proof of some other, carefree life—and lie on my rug, staring at the ceiling and holding my breath, counting longer and longer till I'm dizzy and tired, and barely even hear her come home.

• • •

I awaken, groggy, to the smell of onions cooking.

For a second, I'm fine, and then it all comes back to me.

I don't want to go downstairs, but sooner or later I'll have to face her. It might as well be now.

Mom stands at the kitchen stove. Vegetables are

spread across the counter. A box of pasta stands open next to a pot on the burner with steam rising from it. She has her back to me. She hasn't heard me come in.

I sit quietly at the table. Part of me is afraid of what she's going to say, but, mostly, I don't care. I already know she doesn't like me. So what if she's mad?

I watch her thin shoulders move up and down as she chops celery and throws it into the sizzling pan. Finally, I clear my throat.

She turns her head. Her eyes look watery, but maybe it's just the onions sizzling.

"I got your note," I say, and pause for effect. "We went to the beach, not the mall. To the ocean where Simon drowned. Before the movies, I mean. We did go to the movies, that part is true. But first we went to the beach."

She whirls around and glares at me. "The beach?"

"Yes. The beach. In fact, I go there all the time. With Frankie and Mrs. Schyler. I like it there, too. It makes me feel closer to Simon."

She cuts me off. "My God, Francesca, do you know what could have happened?"

"No," I say, rolling my eyes, "I don't know. Why don't you tell me? Oh, wait, you mean what's *already* happened? Because I doubt that's happening again. Maybe something else, but not that one. Simon's dead. He can't re-drown now, can he?"

I'm being mean. I'm trying to hurt her. I'm not sure why.

"Jesus, Francesca, don't say another word! You know better than anyone . . . And I wouldn't even have known where you were! You think that's smart? You think *that's* a good idea?" She's screaming now, her voice shrill, her lips trembling. Tears fall, but they're not about me. As always, they're for Simon.

Still, her anger frightens me a little. I'm suddenly afraid of what she'll really say. What she hasn't said, but has wanted to, since the day that Simon died. What she's always thought. That it's all my fault that Simon died.

Why doesn't she just come out and say it? Blame me. Get it over with. Tell me what I've already known for years.

I bite my lip to stop from crying. I won't give her the satisfaction.

The sharp smell of burnt garlic and onions singes the air.

Still, I goad her more, willing her to say it already. "In fact, guess what, Mom? People swim all the time. Every single day, people are out there swimming. And not everyone drowns. Do you hear me? Not everyone drowns! In fact, almost nobody drowns!"

I shift gears, making my tone formal and singsong, as if I'm delivering information for a public-service announcement: "Did you know that less than one in one hundred thousand people drown in the United States every year?" I'd enjoy it more—the horrified look on her face—except my voice breaks, and the tears betray me and start to fall. "That is a very, very small percentage. Safer than, well, pretty much everything there is. But go on! Keep devoting your life to . . . " I stop, totally choked up.

"To what, Francesca? To what? Trying to make some good come from your brother's death?"

I shove my chair back and stand. She's hurting now, I can see it, but I don't want to stop. It's like I want to enrage her. I want to push her to say what I need to hear.

"Make good come? You spend your whole life in some dark basement trying to keep people out of the water. Me, out of the water! You don't want me to swim. You don't want me to drown. But we all know the one person you cared about has already drowned!

"And, still, you want me to be afraid. Of everything. To stay frozen in that day. Well, guess what, Mom? I'm not! I'm sad and I'm sorry, but I'm not afraid anymore, and I don't want to be. I don't ever want to be like that again! I love the water. I love to swim. Can you believe it? I swim practically every day. With Frankie at the club. And in the ocean! But you're right. I *don't* tell you. I *can't* tell you. Because you'll give me that look, that scared, pathetic look, like it takes all your effort to get up out of bed in the morning and just breathe.

"Well, here's the thing: I don't want to be like that, like you. And just because Simon died doesn't mean everyone else is going to. So I don't care if you give me that look anymore, that look like you hate me. I'm used to it by now. I *know* you hate me. I know you do. For everything. For letting Simon drown."

"Francesca, my God—"

"God, what? There is no God, remember? There's no nothing for you. No faith, no love, no Simon, no me, no Dad. No nothing! Oh, right, wait. Nothing but your stupid Drowning Foundation. So nobody ever, in the history of mankind, drowns again! Good luck with that."

I've said enough. I should stop. But I can't. I can't stop myself from crashing.

"So go ahead! Keep walking around here in your miserable, sad, ghost bubble until no one can take it anymore. But trust me, I'm done. And Dad is done, too. Not even Dad can take you anymore!" My eyes shift to the window, and I feel myself tumble over the last cliff, the one from which I can never return. "No wonder he's always with Mrs. Merrill! No wonder he's cheating on you! Even Dad can't stand you anymore!"

Mom drops the wooden spoon she was holding and walks over and slaps me across the face.

Which, at least, shuts me up.

I don't move. The air between us buzzes with the silence. My cheek stings where her fingers struck.

"Francesca?"

I turn. Dad stands in the doorway. I have no idea how long he's been there.

But I can guess. Because I've never seen him look so hurt and upset. Not since the day that Simon died.

I didn't mean to hurt my father.

"Great, you can both hate me now," I say, and storm out, slamming the door so hard, it echoes.

▪▪ *thirty-four* ▪▪

I've walked around our neighborhood for at least an hour, but I don't want to go home. I don't know what I'll say if I do.

I feel sick about everything. Not just about what I said to Mom and Dad, but about telling on Dad, and even ratting out Mrs. Merrill. Part of me thinks she deserves it, but part of me feels bad because there's something that seems sad about her, too.

Anyway, how could I have told Mom about Mrs. Merrill when I don't even know if it's true?

How could I tell her if it is?

It occurs to me that maybe I want it to be true. Maybe I want Dad to have done something terrible and wrong like that, because even if he did, I'd still love him and I'd still want him to be my father. Even if he screwed up, I'd still think he was a good person.

Maybe that's what I'm secretly hoping for. Because if Dad could make such a huge, horrible mistake and still be a good person, then that would mean, technically, I could be, too. I could still be worthy of loving, even if I let my brother drown.

I stop shy of the front of our house. Mom's and Dad's

cars are both in the driveway, so at least they're not driving around looking for me.

Maybe nobody cares if I'm gone.

My eyes shift across the street to Mrs. Merrill's house. Her car is there. And her husband's Maserati.

I take a deep breath and, without thinking more, move in that direction.

I slip around the house to the deck stairs and knock quietly on the back door. Through the window I can see Mrs. Merrill in the kitchen. I knock a little harder and she turns around, a look of alarm crossing her face. She holds up a finger—*one minute*—and disappears around the corner.

She returns with a box of tissues and a light sweater and comes out onto the deck. She wraps the sweater around my bare shoulders and says, "Let's go sit over here."

I follow her down the steps and into the garden. There's a bench by the roses in the back corner. She glances nervously up toward the house, to the window that looks in on the living room. I can see the TV's blue glow from here.

"Now," she says, putting her hand on my shoulder, "tell me what on earth has happened."

"I told her," I say. "I told my mother about you."

The alarm returns to her face, but she works hard to hide it. She scratches at a speck of thread on her linen slacks and waits.

"It's just that we got in a fight, and this afternoon

when I was at the club with Frankie, I saw it. I saw where the key goes." My heart starts up when I say this, but she gives me a puzzled look, and I remember that the last time I was here, I never actually showed her that I have her key.

"Oh, I have it," I say. "I have your key. I mean, my dad had it in his car, and I thought it was yours and, well, that's why I came here that day. But it doesn't go to your house, because it's too small, but it goes there, to your cabana at the club. And, well, I'm not an idiot, you know."

She closes her eyes for a moment and squeezes my shoulder, then leaves her hand there. I want to shake it off, but I don't.

"I see. Of course not," she says. "Nobody thinks that you are."

She rubs my back, which only makes it worse. I don't want to feel comforted by her. I want to hate her. And I don't want her to be kind. I don't deserve it.

"So," she says quietly, "tell me, what exactly happened with your mother?"

"We got in a fight. Because I went to the beach and didn't tell her. Because she wouldn't have let me go if I had. Because of how my brother drowned."

"Ah, yes, Simon. That must be so incredibly hard. For both you and your mother."

My breath catches when she mentions my brother by name. As if his name is sacred and not hers to say. Then again, there's something soothing about her knowing it, too, and wanting to talk about him. She makes it seem okay to talk, instead of it feeling taboo.

"I know it's hard for her," I say, "but it's hard for me, too. And she blames me. She's always blamed me. Like all of it was my fault. And maybe she's right. I mean, it *is* my fault that Simon died . . . " But I can't talk anymore because I'm crying too hard.

She pulls me in and hugs me now, rocks me, and says, "Oh, you poor, poor dear," and holds me there until I'm all cried out and exhausted.

When I finally calm down, I pull away, a little embarrassed, and look past her at the roses, now shadowy in the twilight. Her whole backyard smells of them.

"If my dad leaves us, I'll have no one," I whisper. "My mother doesn't love me anymore."

She laughs gently, but not in a funny way. "Your dad isn't leaving you, honey. I told you that already. I promise you that. I do."

"How do you know?"

"We're friends, Francesca. That's all. We talk. That's all I'm going to say. I'm not going to go into further details with you, because it's not your business, or at least it's not mine with you. That's between you and your dad. You have every right to ask him if you want." She pauses and smoothes her slacks. "Suffice it to say we're friends, we've become friends — well, good friends — perhaps better friends than we should have. We'll have to be more careful about that." Her eyes dart away to the house again, to the window with the blue glow of the TV.

"Life is hard, Francesca; you of all people know that. It's full of tragedies. Some big, some small. People hurt, they get lonely, they make mistakes. Even grown people. That's not an excuse. I'm just telling you how it is. I'm not saying it makes it all okay. Understand that. I'm not making any excuses. For anyone."

She stops because she's getting choked up. We both sit quietly until she can talk again.

"Your dad and I are friends, that's all, and I need to work harder to keep it that way. Because our friendship matters to me. He's a good man."

She tips my chin up so that I'm looking at her and makes her voice brighter, but somehow still stern. "People make mistakes, Francesca, but if they're lucky, they figure it out before it's too late. Maybe you and I have that in common." She brushes back a strand of my hair. "Do you understand?"

I nod, even though I'm not sure whether she's talking about her and Dad or me and Lisette and Bradley. Either way, it doesn't matter.

"Good. Now, about you and your mother." My heart sinks. *My mother.* God, what was I thinking? I've told my mother all sorts of stupid, horrible things. I press the heels of my hands to my eyes to stop new tears from coming, but Mrs. Merrill pulls them away and says, "Sometimes we just need a good cry. If you let them all out, maybe they'll stay away for a long while."

So I do. I give in and let them flow again. When I'm finished, she pats my knee. "See? That's better. Now, let's get a few things straight. It is not your fault that Simon died, Francesca. Your mother knows this, and your father knows this. The whole wide world knows this. You were not the grown-up there. You were not responsible. Do you understand?"

I nod, even though I'm not sure my mother would agree with her.

"And one more thing: I know your dad loves you. And I'm sure your mother does, too. She's just not as strong as you and your father are. Is that possible, to view her as not as strong?"

I shrug, and she smiles.

"So, then, here's what I think. You go home and trust me that everything will be okay. Maybe messy for a while, but sometimes messy is okay. You apologize to your mother and tell her that, from now on, you will speak only the truths that you know. No more rumors or gossip. No more half pieces of information. And you do your best to right things between the two of you. Okay?"

I nod, and she stands up, letting me know that we're finished. I stand up, too, and we walk together across her backyard.

When we reach the deck stairs, she stops. "It's hard, I know, but you try anyway, Francesca, you promise me? You keep on trying the best you can. And you know what? Sometimes life surprises you and rewards you for it more than you know. You never actually know what life will bring." I nod. "Okay, then. Go on home and do what you need to do."

I watch her walk up the stairs, back straight, head high. She's poised, but now I see how sad she is underneath.

I walk slowly across the street. At the curb, I stop and stare at our kitchen window. The lights are on, but I don't see Mom or Dad. They're in the house somewhere. I'll have to find them and talk. But I don't know what I'll say.

I cross our lawn toward the stoop. Nothing to do but push forward.

⣿ *thirty-five* ⣿

The kitchen is empty and clean.

Dad's voice drifts in from the living room, low and soft, but he stops talking when I walk in. They're both in there. Mom and Dad. Maybe not for long, but for now.

"Hey," I say softly, careful not to look at her.

Dad jumps up from the couch and walks toward me. "Beans, are you okay? Where the heck did you go?" I can tell he's mad but trying to control it; that, for the moment, his anger is overshadowed by concern.

Or maybe he gets that I'm the one who should be mad. He's the one sneaking around. He's the one betraying us.

Mom stands, too, arms clutched to her waist. Her eyes are puffy from crying. But the look on her face isn't anger or hatred or disappointment. It's something different this time.

I'm not sure what, but I can't bear it. And I can't talk about it, either. Not now. Maybe in the morning.

I turn away and veer toward the stairs. "I'm going to bed," I say.

No one stops me. No one grounds me. No one yells.

I could just keep going, but I promised Mrs. Merrill.

A few steps up, I turn. "Mom?" Her head jerks up to look at me. "I was wrong," I say, shifting my gaze away. "I'm sorry. I was wrong about everything I said. I was angry, so I made it up. I didn't mean it. I'm sorry I said such horrible things." I try to look at her so she knows I'm sincere, but I can't stand seeing her look so hurt and broken and small.

I start up the stairs again.

"Francesca!" she calls. I keep going, my back to her. I kept my promise to Mrs. Merrill. There's nothing else I need to say right now. "Frankie, please!"

I stop. I stop because she calls me Frankie.

I turn and look at Dad. He's nudging her forward. Holding her hand.

Her eyes meet mine and dart down. Dad nods. Finally, she speaks, her words slow with effort. "Frankie, listen. I was the one who was wrong. Who's been wrong. I'm so, so sorry for that. You don't know how sorry I am. We're all hurting, yes. It's been hell to try to get past the terrible thing that happened. But no one is hurting more than you. I should have known that. And I should have been there for you. I haven't been here for you . . ." Her voice cracks, and her eyes fill with tears. "I haven't done a very good job. And for that, I'm truly very sorry."

My eyes well up, too, but for some reason I don't cry. Maybe Mrs. Merrill's right. Maybe I'm all cried out for now.

"Okay," I say, because I don't know what else to say, and I start again up the stairs.

"I want you to be happy, Frankie," she calls up after me. "Please. I should have done a better job."

• • •

I'm so tired, I don't even take off my clothes or bother to get under the sheets, just lie on my bedspread and let my body tumble into sleep. As I drift off, the last thing that occurs to me is that the sand is gone. Mom has been in here and vacuumed. The room is straightened and clean.

And Fisher Frog is back on my bed.

▪▪ *thirty-six* ▪▪

I awaken with a start, feeling odd. The house is quiet and gray.

I roll over and glance at my clock — 5:05 a.m. I sit up and stare around my room, but everything seems normal. It's not, though. I remember.

Maybe Mom forgives me, but how will she forgive Dad? I may have tried to make things right, but she's not stupid. I wonder what he told her about all the horrible things I said.

I slip out of bed and tiptoe down the hall past Simon's door to their bedroom. Their door is ajar, like always. I peek in. For now, they're together, sleeping.

I walk back down the hall, stop in the bathroom and brush my teeth, and stare at myself in the mirror. I'm a mess of tangled hair and smudged eyes. Not to mention in yesterday's clothes. I wash my face and inspect again, brushing my fingers across my lips. I close my eyes and imagine Bradley's fingers there instead, and then his mouth pressing down on top of mine.

Imagination and memory are all that I have left of that.

I turn off the lights and head back down the hall to my room. At Simon's door, I stop. The door is open a little. I slip in, my heart racing, as my eyes scan the room. I quietly close the door behind me.

His bed looks sad and empty without Fisher Frog. I sit and it creaks softly. I lie back, resting my head on Simon's pillow, and stare out his window at the top of the trees, remembering the spill of sunlight that filtered in that very first day I met Frankie Sky.

Frankie Sky and Simon. *Is Simon Frankie Sky?*

I close my eyes and try to sort out what is real and what is merely wishful thinking, then sit up with a start. I don't know why, but I feel like something important is in here. Some clue. Some answer.

"Simon, what do you want to tell me?" I whisper, sitting perfectly still. I feel my brother in the room. The air smells of him, of peaches and sunshine and the ocean.

I flip the switch on his table lamp, my heart beating hard as the train with the little frog engineer circles the base. I switch it off quickly, before it circles again and lets out its faint, hollow whistle. The sound of distance and longing.

My hand drops to the night table drawer. I know beyond a doubt something's in here.

I tug at the knob. The drawer sticks in its track. Objects rattle inside.

I kneel down and work the drawer out slowly, then remove items one by one: Simon's baby book. A tube of half-used diaper-rash cream. A Raffi CD. A piece of cardboard with his first lock of blond hair taped to it.

I place them carefully on the bed, but there's nothing unexpected in there.

I slide the drawer closed, but as I do, something rattles, so I yank it open again further, reach in, and feel around with my fingers.

My heart nearly bursts when I feel the smooth round disk in the back. Even before I pull it out, I know.

A sand dollar. *God's fingerprint in a lowly little shell.*

I stare at it in my hand. It looks exactly like the one that Bradley gave me.

I put everything else back the way I found it and straighten up Simon's bed. When I'm sure it looks the same, I close the door and tiptoe back to my room.

Sunlight creeps in through my bedroom window. I study the sand dollar. A perfect, white, five-pointed flower. I turn it over and look at the base. Pinprick holes that stretch toward the edges like a starburst.

I glance at the clock again. It's still hours before I'm due over at Frankie's. An hour or two before Dad will get up and leave for work, before Mom will leave for the Foundation.

Was the shell always there, or is it some weird sign from Simon?

I flip the shell to the front again, to the five white petals, and try to remember the words to the song. The part about the petals like white doves.

Now break the center open
And here you will see...

No, not *see*. *Release.*

Now break the center open
And here you will release
The five white doves awaiting
To spread good will and peace.

I close my hand around it and wonder, but I won't break it open. I can't.

I walk to my desk, open the secret drawer, and take out the sand dollar from Bradley. I place them side by side on the desk in front of me.

There's no way it's just a coincidence. There's no way it isn't a sign.

But a sign of what? That Frankie is Simon? Or that I'm meant to be with Bradley? Of course, both are nothing more than wishful thinking.

And yet.

I press Simon's sand dollar to my cheek. I swear I can feel his breath.

My cell phone buzzes and startles me. A text from Lisette.

> Hey, Beans! Sure ur sleeping. Just saying
> good-bye at this UNGODLY (hah!) hour. Wish
> me luck, I just used a real toilet for the last

time till I get back. Will try to sneak texts but
if not c u soon. Luv u, Zette.

Ungodly.

I stare at the sand dollars again and wonder if Pastor Sutter knows something I don't. If it *is* possible that life isn't ungodly. That there are things unseeable—powers, miracles, karma, souls, *God*—bigger than we are, orchestrating how everything unfolds.

I press ignore on Lisette's text, reminding myself to respond later. If I do it now, she'll ask why I'm up so early. Instead, I turn on my computer.

My phone buzzes again. I almost don't bother to look, but it's not from Lisette. It's from a number I don't recognize.

Hey, *Beans* LOL! Was doing some research
and found out that fewer crabs died on Xmas
Island this year than last. Seems like a good
thing, so I wanted u to kno. Bradley.

I stare at the note in disbelief, my heart going crazy. He's texting me at the crack of dawn. I shouldn't respond, but there's no way I can ignore it completely.

Good to know. Thanks, I type back. In three seconds, a "☺" appears.

I press the phone to my heart. I should leave it at that.

No Bradley.

No cookies.

No more betrayals.

I put my phone down, push it away from my needy, disobeying fingers, and do what I was about to do anyway: type *Christmas Island crabs* into the search bar.

I turn the volume low and click on some video from a nature channel. Classical music plays as a sea of red crabs crawls across the screen, just like Bradley described to me. A British guy narrates how, every year, over one hundred and twenty million crabs migrate to the ocean to breed even though they don't know how to swim. He explains that they lay their eggs in the water, but then have to return to where they came from. And that, even though they try to close roads and put up roadblocks, over a million red crabs get killed every year.

"It appears for these small creatures, at least, an innate sense of purpose, a higher calling, if you will, overrides logic or good sense."

I watch amazed as the mass of tiny red crabs crosses streets to the music, crawling up the sides of curbs, through drainage tunnels, over bridges. Bradley wasn't exaggerating; it's freaky, but mesmerizing. A moving red carpet of crabs.

When it's over, I'm still not sure what to do with myself. It's not even six thirty, and everything feels upside down. Sooner or later, I'm going to have to deal, though. And I'm hungry, so I head downstairs.

As I walk into the kitchen, I see the note folded

on the table. Propped like a greeting card, my name—
Frankie—on the front in Mom's tight, perfect script.

I sit down and slide it over, even though I don't know
if I really want to read what's inside. What if it's a good-
bye? Or worse, what if she explains how, now that she
knows about Mrs. Merrill, she just can't let Dad live
here anymore?

My beautiful Frankie,

*1. I just wanted to tell you that you
were right. I have buried myself in the
Foundation and the past and all that
was lost, instead of all that I still have
to live for, including you, my bold and
beautiful daughter.*

*I'm sorry that it's taken me so long
to realize this, and that I haven't been a
better mother when you needed your mother
the most.*

*Please know that I'm not angry with
you, nor do I blame you for Simon's
death. Nor have I blamed you, ever. Your
brother's death was MY fault, Frankie,
and your dad's fault, but certainly it was
never, ever yours. You were the best big
sister that Simon could have had. He
loved you very much, and I do, too. You
make me proud every day, and I've done a
horrible job of letting you know. But it's*

the truth, and I'm going to try harder to show it.

2. If you ever lie to me again about where you are, or where you are going, you will be grounded for life. Seriously.

— Mom

I sit for a long time, staring at her words, and at my name like that—the good way, *Frankie,* like she used to call me. Then I walk to the window and stare out across the street to Mrs. Merrill's house like I did that last day of school. The day I saw my father drive by. The house is quiet and still, her black Mercedes and the silver Maserati asleep, side by side, in the driveway.

I think about how Mrs. Merrill has lived here for years, and I never even knew her before. Is it really just a coincidence that all this happened? That, for better or worse, she suddenly came into our lives?

I skip the food, take the note, and tiptoe back up to my room. I fold it in half again, slip it in my desk drawer, and take out the silver key instead. I pad back downstairs and out the front door and return the key to the console in Dad's car.

There are just some things you don't need to know for sure.

■■ *thirty-seven* ■■

With Lisette away and the drama with Mrs. Merrill seemingly over, it feels like everything slows down. I focus on Frankie and my job and try hard not to pine like a fool for Bradley.

It doesn't help that he keeps texting me, things like Did u kno Xmas Island crabs aren't edible? or According to Wikipedia, an accidental introduction of the yellow crazy ant to Xmas Island recently killed 15-20 million crabs ☹, which make me totally melt with desire.

I try to use willpower like Frog did, and respond only with things that don't invite conversation, like Thanks, I didn't kno or That's sad about the crazy ants, but I can't bring myself to tell him to stop, so he keeps sending cute and heartbreaking messages.

Mrs. Schyler, at least, is happy. Thanks to her new boyfriend.

On one of our beach days during the second week Lisette is gone, she tells me about Joey while Frankie is busy driving trucks in the sand.

"He owns a woodworking shop. You should see his stuff, Francesca. It's beautiful. He made me this," she says, all dreamy, slipping a pendant from her neck. She hands it to me. It's a solid wood heart the color of coffee beans, with lighter, golden lines that spiral in toward the center.

"He calls it Love Infinity," she says.

"It's so pretty," I say, hoping one day someone will give me something as beautiful—not that a crab leg isn't special.

I hand the heart back to Mrs. Schyler and get up to go play with Frankie. He's been calling me for ten minutes. I've been stalling here with Mrs. Schyler because I can see from here what he's doing.

Which is, making a sand castle.

With a big, fat moat around it.

All kids make sand castles, right? Still, I feel queasy.

"Get some shells to decorate, Beans!" he says when he sees me coming.

I wander in the area, kicking at sand, bending to pick up an occasional shell, but no way I'm walking away or taking my eyes off of him. The jingles are out like crazy this summer, so it's easy to gather a bunch right here.

Every few seconds I glance over at him, head down, blond curls lit by the sun.

I was gathering shells just like this the moment that Simon disappeared.

"Here you go." I drop to my knees and hand him the small supply of jingles. He nods. My breath feels rapid and shallow. A trickle of sweat slides down between my shoulder blades. "That's a good castle, Frankie," I say.

It looks just like the one I was building with Simon. I have to get a grip on myself.

He squints up at me in the sunshine. "Yep, I builded it myself," he says proudly.

"You did, Frankie," I say, thinking of Simon and wondering if it's exactly true.

We press shells around the castle until it looks festive and beautiful. When we finish, Frankie says, "Is really a good castle, Beans, right?"

"Yes, Frankie. It's a really good castle." Another bead of sweat slips down my back.

"Good," he says, taking my hand with his and lifting a pail with another. "We need to fill the moat up with water."

"What?" I whisper, my throat dry.

He pulls me to stand. "Yes, Beans. We have to. We have to get water and fill the moat."

I stare at his face, but everything slips out of focus. I can't hold on to his features. I think there's something wrong with me. I glance back at Mrs. Schyler to see if she'll help, but she's facedown on her blanket, asleep.

"Beans, we have to get water."

"We can't, Simon! We can't get water!"

"We can, Beans. Is really okay."

He lets go of my hand and picks up a second pail and places it in my grip, then holds my free hand again. "Let's go, Beans. Let's go now and get the water. We have to."

"But it won't fill up the moat!"

"It will. We need to."

My legs tremble as he pulls me toward the water. My breakfast sloshes in my stomach, rises bitterly in my throat. I don't know why I let him take me, or why I follow.

It's as if I can't stop myself. As if I can't stop him.

"Come on, Beans. Is okay," he says.

At the water's edge, sunlight glints gold off the slick sand. The water, calm a minute ago, has kicked up. Larger waves break against the shore.

I clutch Frankie's arm as he scoops, filling his pail, then mine. We walk back to the moat and dump them both in.

The water holds for a second, then bubbles and sinks down, disappearing into the earth.

"See?" I say. "The water doesn't stay. It gets absorbed by the sand. It won't work. I told you. No more of that now, okay?"

"We have to. We have to go back, Beans." He tugs my arm, making me.

Back at the sand castle, he dumps his pail, then mine. The water holds, burbles, sinks, and starts to disappear. Relief washes over me. "I told you, Frankie. I told you—" But he points, because the water has stopped draining two-thirds of the way down. I stare, waiting for the rest to leak away, but it sits there at the base of the moat.

"See?" He grabs my arm and drags us back down to the water.

I clutch his arm tighter. By the third trip, the water is halfway up, and by the fourth, it's almost all the way full.

By the fifth, the water swirls at the top.

"I tolded you, Beans. I tolded you."

We drop to our knees, and Frankie gives the water a splash with his fingers, and then we watch as it circles, as if pulled by an invisible current, an eddy that shimmers and sparkles in the sunlight.

Frankie leans across and picks up the few remaining jingle shells, drops them in, and stirs them with a piece of driftwood. They float and spin at the top, like little pastel petals of impossible hope.

He tosses the driftwood away and leans against me. "Is magic, Beans, right?"

"Yes, Frankie," I say, leaning back on him. "I think that maybe it is."

Part V

◼◼ *thirty-eight* ◼◼

The following Monday, Mrs. Schyler answers when I ring the bell.

She ushers me in, sits me down, and tells me they're moving to Cape Cod. To give it a go with her boyfriend. The one I stupidly told her to go out with.

"We're gonna give it a go, Francesca." That's how she says it, like it's no big deal. Like it doesn't mean I'm losing Frankie Sky.

My body drains of every ounce of enthusiasm.

"I know, sweetie." She touches my cheek and keeps her hand there. "You have no idea how very much we're going to miss you."

I wrap my arms around myself and stare at the floor, but I don't know if I can keep from crying.

"I wanted to give you a heads up, let you know first, but you do need to keep quiet a few more days. Until I iron out plans for sure. Then I'll tell my father and Frankie. Which I haven't quite found the nerve to do."

"You haven't told Frankie?" My eyes dart beyond the kitchen, wondering where he is, why he hasn't made his usual appearance. But neither Potato nor Frankie seems to be around.

"No, I was up at the Cape all weekend. My father took Frankie and the dog to his place. He should be bringing him back here any minute. I know it's sudden, Francesca, but trust me, Frankie will love Joey. He needs a father figure, and Joey is a wonderful man. Frankie is going to be so happy there. And, well, anyway, I wanted you to know first."

I blink back tears. I don't know what to say.

"Francesca, please be happy for us. If it weren't for you . . . Well, just know that you've made all the difference in the world. Without you . . ." Her eyes move away, then back to mine. "Without you, I don't know if I would have made it through this summer. You're a very special girl."

She squeezes my arm and I nod, sick to my stomach. I don't want to have helped her be happier if it means she's leaving and taking Frankie Sky.

"We won't go until the beginning of September," she says. "Who knows if the plans will even hold until then? But he's asked me to go be with him, and I want to try." She laughs nervously. "We can always come back, right? Besides, with school starting, you'll be so busy, you won't even have time to help me in the fall."

"Yes, I would," I say.

She pulls me in and strokes my hair, then holds me back and stares straight into my teary eyes. "Sweet, sweet, Francesca, don't you worry. With my father here, we'll be visiting all the time. All the time. And in the summer, you could even come up and stay with us. Wouldn't that be wonderful?" She tips my chin up and makes her voice stern and sincere. "All the time, Francesca. We'll find a way to get together all the time."

"Okay," I say, but I can actually feel my heart breaking.

•   •   •

After that, it's hard to be with Frankie because it hurts too much to think about being without him. I know I'll get to see him when he visits, but that's just not the same.

Still, I do my best to be happy and to have fun with him, and keep my word to Mrs. Schyler by not saying anything to him yet. Sometimes I think I should, like when we're at the club and Frankie is suddenly talking about winter out of the blue. I swear, it's like he senses something is changing, and he wants to make plans that might stop it.

"And when it snows," he says, watching me through his cobalt sunglasses, "we can sit on the sled and slide all the way down the hill. I do that all the time with Potato in the winter, and he likes it!"

I can picture poor Potato, dog lips peeled back in the wind, as he and Frankie go whooshing down the hillside, so I laugh, even though I really want to cry.

"I bet, Frankie," I say. "Maybe we'll do that. It sounds like fun."

"Not maybe," Frankie says. "We will definitely, definitely do that, Beans."

"Okay, Frankie, we will definitely do that," I say.

I study Peter Pintero up on the lifeguard stand, thinking about the day he first let me into the club. Today, he wears orange board shorts and a navy T-shirt with one of those old Wacky Packages graphics on it. A Cracker Jack sailor guy smiles from the old-fashioned red-and-white-striped box, but with greasy long hair and no teeth, a skateboard in his hands. The box reads *Slacker Jacks*. Peter nods at me like he always does, and I half wish I really liked him, because that would make life easier around here.

I think about Lisette, who should be coming home tomorrow, and how hard it will be to see her with Bradley again. Especially once school starts up. Especially with Frankie gone.

"Beans is blue again?" Frankie says.

"Blue and blue," I say. "Come on. Let's blow this Popsicle stand and go to the playground."

Frankie follows obediently, but slowly, shuffling his feet. I've noticed these last few days that he's been perfectly behaved, like he's trying to make things easier on me. But today he seems quiet and subdued. Like when we reach the playground, and I yell "Race you!" and take off toward the merry-go-round, Frankie just drags behind.

"You okay, dude?" I call, stopping to wait for him. He takes my hand.

"Yeah. Just tired. Dumb Potato bugged me all night in my bed."

"He did?"

"Yeah. And my head hurts."

"It does? Do you want me to call your mom to take us home?"

"No. Is okay," he says, "and somebody is here for you again."

Frankie turns and points to the entrance. I look up to see Bradley walking toward me. My heart goes berserk like always. Frankie lets go of my hand and says, "Yep, Frankie will play in the sandbox."

I wait, trying to calm my breath. "Hey," I say when he reaches me, "you got some new important crab part for me?"

He smiles sheepishly, shoves his hands in his pockets, and we head automatically to our tree. "No crabs," he says as we walk. "I just wanted to talk. Can we talk for five minutes, or do you want me to leave?"

"No," I say. "Well, yes. I want to want you to leave, but I don't."

"I know. Me too." He laughs uncomfortably. "Which more?"

Don't, my brain screams. "It's just that we really shouldn't . . ." I say.

Still, when he presses me up against the tree, it's pretty clear I'm not going to stop him. His lips on mine are sunshine and sparklers and everything good about summer. *Let me have this one last time, just to hold on to the taste of him.*

"Honestly, I can't stand it, Frankie." He stops

kissing me and stares hard into my eyes. "I want to be with you. I'll break up with Zette. I was planning to, actually. I just couldn't do it when she was leaving—" But I don't wait for the rest because I'm already kissing him again.

And how can I not—how will I ever be strong and bring myself to stop—if I can't keep my knees from buckling when I'm around him?

Eventually, somehow, I manage to pull back. "Gimme a second," I say. "I need to check on Frankie Sky."

I lean out from behind the tree and take a step toward the sandbox before I register that someone is walking in our direction.

Lisette.

Lisette is headed through the playground gate in our direction.

She walks head down, texting.

Is she texting Bradley, or me?

"Shit!" I whisper, shoving Bradley behind the tree. "Please don't move. Lisette is here. Oh God, please don't move." Panic surges in my throat. I try to walk calmly toward her, fast, but like normal.

I need to get there before she gets too close.

"Hey, Beans!"

She waves, happy to see me. I force a smile, fake and stupid, on my face. How can I smile when I'm about to destroy our friendship? Because this I know: she will never, ever forgive me.

I twist back toward the tree. I can see the edge of Bradley's shirt sticking out from the side, but otherwise, he's pretty well hidden. *Please just let me get out of this.*

I jog the rest of the way to catch up, keeping her at a safe distance. Geez, she's practically skipping to me.

How could I do this? How could I cheat on my best friend?

Tears creep into my eyes, but I fight them. I need to get a grip. I need to stay calm and get Lisette to leave without seeing Bradley. Then I'll make him go home, and I'll never ever talk to him again.

If I can just get through the next few minutes, I swear I'll never kiss Bradley Stephenson again.

"Hey, missy miss! When did you get back? And what are you doing here? I thought you were back to-morrow?" My knees shake. I hope my voice doesn't be-tray me.

"Aren't you happy to see me? I've been trying to reach you for days."

She has? I try to get my brain to focus. Did I miss texts from her? Did I ignore them? Did she try to call? With everything that's gone down with Mom and Dad and Mrs. Merrill and Frankie Sky, I don't even know what day it is.

"Earth to Beans! I said, what have you been up to?"

I force my eyes back to her. *Ask her about Bible Camp. Make small talk. Get Frankie Sky, and get us the heck out of here!*

"Nothing much, just working. How was camp?"

"Good! Well, great! Well, actually, amazing! I've been trying to tell you about that."

I fight every bone in my body not to turn around, not to look behind me toward the tree. I have to trust that Bradley will stay put. Or, better yet, maybe he found a back way out.

"Beans, I have so much to tell you! I tried texting you last night, on the way home, and again this morning. I was worried you were ignoring me. I know you've been mad. And I've said that I'm sorry. Anyway, I went by the club, and Peter said you were probably here."

Ah, Peter. "Nice of him," I say.

She rolls her eyes. "I get that you don't like him, and I'm sorry. But he's not a bad guy, Frankie. And I think he's cute. Although he was sort of acting kind of weird." I shift my feet, fight the urge to twist around again. "Anyway, who cares about Peter, right? I have so much to tell you, Beans! Camp was awesome. I hope you're not still mad at me. You'll never believe—"

She stops. Her face changes. She's looking past me, right at the tree.

My heart is about to explode.

"Hey, isn't that Frankie Sky?" she says. "What's wrong with him, Beans?"

For a split second I'm confused, because in my concern about Bradley, I've forgotten all about Frankie Sky. I whip my head around to the sandbox where I left him.

"What's wrong with him, Beans?" she says again, her voice frightened. "Is he hurt or something?"

I race to the sandbox where Frankie lies, curled up and moaning in a fetal position.

"Frankie?" I drop next to him in the sand. His eyes are glassy, his cheeks hot and red. "Frankie, what happened? Why didn't you tell me?" I stroke his forehead. He's burning up, his breath rapid and shallow. "It could be his heart!" I tell Lisette, who's now next to me in the sand. "Frankie, breathe, please!" I say, but his eyes are rolled back into his head.

"I need to do something, Zette. I need to get him to the hospital!" I glance over at the entrance, which now seems miles away, then back to the tree where Bradley is, then back at Frankie again.

I need Bradley's help. I know it. It will be too hard for me to carry Frankie like this all the way back to the club.

"Take my phone, Zette. Call 911. Please. Tell them to get us at the club. Then call his mother. Mrs. Schyler. In my contacts under *S-c-h-y.*"

I shove my phone at her and scoop my arms under Frankie, trying once to lift him on my own. He's too heavy. My eyes dart to the tree again.

"Ow, Beans," Frankie whimpers.

"It's okay, Frankie. I promise. We're going to get you to the hospital." I brush the curls from his face. They're drenched in a feverish sweat. I look at Lisette, but she's dialing, her back to me. The only one not doing anything is me.

"Bradley!" I yell. "I need you. I need you to come out right now. Frankie is sick. I need you to help me right now!"

He steps out, confused, and walks toward us, tentatively at first, then faster. Lisette jerks her head around, her eyes darting from Bradley to me and back again.

"I'm sorry," I say. "I'm really, really sorry. I'll explain later."

She looks at me in disbelief, and she's right. I mean, how will I ever explain?

"Yes," she says into the phone, "we need an ambulance, please. No, not hurt, sick. A little boy. At the Hamlet Dunes Country Club, please." Her voice breaks. "I don't know. His heart, maybe? Just this second. We'll wait for you there."

I look at her, my eyes pleading, as Bradley gathers Frankie. But she won't look up at me. It doesn't matter. I need to help Frankie. I can't worry about anything else right now.

Bradley stands and starts to move, Frankie cradled in his arms. Frankie's head falls back, his body limp, like a rag doll. No way I could have managed him alone.

"What's wrong with him?" Bradley asks as I run alongside him.

"I don't know. He has a hole in his heart . . ." But I'm winded and scared, and I can't even find words to explain.

At the entrance, I swing open the gate. As it closes behind us, I glance back and look for Lisette. She stands where I left her, at the sandbox, too far to make out whatever heartbreaking expression is on her face.

As we cross the street to the club, I grab hold of Frankie's hand. I lean in close and whisper, "Frankie, *non vel ocean mos somniculous nostrum animus.* Saint Florian will protect you."

He whimpers and squeezes my fingers.

thirty-nine

The ambulance comes in five minutes.

I insist that I ride with Frankie, but the paramedics won't let me. "Immediate family only, hon," the EMT says, whisking Frankie, now strapped to a stretcher, into the back. "Don't you worry, though, we'll take good care of him, I promise." He jumps in and pulls the doors closed along with him.

I stare as the ambulance speeds Frankie away.

"You come with me, child," Mr. Habberstaad says. He nods toward his fancy red sports car that's parked right up front. "I used to do some racing in my time. We'll be there before the ambulance. You watch me. You've called Brooke, yes? I'm sure she'll meet us there."

I turn to Bradley, though it pains me to look at him.

"Do you want me to go with you?" he asks.

I shake my head and look away. "Go check on Lisette. And thank you for helping me."

He reaches out as if he's going to grab my hand or something, but I say, "Please, Bradley, just go," and I slip into Mr. Habberstaad's car.

• • •

As promised, Mr. Habberstaad drives like a lunatic. The ambulance beats us there, but not by much. When we pull into the emergency parking area, it's still at the entrance, siren silent, back doors open, lights flashing.

I feel frozen, unable to face it if anything bad has happened.

Frankie is inside, being helped by doctors and nurses, I tell myself. *He'll be okay. Please, God, let him be okay.*

As we enter, I swipe at the tears. I don't want Mr. Habberstaad to see me cry. I don't want to explain to him how, one way or another, I make everyone I love leave me or die.

"Francesca! Here!" I whirl around to where Mrs. Schyler runs toward us, teary-eyed and small.

Mr. Habberstaad puts an arm around her and says, "Now, now, Brooke, don't you worry, my dear, you know how resilient that boy of yours is."

"I prayed to Saint Florian," I whisper to her, "even the Latin. I prayed to him the whole entire way."

"Thank you, Francesca." She smiles sadly and takes my hand, and we head into the hospital together.

At the nurses' station, a doctor walks toward us, a look of concern on his face. "Mrs. Schyler?" he says. "The boy's mother?"

"Yes."

"Come, let's speak over here."

My chest tightens. I can tell something terrible has happened, that Frankie Sky is gone. "Your son came in here with a high fever . . ." the doctor says, steering her away. I can't bring myself to listen to the rest.

I close my eyes and repeat the words at the base of the statue over and over in my brain: *Non vel ocean mos somniculous nostrum animus, non vel ocean mos somniculous nostrum animus,* until the hospital room sways and constricts and everything swirls and falls away.

■■ *forty* ■■

"Francesca?"

"Francesca!"

One voice soft, girly. The other deep, louder.

"Francesca!"

The deep one again.

I blink and raise my arm to my forehead. There's a wet cold weight on it.

Not a weight. A cloth. There's a washcloth on my head.

I open my eyes. Fluorescent lights widen in a blurry halo above me. Mrs. Schyler's blond curls bob there, too. "Are you okay, sweetie?"

A man in the corner. My father? No, not my father. Mr. Habberstaad.

I'm in the hospital, but why?

Frankie Sky! Oh, God, please don't let Frankie Sky be dead.

"Francesca." Mrs. Schyler touches my forehead. She's smiling. But it feels hard to trust what I see. "You frightened us! Did you hear the doctor? He said Frankie is doing just fine."

I sit up dizzily. Mrs. Schyler puts a hand on my

shoulder to steady me. She brushes the hair from my forehead. My body is drenched in cold sweat.

"You fainted, sweetie," she says.

I search my brain, trying to make sure I'm not dreaming or hallucinating.

"Frankie's okay, then?" She nods. "But what about his heart?"

She shakes her head. "It isn't his heart. Just a fever. A run-of-the-mill old virus. He spiked a high temp and got dehydrated. They've got fluids in him now, and he's resting comfortably in triage. Come, I'll show you."

I stand up, but Mrs. Schyler holds tight to my arm. A nurse brings a plastic cup of orange juice and places it in my hands. "Drink this, doll," she says. "Let's get some sugar in you."

I drink it as Mrs. Schyler leads us down the hall.

As we walk, she explains more how Frankie has a virus that they think was exacerbated by sunstroke. "Add to that some minor dehydration and we ended up here. Once he gets hydrated, they say he'll be feeling much better."

"It's my fault," I say. "I should have made sure he was drinking."

"It's not anyone's fault, Francesca. Just one of those things." Her red heels click across the linoleum. Mr. Habberstaad walks on her other side. He's been so sweet and fatherly, not at all the gruff man I met in his office that first day. "Of course, they'll want to hold him here for a few hours to run some routine tests and keep a general eye on things, make sure his temperature goes down. And they do have to make sure there's no infection—that it wasn't an episode of endocarditis." I turn to her, alarmed, and she adds quickly, "But they doubt it was, and they don't seem worried at all. At any rate, if all his blood work comes back negative, they'll discharge him this evening, or first thing in the morning, latest."

"I want to stay with him."

"Don't be silly, Francesca. Frankie's grandpa is on his way. You say a quick hello to him and then let Mr. Habberstaad take you home. You must be exhausted."

"But what about his heart?" I ask cautiously.

"Other than confirming that there's no infection—and there won't be—so far everything sounds quiet on the EKG."

"Everything?"

She nods and shrugs. "Absolutely no evidence of a tear." My eyes widen and I open my mouth to ask more, but she presses a finger to her lips. "Shush," she says, smiling, "never question a good thing when you have one."

We reach triage. Frankie sits on the stretcher with his sunglasses on. "Beans!" he says when he sees me. "You is blue again!"

"Believe me, Frankie," I say, hugging him, "now that I see you, I am the total opposite of blue."

● ● ●

I lie in bed and stare out my dark window, then glance at my cell phone on my nightstand—3:04 a.m.

Lately, there's been a whole lot of not sleeping going on.

I pick up my cell, grateful that Bradley dropped it home to me. I check for a text from Lisette, but there won't be any. There were none at midnight, and I'm sure there won't be any now.

I grab Fisher Frog and hug him to my chest. Of course, I'm happy and relieved that Frankie is okay, but that doesn't solve the mess I've made with Lisette.

Lisette, my former and only best friend, ever, in the world.

Not a single text from her since this afternoon.

I raise Fisher Frog above me and whisper, "How do we make such big messes of things, Fisher Frog? That is what I want to know." But he just dangles his arms and legs, one plastic eye glinting at me. "Lots of help you are," I say, tossing him to the foot of my bed.

Maybe I should send Lisette a note, try to explain things. But I don't know what I could say that would possibly make anything right.

Hey, Lisette, real sorry I kissed your boyfriend, but you've had plenty of them, so what's one less, right? Plus, I think I'm in love with him, so could you maybe go easy on me?

Geez, who could blame her for hating me?

I turn on the light, walk to my closet, and slide out my old wooden step stool. On the high shelf is a small shoe box where I keep my most prized possessions. My baby-name bracelet strung with pink and white square letter beads. A ribbon I won for a poem I wrote in third grade. A piece of ruby beach glass I found before Simon died.

Only one last thing to do.

I carry the box over, place it on my bed, and find my half of our hot pink enamel heart pendant. They were a present to each other the first Christmas Simon was gone. Lisette's mother had taken us to the mall to go shopping.

"See? Our hearts are one together," Lisette had said giddily, latching my half around my neck, still at the store counter.

"And broken if separated," I had answered, latching the other around hers.

With them secured around our necks, she had moved so close to me that our breath mixed, so she could hold her half against mine. They fit together perfectly, like puzzle pieces.

"Let's always wear these, even when we're old, okay? And let's never fight or do anything mean to each other, like keep secrets, or break promises, or anything bad like that. If we do" — Lisette fake snapped them apart in a dramatic motion and stepped back — "each of us will have our hearts broken. So we have to promise, Beans, okay? We have to swear never to break the other person's heart."

I had panicked. "But what if we do, Lisette? What

if I hurt you and don't mean to? What if I can't be . . ."
I had stopped, dumb tears filling my eyes, but we both
knew the end of the sentence: *What if I can't be trusted?*
And how could I be trusted when I had just let my own
brother die?

"Don't be silly, Beans. Of course you can!" She
pulled me back in and pushed our pendant halves together. "See, each of our pieces is nothing alone. But
when you put them together, they're totally perfect, like
we are."

"But what if I do, Zette? What if I mess up? I have
to know. I'm not keeping mine unless I know."

She had dropped my half and rolled her eyes. "Okay,
fine. If you ever mess up—if either of us does—"

"Even by accident."

"Even by accident, then we give our half back to the
other person. That way we don't have their heart anymore, and they can give it to a new, better friend. How's
that? It's a perfect solution."

"Good," I had said, but I'd made us pinkie swear
before I could feel relaxed again.

Then, at the beginning of ninth grade, we decided to
take them off, that they were juvenile, so we put them
away for safekeeping.

"For our thirtieth birthdays, we'll take them out
and wear them," Lisette had said as we ceremoniously
wrapped them and sealed them away.

Now the thought of sending my half back literally
breaks my heart, but I know it's what I have to do. She'll

know it's permission, and I owe her that. She'll know exactly what it means.

I walk to my desk with the pendant clutched so tightly, it leaves indents in my palm, and pull a piece of loose leaf from my drawer. I stick the pendant to the center with Scotch tape, then fold the paper around it and fasten the sides.

On the front I write, *Lisette, please know that I am sorry, Beans.* Then I leave it on my desk, turn out my lights, and pray I can sleep until morning.

forty-one

I bike over to Lisette's house early, drop the package in her mailbox, and go home to wait for her to text or call. Better yet, for her to march on over, hands on hips, toss the package back at me in exasperation, and say, *You know, Francesca Beans Schnell, you are so very stupid. Of course we are still friends. We have always been friends, and we will always be friends. Just because you made a mistake doesn't mean I'll never forgive you.*

I check the mailbox fifty times.

I check my cell phone.

I check e-mail.

But there's no marching back.

Nothing from Lisette comes all day.

And why would it? I screwed up. I betrayed her. We're not little kids anymore.

Lisette is done with me, and has every right to be.

I've got no one to blame but myself.

●   ●   ●

By the next morning, I still haven't heard from her. Somehow, I need to go on with my day.

I call Mrs. Schyler, who says Frankie's fever is gone, so it's okay if I want to come over.

I do. I am desperate to see Frankie Sky.

Not to mention to get out of the house. Mom and Dad keep giving me endless concerned looks. But I don't know what to tell them. The truth is, I'm worried about me, too.

I'm heartbroken about Frankie and Lisette. Plus, Bradley keeps texting, and I'm trying (trying!), but I'm heartbroken about him, too. How can I want to be with a person so badly, even when I know that it's wrong?

Mostly, I've refrained, only texted back when he checked in about Frankie. And even that was hard to resist:

> Him: How's Frankie doing?
> Me: Better! Thanks.
> Him: Glad to hear.
> Me: ☺ Did u talk to Lisette?
> Him: Sort of.
> Me: Is she okay?
> Him: No. Mad.
> Me: I feel awful.
> Him: Me too. Btw, did u kno male fiddler crabs have a yellow love-claw they wave around to fight off other males? ☺

See? How do I resist that?

Yet, somehow, I do. Since then, we haven't texted at all.

So, then, I'm turning over a new leaf.

Doing the right thing.

No more cookies for me. No matter how delicious they are.

Not today. Not tomorrow. Not ever.

So why do I feel so awful?

• • •

I walk up the Schylers' driveway. Frankie watches me from the window.

I can see from his face that he's feeling better, but also that Mrs. Schyler has told him that they're moving away. Don't ask me how I can tell such things from the window like that. It's just how it is between Frankie Sky and me.

Still, I'm glad he knows, because I feel too sad about everything to keep faking it.

I walk slowly up the front steps, feeling the weight of the fact that there will only be a few more times I get to see him.

He opens the door, but doesn't let me in, rather steps out and shuts it quickly, squishing Potato in half. The dog yelps. "I said no, Tato!" he says, opening the door again so Potato can squeeze back inside.

Frankie stands on the stoop in his bare feet, blue Batman underwear, and no shirt, looking a lot like the first day I came here. Only today he has no towel cape, which I guess means he won't try to fly.

He puts his hands on his hips and looks at me. There's a tattoo on his stomach — one of those press-on kinds — Superman, arms raised in the air. And a second on his arm of the Incredible Hulk or the Green Hornet, or some other superhero who is green.

"Hey, Beans," he says. "I seed you from the window."

"I seed you seeing me, Frankie."

He nods approvingly and sits on the steps with a loud sigh. I sit down next to him.

"Frankie Sky is moving," he says.

"Yeah. I heard. It makes me pretty sad. But also, I'm happy for you, too, you know? Because you'll like Joey a lot, and your mom likes him so much, and that makes her happy, which is good."

"Yep," he says. "But I is blue. And Beans is blue. And not the glasses kind."

"A little," I say, leaning against him.

He rests his elbows on his knees and his chin in his hands and he thinks like that for a while. "Don't be blue, Beans," he says finally, "because Frankie Sky knows how to swim. And Beans teached him just like she said."

"Taught," I say. "I taught you how to swim." Even though, as I say it, I doubt that it's true, that I had anything to do with Frankie knowing how to swim.

"Taught, right! Beans taughted me."

I giggle. "Well, I think you pretty much taught yourself how to swim, Frankie." He nods, but doesn't say anything.

I look out across the street and think of the first day I met him, and the day at the club when he dove in and nearly drowned. How I dove in after him without even knowing if I remembered how to swim. I think of the way the sun sparkled down on us as he moved through the water like a frog, and how he smiled at me.

It's only been a few weeks of summer. How can it feel like I've known Frankie Sky forever if he doesn't hold a piece of my brother?

"And I doesn't have a hole in my heart anymore, Beans," he is saying, "because it was just a fever sick, but not a scary heart sick. So Grandpa Harris says I don't need to know how to fly. Well, only in a plane to Cape Cod, but also we can drive in the car if we want to."

"Well, that is the best news, Frankie, because it scares me when you try to fly."

"I won't. Only if Beans is there, ready."

"Okay, good." I reach out and poke the tattoo on his belly, and he giggles. The superhero wrinkles and disappears into the folds. "Want to hold my hand, Frankie?" I ask.

"Yep," he says. "Yep, I do."

• • •

On my way home, I run into Mrs. Merrill. Okay, lie. I walk into her backyard to find her.

I'm not sure why. I just feel like I need to talk to her. Maybe it's because I haven't seen her at the club, or even leave the driveway much, for that matter, so I'm guessing she also lost a friend.

She kneels in front of a yellow rosebush, pruning off dead buds. I take a deep breath and cross the grass to talk to her.

"Hello, Francesca!" she says before I realize she's seen me. "To what do I owe this pleasure?" And I can't help but smile, because I've been a thief, a cheat, a liar, and, worse than all of that, a snitch, and yet somehow she actually seems genuinely happy to see me. Which makes me feel a little bit like a traitor.

I sit on the ground next to her, kick off my flip-flops, and run my toes through the grass. "Your flowers are so pretty," I say.

She sits back and pushes a wisp of hair from her eyes. "Thank you. I try. It's a lot of work, but they make me happy." She sighs, which makes me wonder how happy she really is. "So, how are you, Francesca? I haven't seen you for a few days. Everything okay at home?"

"I think so," I say.

"Well, good then." She looks at me hard. "You don't look so happy."

"No," I say. "Frankie Sky is moving. And Lisette found out about things."

"I see," she says gently. "That's tough." She leans away and snips a few more blossoms, then turns to me and slips one behind my ear. "So, what are you going to do?"

I pull the rose out and look at it. It's a perfect chiffon yellow. Fragile, but so very fragrant. I hold it to my nose and breathe in its scent, which is less sweet and more lemony than I'm expecting. I slip it back behind my ear and stand up.

"I'm going to try to fix things, I suppose."

﹏ *forty-two* ﹏

I sit at my desk and stare at the yellow rose from Mrs. Merrill that I tacked to my bulletin board last night. The edges have started to turn brown.

Covering the rest of the board are a few year-end exam reminders and other school stuff I never got around to taking down, plus an endless array of photos of Lisette and me, stuck up there with pushpins. Some are so old that she smiles beneath two long, blond pigtails tied with pink ribbons, and I sit next to her, my face framed by a hideously short boy haircut that barely reaches over my ears.

There are a few from middle school, and last year, too, near our lockers, and even a few from this summer, the day with Alex and Jared at the beach. In one, our sunburned cheeks are pressed together, the sky blue and bright behind us. I cropped the water out so my mother wouldn't know where we were. In the other, it's turned dark, and our faces are lit eerily by the bright white sparklers that we're holding.

That was right before I made the wish about Bradley.

I look at the red crab claw that sits on the corner of my windowsill. It makes my heart hurt. The thing is, I want to be sorry that I let him kiss me, and *part* of me really *is* sorry. But another huge part of me isn't sorry. Because in spite of what happened with Lisette, I wouldn't give up those kisses with Bradley.

I pick up the crab claw and use it to slide my cell phone over, but still no messages from her.

I think about reading through all the old ones from Bradley, but it will only make it harder to do what I have to do. I slip my cell phone in my pocket, throw on sneakers, and head downstairs.

I *owe* Lisette this. Whatever happens, I owe her a real apology. She needs to hear in person how much she matters to me, even if it's all mixed up with other things.

It's still early, so I walk slowly, trying to make it take as long as possible. But eventually I'm on the hill that's her street, and her house comes into view.

I walk across her lawn and up her front steps and stand for a minute before I can bring myself to ring the bell.

She answers a few seconds later. Pulls the door open and stands in her pajamas, hands on hips, glaring.

I clear my throat. She waits.

She's not going to make this easy for me.

"Hey, Zette," I manage. My voice shakes. I can barely look at her.

"So, did you want to come in or what?"

"Can I?"

She holds the door open and moves aside.

I follow her inside, and this feeling comes over

me like it's been forever since I've been in her house, which, in a way, it kind of has. So much has happened since the last time I was here. For a second, I long to time travel back to when both of us were little and silly and everything felt lighter and easier.

But the truth is, nothing has been easy for me, not since the moment my brother died. And yet, somehow, I do feel lighter now. Somehow, despite everything, some sort of weight has been lifted. Obviously not about Lisette, but the blanket of my brother Simon's death.

"Um, Frankie, did you want something?"

My eyes snap back to her. She looks so hurt and angry. "Could we go to your room?" I ask.

"Sure, I guess, but you'll have to make it fast. I have stuff to do."

When we reach her bedroom, she shuts the door and sits on her bed. I stand awkwardly, not knowing if I should sit next to her.

"You seriously should have told me, Beans," she blurts, throwing me off from what little order of explanation I had crafted at home. "You should have told me something happened with you and Bradley instead of fooling around behind my back."

I start to stammer something about wanting to, or trying to, but it's a lie, so I stop. I didn't come here to lie. I came here to tell her the truth.

"You're right, Lisette. You are. And I'm so very sorry. Because I love you, I swear I do. You are the best friend ever, and I should have found a way to tell you. Or not do it. I think I didn't tell you because even I couldn't believe it."

She rolls her eyes a little. "Believe what?"

"That anyone like Bradley could truly like me. I mean, could actually know about Simon and what happened and still truly like me. That I could possibly deserve to be liked." I choke up, no matter how hard I'm trying not to.

"I do," she says. "I've told you that."

"I know, Zette, but it doesn't matter how much you tell me if I don't believe it myself."

"Well, great," she says. "So I guess you do now. Hooray for that. Really. But it still didn't give you the right to do what you did."

"I know."

"That's it? You know?"

"No!" I say. "That's not it. Because I'd never want to hurt you. But I'm confused, too, Zette, because I really like Bradley. I mean really, really like him. And, believe me, I know that shouldn't matter, because you're my friend and that's the only thing that should matter at all. And it *is* the only thing that matters in my head. Except, somehow, I can't stop feeling the way I do. So I'm having a hard time, even though I know that makes me a terrible person." Tears spill down my cheeks. "You have every right to hate me, Lisette. I think I would hate me, too."

She closes her eyes, and I figure I should go. I've said what I came to say. I can't ask her not to be mad at me. I turn to leave, but pause at the bedroom door. "But I hope you don't hate me forever, that you'll find a way not to, one of these days."

"Beans."

"Yeah?"

"You're not a terrible person." She walks over and pulls me back by the arm. "You should have told me, that's all. I would have understood."

"But I . . ." I stop and stare at her. "What do you mean you would have understood?"

"Beans," she says, sitting and pulling me down with her, "you're my best friend. You always have been. And you always will be. You should have told me how you were feeling. You shouldn't have lied to me. That way maybe I wouldn't have been so mad. Or maybe I would have been a little mad, but I'm pretty sure I would have tried to understand."

"But he's your boyfriend."

"True," she says thoughtfully. "Or was."

"What do you mean?"

She holds her finger to her lips and lowers her voice a little. "Okay, so I've been trying to tell you. I don't even like Bradley anymore. Not *that* way. I mean, he's a great guy and all, and you two should be together. But I'm dating somebody else. I met him at camp. I'm totally crazy for him." I raise my eyebrows in shock a little. "I could have told you that and spared you all the drama," she says, "if you would have answered my texts. I was trying to tell you, Beans."

"You were?" My mind's racing to other places like, does Bradley know? Still, I manage, "So, wow, that's great I guess. Tell me about him. Who?"

"His name's Tyler. Tyler Dittman." I must make a face because she laughs. "I know, right? But trust me, he's way cuter than he sounds. Anyway, that's why I came to the playground to find you the other day. I was so excited, and I wanted you to be the first to know. But then all that stuff happened. And, anyway, that's beside the point, because, if you must know, I am totally, truly in lust with him."

"Tyler," I say. "Dittman."

"Right. You'll see. Oh, and guess what? Turns out he goes to Longacre. Longacre, Beans! That's only, like, twenty minutes from here. But, still, even if I hadn't met Tyler, I want some credit. Because, believe me, I know everything you've been through, and you deserve to be happy. You deserve something really good to happen. And if that something good is with Bradley, well, you should have known I'd be happy for you. Or at least I'd have tried to be. I mean, there's no one who knows better how hard it's been for you since Simon died." I look away. It's still difficult to hear this about me. "Not that any of that gives you permission to go around kissing other people's boyfriends." She pushes me affectionately. "So tell me, how was it?" she says.

I blush. "Like a sparkler. Just like you told me it is."

"See? Oh, speaking of which, I forgot to give you this."

"What?" She walks to her dresser and comes back with her hand in a fist. She opens it and drops my half of the pink heart pendant out on the bed. I look at her, tears welling in my eyes. "You sure, Zette?"

She rolls her eyes again, but hugs me. "Yes, Beans, of course I'm sure. You'd better keep it. I mean, seriously, who else but us would wear such a cheesy thing?"

◾◾ *forty-three* ◾◾

Two days before school starts, it's raining out and I'm lying on my bed.

I fiddle with the pendant around my neck—not my half of the heart pendant from Lisette (that's back in my closet), but a small wooden heart that Mrs. Schyler had Joey make for me. It came in the mail just yesterday.

> Dear Francesca,
>
> We're settled here and it's wonderful, but, oh, how Frankie and I miss you! The good news is, we will actually be back for a visit mid-October and do <u>expect</u> to see you plenty then!
>
> Meanwhile, a small gift is enclosed. I asked Joey to make this piece especially for you. I love how the heart is imperfect, don't you? And yet, the circles within never break or disconnect.
>
> This one is made from the wood of a yew tree, so it made me think of you completely . . .
>
> With love and gratitude,
> Brooke

I hold the heart up to the light from my window so it shines around its pale blond edges. A yellow ring the color of Simon's hair. The inner wood is darker, a pretty pinkish brown with fine bloodred veins that meet at a point in the center.

When I got it, I looked up yew wood on the Internet. The first website I opened said that a yew tree is a sacred tree of rebirth and transformation, and that botanists believe that one single yew tree can give birth to so many new trees that the seed of that first tree may span all of time and history.

I can't say it really surprised me. Think what you will, but I know that Simon is like that tree, and that he and Frankie are connected. I know in my heart that Simon's soul is living in Frankie Sky. And when I wear my pendant, I swear I can feel Simon near me.

•　•　•

Dad's off to work and Mom's at the Drowning Foundation. Well, the renamed Simon A. Schnell Foundation for Water Awareness and Safety.

Hey, it's not a huge change, but it's an improvement.

I lie on my bed. On one side of me is Fisher Frog, and on the other side, Bradley J. Stephenson.

Did I forget to mention that? He's been here pretty constantly the past few days.

In other news, today I turn sixteen, which is why the remains of a birthday cupcake sit on my nightstand by my bed. Bradley bought it for me. It's a mess now, half-eaten, but before, it was the coolest cupcake you've ever seen. A red crab covered in fondant, with two fat pincher claws and black-and-white googly eyes.

"The only kind of Christmas Island crab that's edible," Bradley had said, handing it to me. Now, as he kisses me, his mouth still tastes like cherries, red velvet, and sugar.

Next to the cupcake wrapper are my two sand dollars, and next to those, a framed photograph of Frankie Sky and me together by the pool. Beside that is the small plastic statue of Saint Florian. Mrs. Schyler gave that to me, too, but she promised to get Frankie another one as soon as they were settled.

Yes, they live in Cape Cod now, but they're coming home to visit in October.

I stop kissing Bradley for a minute to glance at the man in the funny hat with the feather and the ivory robes with all the folds.

Not even the ocean can drown our souls.

That's the truth, I think. *Not even.*

The End.

Acknowledgments

Thank you to: Elise Howard, for loving this story as much as I do, and making it shine;

Jim McCarthy, for his guidance and patience, and for fielding my constant frantic emails;

Emily Parliman, Brunson Hoole, and Kate Hurley (who knows a sand dollar is *not* really a shell), Eileen Lawrence, Emma Boyer, and all the other amazing people at Algonquin Young Readers who worked so hard, and keep working, to make this a beautiful book and share it with the world;

Lori Landau, for her talent that inspires me to look more closely at the world;

Annmarie Kearney-Wood, who has read this book more times than I can count;

Kelly Hager, my tireless cheerleader who promised me the book would sell;

My early, insightful readers: Holden Miller, Lori Landau, AKW, Becky Kyle, Heidi Peach, Jeff Fielder, Paige, Mom, Dad, David, and Solea, who changed her mind and kept reading, making me believe the story held some magic . . . and Amy Fellner Dominy, who always reads with a keen, expert eye;

Paul W. Hankins and members of the Nerdy Book Club, who endlessly honor me by sharing my work;

James King, and all the *Graduates*, for their humor and understanding, and all my Facebook friends who cheer on every excerpt.

And lastly, Frances Foster, who believed in me first, and gave me a chance.

If I've left you out, please know it's because my memory is not as good as it used to be. I am forever grateful for your encouragement and support.